LEAGUE OF INDEPENDENT OPERATIVES
BOOK 5

DEFENDER

KATE SHEERAN SWED

Join my mailing list to get an exclusive *LIO* prequel novella —
plus access to an entire library of short stories and goodies.

Join here: https://www.katesheeranswed.com

To all the heroes who work in healthcare:
you are our true defenders

1 / CALDWELL

United States President Fredrick Caldwell owed his position to accident as much as anything else. He'd ascended to office after the scandalous resignation of his predecessor, and even now—two years out from the next election—his political career hung by a thread. His party wasn't convinced that he'd been innocent with regards to the former president's crooked machinations—savvy of them, since he'd been knuckle-deep in that pie himself—though they'd yet to drum up any evidence against him. So that was one reason to hope.

On a typical morning, Caldwell would have arrived in the Oval Office before dawn. It was an unlikely place to get any actual work done—the weight of all that pomp hung over him like a yoke—but that wasn't the point.

The point was to arrive ahead of his staff. So that later—much later—when they were interviewed for documentaries about his triumphant administration, they'd talk about his dedication, his work ethic. Always in the office first. Always there last. Always working.

Mostly, Caldwell sat at the behemoth of a desk and worried that the secret service agents outside could see the classic sitcoms he was watching on his phone.

This morning, Caldwell's early-rising rhythm woke him early. Just like always. Only today, he couldn't head over to the Oval Office, because he'd stayed the night in a bunker.

He swung his feet around the side of the cot, the concrete floor like ice on his toes. He craved his morning coffee—two creams, two sugars. He craved the gentle laughter of *Bewitched* and *Leave It to Beaver*.

A secret service agent slept on another cot, just a few paces away, while others milled about by the door. They spoke commandingly into radios and listened back as tinny voices provided updates from aboveground.

Caldwell wasn't sure he wanted to hear those updates.

Two days ago, a space invader, who called himself Sever, had installed an impenetrable dome of energy in the middle of Washington, D.C. Over the top of it, actually. Like a big, glowing, onion-shaped cap.

He didn't know if anyone'd been able to measure it yet, but the thing had to be at least a mile high. It pulsed out from a central point by the riverfront, not four miles from where Caldwell had been eating lunch in the White House—Cobb salad, breadsticks on the side—and anxiously anticipating a call with the UK's Prime Minister, who always had to make a snide dig about Caldwell's bald spot.

When the agents had rushed in to shepherd him away to safety, his first feeling had been relief at avoiding the call.

Caldwell hadn't wanted to be president. He'd only wanted to wave and smile, shake some hands, cut some ribbons. Make a name for himself.

All right, and maybe a tidy profit. Something to retire on, write books about. Perhaps a fictionalized portrayal of his life, with a handsome actor to play him. Parker Chapman, maybe. Or Jeff Hayes.

But no. Jeff Hayes hated him. Or at least, he hated that

executive order about registering enhanced abilities. Hayes would play Caldwell as the villain.

Given that the entire Enhanced Abilities Enforcement Association had just gone up in flames, Caldwell was inclined to hate the executive order, too. Just a little bit.

Caldwell rubbed his face, hoping to God that someone had thought to install a Keurig down here. At least he didn't have a spouse, or any children, to inconvenience with this whole debacle. That'd almost kept him off the ticket as vice president, but in the end his bachelorhood had appealed to the younger voters.

The radio chatter, which had been a consistent white noise in the background, suddenly erupted into shouts. The secret service agents started pointing to doors and shouting commands, and one of them even headed toward Caldwell with a determination that made him wonder if there was another, even secret-er bunker to hide in.

The voices increased to a frenzy, and Caldwell had a split second to catch his own VP's name paired with the word 'taken' before the wall turned orange.

It looked like it was on fire, but it didn't bring any heat with it—only a sinus-resonating beat that made his molars ache. In the instant he recognized this, the wall of energy rushed straight toward him, as if it had been peeled away from the concrete.

Caldwell leapt to his feet as an agent dove to shield him, but not even the secret service could save him from a tsunami of glowing energy. The deep-toned buzz vibrated through the floor, and the orange wall jolted through him with a teeth-rattling pulse.

The concrete remained in place. Caldwell blinked. "What was that?" It was a ridiculous question, one he already knew the answer to.

"It was the alien's forcefield, sir," one of the agents said. To his credit, he didn't roll his eyes at Caldwell's apparent ignorance. "The dome's range extended. We need to get you out of here."

Caldwell had to admire the stalwart calm of the agents. They were like fighter pilots, these guys. Stoic to the end.

He'd have to do them the courtesy of showing the same mettle. Caldwell pushed to his feet, his knees threatening to buckle. It felt like every cell in his body had just been thrown into a blender. "I'm not much for strategy," he said, "but I think it might be too late for that."

As if summoned by this statement, a golden line sizzled through the air. It was like the energy field, and yet it was completely different; the wall had been fire, while this looked more like liquid gold.

The line expanded, like an open wound, until it was big enough to expel a person.

Or, more accurately, an alien. He stepped through the portal like a ballet dancer at curtain call, come to take a bow. He lifted his cloak with an elegant flick, keeping it away from the edge of the impossible doorway. He was shorter than Caldwell by a full head, his hair thick, his nose long. With the cloak, and the silver-tipped boots, and the snottish tilt of his chin, Caldwell half expected him to start spouting Shakespeare.

Of course, the spots of fire in his eyes made him rather too alien, even for the theater.

Caldwell didn't want to believe it, that a man who looked so ordinary—fiery eyes aside—could be so powerful. Yes, enhanced humans existed. The League of Independent Operatives, the Pearl Knife. They had strongmen and invisibility, fire powers. Things like that. Extraordinary, yes, but familiar. And, though Caldwell little deserved it, friendly. For the most part.

This man was something else.

The secret service agent who'd tried to protect Caldwell moved toward them, as if to shield him again. But Sever lifted a hand, and the man stopped. He didn't fall. He didn't disappear, or implode. He simply halted, one foot in front of him, one hand halfway to his weapon.

After the way Sever had torn the EAEA agents apart in the restaurant, Caldwell was glad the alien had only stopped the agent instead of snapping his neck. With a twinge, he realized he didn't know any of these men's names. Not one.

"How did you find me?" he heard himself ask. "I don't even know where we are."

Sever flexed his fingers, then inclined his head toward the portal with a flourish. Like a magician revealing his trick. Only he hadn't revealed anything at all.

"Mr. President," Sever said. "I've come to invite you to a diplomatic summit."

Caldwell went without a struggle.

A neighborhood in Alexandria, Virginia vanished today after residents took up arms against the arrival of the D.C. Dome. Over a distance of six blocks, they attacked the oncoming forcefield with axes, kitchen knives, and lawnmower blades.

The Dome has passed over other areas harmlessly, with only a pulse of energy. Yet aerial images show the combatant neighborhood blinking out of sight as the Dome engulfs the resisting blocks. Analysts say the area now resembles a large, empty lot, as though the neighborhood had never existed.

The Dome now extends to the Capital Beltway, with a circumference of sixty-four miles...

━━

Fire cages the streets of Philadelphia after a rogue enhanced human descended to quash local protests against the D.C. Dome. Our reporters identified her as Jenna Carpenter, who unveiled the existence of the League of Independent Operatives just under one year ago. She's calling herself the Daughter of Fire...

━━

D.C. residents, and visitors trapped in the area due to the Dome, converged on Nationals Baseball Park today. The man who calls himself Sever has claimed the park as his home base.

"We all know what happened to the League's head-quarters," Baltimore-resident Kimberly Evans told reporters, referring to last night's cave-in at Niagara Falls. "They could all be dead. The Pearl Knife, Coral, Ire. All of them."

Timothy Simmons, who works as a court reporter in the district, agreed. "We figure they wouldn't want us to wait around until this guy decides to kill us," he said. "So we're going to fight."

2 / NATHAN

CONSCIOUSNESS CAME AND WENT. Nathan was aware of a certain amount of chaos, and a pile of red baseball jerseys pillowing his head. Diana's vinegar scent and Monster's bluish glow, and Dolly's portal light splitting the air at intervals he couldn't begin to measure. He was aware, distantly, of commanding voices and answering footsteps, of newscasters speaking in urgent tones through the TVs on the walls, and of the gnawing fear that gripped his chest whenever he drifted awake and remembered what had happened.

HQ in ruins, and Niagara Falls with it. Tally lying dead in a pool of blood. And Mary, injured, watching helplessly as Sever dragged Nathan away.

Was she alive? Had Eloise gotten everyone out before HQ collapsed on top of them?

Nathan's stomach and ribs ached where Monster had kicked him during the fight at HQ, and he wouldn't have been remotely surprised to lift his shirt and find a bruise covering his torso. If he had the energy to do that much. Whenever he woke, even briefly, he tried to assess his pain level, tried to determine whether he might have internal bleeding. But there was a reason people didn't perform first aid on themselves as a matter of course. He couldn't tell.

Slowly, consciousness overcame unconsciousness. Slowly, the footsteps around him calmed, the voices faded, and the chaos subsided into silence.

He sat up and his stomach clenched, black spots crowding into his vision and threatening to push him back down. He breathed in, and pain seared through his lungs, as if they'd been subjected directly to Jenna's fire. He breathed out, and his ribs practically creaked in protest at the movement. Even his face hurt, as if there were a stinging bruise clapped across the entire right side of his face. There probably was.

Nathan forced himself to look around, moving his head carefully. He was sitting on the floor of a souvenir shop, of all places. The red, white, and blue pennants, mugs, foam fingers, and jerseys all pointed to Nationals Park in D.C.

Moving slowly, Nathan pushed himself up on all fours and used the closest T-shirt rack to help him to his feet. It was strange that no guards hovered over him, no LIO retirees came to kick him back down, and no sadistic aliens decided it was time to freeze him in place.

By the time he managed to straighten all the way, he realized that the shop wasn't quite as silent as he'd thought. He could hear voices in the distance, almost like a crowd in the background of a baseball game—ironic—but without any commentary.

And the crowd was shouting.

Nathan took a step toward the front of the shop. When he didn't fall over, he took another.

No one showed up to stop him. So he walked right out the front door.

Sever stood in the middle of a kind of courtyard, likely the main entrance to the stadium, with Morik at his side and his

LIO-retiree allies behind him. Dolly, Monster, Diana, Rocker, the twins. Goldi, Ranger, and Carlisle. Plus Jenna, just for good measure. Clouds obscured the sky, and he couldn't tell whether it was morning or afternoon.

A row of turnstiles separated Sever from an enormous crowd of people.

That explained Nathan's lack of guard, he supposed. With Sever posed out front like a diminutive historical general, it was difficult to tell whether he was meant to protect the retirees, or the other way around. These people might not pose much of a threat, but Nathan certainly posed less.

He'd have expected the crowd to be louder than it was, given how far they spilled out across the concrete and down the steps that led into the park. None of them had crossed the turnstiles—not yet—but they stood flush against them, as if ready to storm the place. A couple held signs, but mostly they stood there, shoulder-to-shoulder, like they believed strength in numbers could save them.

Maybe it could.

Sever lifted a hand, like an emperor greeting his subjects, and for a moment Nathan was afraid, deeply afraid, that these people had come to support him.

But then Sever said, "You are here because you have questions. I understand. So, ask. What would you like to know?"

Silence. Not complete silence, but crowd silence—shuffling, murmuring, whispering. One of the signs caught in a breath of wind and folded itself in half.

It was difficult to rail against a dictator who sounded so reasonable. So fair.

"When are you going to free us?" a man shouted, one of the people closest to the turnstiles.

"Why are you keeping us prisoner?" someone else said, apparently emboldened by the first guy's courage.

They were all courageous, as far as Nathan could tell. He wouldn't have blamed them for locking themselves away, finding a place to hide until the danger passed.

Not that hiding would save them from Sever, if he decided to incinerate Earth.

A volley of other questions followed the first two, along with a few shouted curses. They were from other states, other countries. The dome had them trapped. Or they were residents of D.C., desperate to know what Sever planned to do to them.

"Free you." When Sever repeated the first man's phrase, his voice echoed much more loudly than physics accounted for. But his tone was calm. Not placating, perhaps, but almost... disbelieving. "I am *trying* to free you. From the influence of the Blade of Starlight."

Whispers. Did they know what Sever meant? The Blade of Starlight, the Pearl Knife. Probably clear enough. Nathan watched, gripping the door frame, wondering what he could learn. Wondering how, in his current situation, he could help. He scanned the line of retirees. How did they feel about their new alliance with the alien demigod? Were they all of one mind on the subject?

Every alliance came with cracks. Fissures. Nathan only needed to discover what they were. Easier said than done, in his current state. But not impossible.

"Where *is* the League?" the first man demanded. "What have you done with them?"

And are they alive? The question rose unbidden, and Nathan tried to push it down. But it refused to go. He held onto the frame of the door as if his grip could make it so.

They had to be alive. *Mary* had to be alive. The thought skittered across his mind before he could restrain it, an image of her crumpled on the floor of HQ like Tally. Fear added its own volley of pain to his aching body, his chest seizing so hard it was difficult to breathe.

She was alive. She had to be.

"They've run away." Nathan couldn't see Sever's face, but he could hear the derision in his voice. "They're cowards, and they've forsaken you."

Never. But if these people believed that, they might give up. And Nathan wouldn't let that happen. They'd done a brave thing coming here today. They needed hope.

Nathan let go of the door, ignoring the way his ribs twinged as he stepped forward. "They're not cowards."

His voice wasn't as loud as Sever's, could never be as loud as Sever's. It was hard to speak up, hard to tap into his lessons on projecting and crowd control when his throat was dry from thirst and his diaphragm spasmed in pain when he drew a full breath.

But still, he managed to make himself heard. At least by the people in front. He just hoped they knew who he was. Or that some of them did. He might not be as famous as Mary, but maybe he'd been standing next to her for long enough to be recognized. To make a difference.

Monster was standing closest to him, and Nathan made himself continue as the huge man moved to seize him. "I'm alive, but I don't know who else is. What I do know is, they'd never abandon you. Not ever."

As long as *they're* alive. He intended to say the words, but they refused to come. Nathan blinked away the image of Mary, the picture of her dead, bleeding, buried in rock.

And then Monster was gripping his arm, trying to drag him back toward the souvenir shop. When Nathan resisted, Monster kicked him in the shin. It was a simple but painful move, one that nearly dropped Nathan to the ground. Monster dragged Nathan's hands behind his back to restrain him, and his ribs screamed in agony as Monster forced him against the wall.

The crowd exploded into a cacophony of shouts, curses, insults, and questions. Someone in the front threw a phone at Sever's head, but he batted it away with some invisible power before it came within three feet of him. The man who'd asked the first question ducked under the turnstile, and several others made to follow.

Then Sever clenched a fist.

Nathan watched it happen as if in slow motion, the alien's fingers curling toward his palms.

Everything stopped. The people crouched beneath the turnstiles, the ones poised to follow. The waving signs, the shouting. All of it just... stopped.

There had to be hundreds of people in front of the park, and none of them moved. They were frozen in place, every one of them. The angry man from the front was on his hands and knees, crouched halfway through the turnstile. A woman beside him had one foot off the ground, her hand on the silver gate, as if she'd planned to vault over it.

Nathan had seen it before. Sever had done this to the Enhanced Abilities Enforcement Association agents in the restaurant fight—had that been yesterday? the day before?—but seeing it on such a grand scale made Nathan want to double over and empty his stomach. Or, since Monster still had him shoved back against the wall, all over the retiree. Nathan wasn't picky.

He couldn't wrench his eyes away from the crowd. They looked like an army of wax figures. Even their expressions were frozen. Even their eyes.

"Be grateful for my mercy," Sever said. Nathan didn't know if the crowd could hear; they certainly couldn't respond. Either way, he doubted they would call it mercy.

How long would Sever leave them frozen here? Would they die? Decay? Or would they remain frozen in time for centuries until Sever—or someone else—broke the spell? Like a fairy tale, like Sleeping Beauty. He'd never considered the grotesqueness of a story like that, until now.

Taking hold of his cloak, Sever turned on his heel and swept back toward the shop. "Find a secure place for the prisoners," he told Morik.

Pain radiated through Nathan's body, his face, his ribs, his stomach. He couldn't look away from the frozen crowd, the cruel display of Sever's power standing there like corporeal ghosts.

Nathan needed to pay attention. He was here, so he needed to learn what he could. Ribs smarting, pain blackening the corners of his vision, he played back Sever's last words.

He'd said prisoners, plural. Who else had Sever captured? Unless he meant the frozen crowd. But if so, then why not just freeze Nathan along with them? Why not just freeze the other prisoner, or prisoners, whoever they were? Seemed like that might be easier.

Nathan looked out at the crowd again. Sever had frozen him briefly in the restaurant, too, and he'd come out of it alive. He had to believe these people were alive, too, at least for now.

Morik nodded, his fat curls bobbing as he followed his master. "And the people?"

Sever didn't even glance at the crowd, still standing motionless behind him. "Leave them."

3 / ELOISE

It seemed to Eloise that someone had written up a manual that dictated exactly which rooms needed to exist in a secret hideout. Well-stocked pantries, labs full of mysterious instruments. And a fully equipped training room, of course.

Wave's Yacht might be drifting in the middle of the Pacific somewhere, but its training room reminded Eloise eerily of the one at HQ. Mats, mirrors, targets. Punching bags. A line of fire extinguishers. It even smelled the same, like new plastic and lemon air freshener. The scents brought back an immediate rush of memories from her youth, hours spent sparring and training and sparring some more.

Her heart resisted the idea that HQ's training room was gone now. Her home. Her stomach seemed to know it, judging by the tight knot there that refused to loosen.

But her heart had cried its eyes dry last night, with Steve's arm around her shoulders. Today, it was Mary who needed help.

Mary sat in the middle of the training room with her legs crossed, one palm pressed into the mat in front of her, the other cradled in a sling to stabilize her injured shoulder. She was staring at her hand, her face pale, her curls hanging limp around her face. Eloise couldn't have said how long she'd been sitting there, or why she'd even come. She looked as wrecked as HQ.

Eloise crossed the room and sat down on the mat beside Mary. Her friend, her sister. She had no idea what to say.

It was Mary who spoke first. "His book." Her voice sounded thin, like a rubber band about to snap, a parchment paper about to tear. Far away, too. Like an echo of itself. "He was reading some book, I don't know, and he was marking his place with a slip of paper. It was almost to the end."

Unsure where this was going, Eloise kept her expression carefully neutral.

"I have no idea what book it is," Mary continued. "Was. I know it had aliens, because we joked about it, but I can't think of the title, and I can't get it back for him because it's buried under rock."

She was in shock, and it was no wonder. Her home destroyed, Nathan snatched away. A recruit was dead, the retirees were free, and it all seemed like some kind of a cruel joke. Like it couldn't possibly have happened.

Eloise had grown up in that place, too. It was home, pure and simple. A part of her would always see it that way.

They'd *all* lost yesterday, and badly. Eloise couldn't shake the image of Tally leaping to save Mary, the sound of her neck snapping her soul away. Eloise couldn't help feeling that she'd failed Tally. Failed them all.

That grief was raw, and deep. And then, after all Mary had been through, after all she'd had to sacrifice, for her to lose Nathan, too... It was too much to bear. For Mary, for Eloise. For the entire League. They were ragged, and they were broken, and she had no idea how to fix them.

So Eloise did something she'd rarely done since she and

Mary were kids. She put her arm around Mary's shoulders, careful not to jostle her hurt one.

"We're going to get him back," Eloise said, the words coming out more fiercely than she'd intended. She wasn't supposed to be the one on the edge of tears. She was supposed to be the one keeping everyone together.

"How?" Mary whispered. "When?"

Eloise stood and offered Mary a hand to help her to her feet. "There's no time like the present," she said. "Let's go see the Committee."

4 / MARY

MARY DIDN'T KNOW if Wave's ruling Committee had slept, if they ever slept, or if they simply sat in that little semi-circle of chairs all the time. Tapping their feet, steepling their fingers, and looking about as high-and-mighty as a jury of hawks facing an accused band of chickadees.

Not to judge, but really, was it any wonder everyone thought Wave was evil?

The Committee watched in silence as she and Eloise crossed the space, which kind of made her think of a throne room. Or, given that they lived on a cruise ship, maybe a repurposed buffet. It certainly had the ugly carpet for it, zig-zagging patterns and all.

She couldn't tell if the Committee members were upset that she and El had burst in unannounced—they didn't appear to feel a need to guard the doors on their fortress of a ship—or if they'd expected it, or if they didn't care. Or if they each felt differently about it. Or if they simply wanted a nap.

Mary felt like she needed one, like she could collapse into a bed and sleep for days. She'd only just woken, after sleeping with the help of a pill—and her body's inability to go forty-eight hours without rest. Everyone had their limits.

If she could, she'd sleep until this nightmare ended, until it was Nathan waking her, his cheek against hers, his lips warm with longing.

In the reality of this moment, she was grateful for El's supportive arm, locked around hers. She needed to stay on her feet. Needed to make a plan.

But even after sleep, her brain felt murky, her thoughts drifting by like flecks of dust caught in the sun. As for her feelings, those were locked away in a box she didn't dare disturb. *Grief*, a voice had said in the early hours on the ship—inside her head? or someone on the outside?—but she wouldn't accept that. Couldn't. Because grief meant hope was lost. Grief meant you mourned what was gone. Grief was the enemy to action, and action was everything.

Tally, dead.

HQ, lost.

Nathan.

Mary let the thoughts drift by. Just motes in the sun. Just obstacles to keep her from doing what needed to be done. Her shoulder throbbed, distantly, as though reminding her of how little her body could do right now. She didn't often feel powerless, but she was as close to it now as she'd ever been.

She made her way to the front of the room with Eloise in step at her side, her brain cataloging useless details like the spongy feeling of the ugly carpet under her feet, the four obvious exits—two flanking the Committee, two at her back—and the smell of recently made coffee, the drips still trickling audibly into the pot.

"Mary," the man sitting in the center of the Committee's half-circle said. He wore a suit—what *time* was it?—and some hidden part of her brain that must have been listening when they arrived supplied his name: Jian. "Eloise. How can we—"

"We have to go." Mary hadn't known the words were on the

tip of her tongue, but they came out anyway, as if they'd been waiting for a chance to burst out, and preferably in the form of an interruption.

Silence. The coffee machine huffed.

The elderly woman who sat at the edge of the half-circle leaned toward them, just a tick. She had a cane resting against the side of her chair, her silver hair pulled back severely. Here, Mary's name recall failed her. Betty, maybe. Gertrude? She looked like she could be a Gertrude.

"And you?" she said, her gaze glittering on Eloise. "What do you say about this?"

Still supporting Mary's arm, Eloise hooked her free thumb through her belt loop. A definite indication that she was trying to keep her body language open when she would have preferred to cross her arms. Whether she wanted to cross them because of Mary, or because of the Committee, it was hard to say. "I say there's an impenetrable forcefield around Washington, D.C., and that one of my best operatives is a prisoner inside it."

"So you assume," Jian said.

"He could be dead by now." This young man, who sat at the opposite end from the old woman, lounged with his legs extended, his hands propped behind his head, as if he didn't care one way or the other. But his tone was sharp.

"You could be dead, too," Mary shot back, "but I'm not feeling it today."

She could almost feel Eloise rolling her eyes, but she kept her own gaze locked onto the lounging man.

"You and your operatives came to us," Jian said. "Perhaps you'd do well to follow our guidance?"

"So now we skulk in the shadows while Sever destroys the world?" Eloise abandoned the belt loop, and Mary's elbow, to fold her arms across her chest. "Makes sense, since it's Wave's usual tactic."

"By necessity," a woman with aquamarine-colored hair said, her tone sharp. "Because of your operatives. Because of the League."

"Caution is only prudent. *We* still have a headquarters," the reclining man said.

A jury of hawks. Definitely. Hard not to sympathize with those chickadees.

"How gracious of you to remind us," Eloise said.

Mary took a step forward. El would butt heads with Wave until the end of time, and time was a resource they couldn't afford to waste. "We came here as a courtesy," she said. "I said we *have* to go."

"We'll stop you," the reclining man said.

Mary shrugged. Pain lanced through her shoulder and down her arm, and she wasn't entirely sure she kept the wince from showing on her face. "You can try."

She didn't think she'd have to fight her way out of here. She hoped not; she wasn't entirely sure she'd be up for it. Not a good feeling, when she planned to go directly into another fight. With an alien demi-god who could snap bones from across a room and freeze people in their tracks. Everyone but Mary who, for unknown reasons, could resist his powers.

Oh, yeah, and he thought she was his ex-girlfriend.

She didn't have time to let this conversation devolve into a political tug-of-war. Eloise was on her side, at least. Eloise would help her. And if it devolved into a fight, well, they'd cross that bridge later.

These people all looked ordinary, but Wave's M.O. was to play things close to the vest. Mary would have bet her entire fortune that at least one of them had powers.

Someone peeled away from the wall to Mary's right, and she startled, half ready to attack. Her arm gave a painful spasm.

But it was only Bradley Archer. She'd surveyed the room, and she hadn't even seen him there. It made her wonder if he could secretly camouflage or something. He was wearing his ridiculous galoshes, orange ones today, his hair towering above his scalp like a sculpted yellow weed.

"With respect to the Committee," he said, "I agree with the League."

Eloise whipped her head in his direction, lips parted in surprise. Basically Mary's reaction, too.

"Excuse me?" The lounging man actually un-lounged, dropping the front two legs of his chair to the floor so he could sit up straight. "I think I'll need you to repeat that, Mr. Archer. I thought I heard you say you agree. With the *League*."

"Yes, Matthew, your hearing is as sharp as ever," Bradley said. It was impressive, really, that he could speak such sour words without even a hint of derision. Fun, when it was aimed at someone else. "If we're going to best the demi-god, we need to understand him. And we can hardly spy on him from here."

Matthew opened his mouth, but the old woman raised a hand. "Let him speak."

Mary would have expected the younger man to protest, but he merely inclined his head. Strange interactions. On another day, she might've cared. Or asked El to decipher it for her.

Bradley pointed at Mary. "Sever's powers don't work on her. If we can figure out why, we can leverage that. Use it."

Build a gadget to replicate it, maybe. Not a bad thought. But Mary didn't want to sneak around looking for information. She wanted to get Nathan out of Sever's grasp. Her lungs squeezed with her need for it, shortening her breath as panic tried to yank her distantly numb thoughts into a tornado.

Sever had destroyed HQ. Sever had killed Tally.

Sever had Nathan.

Her arm hurt like hell, her throat pinched painfully with unshed tears, and her muscles were sore and shaky from fighting and fighting and fighting. But she needed to go. She *had* to.

"Her immunity is useful, I grant that, but how do we use it exactly?" Matthew asked.

"I'm standing right here," Mary said.

Bradley smiled, amiable. As if they were discussing dinner plans. Mary couldn't help wondering if these two had a past. "I can't say, can I? Not until we know more."

Jian leaned forward, resting his palms on his knees. "Can the Knife deposit people within the forcefield?"

Eloise bit her lower lip. The Knife had been sparking when they'd arrived here last night, clearly damaged during the fight at HQ. If not before. "I think so." It sounded more like a question than a statement. "The Knife's not too predictable at the moment. I can try."

The Committee members exchanged glances, eyebrow twitches, minuscule head shakes and nods. Did they have some kind of silent communication method? Interest sparked in Mary's stomach, but she tamped it down. Silent communication wouldn't save Nathan—at least, not immediately—so it would have to wait.

It was more likely that they simply all knew each other very, very well.

"All right," the old woman said finally. "Mary will go. Bradley will go. Any more than that, and you'll risk detection. We can't take a chance that the Knife might get trapped inside that forcefield with Sever."

Eloise scowled, but Mary suspected she'd have said the same thing if given the chance. Mary didn't like the idea of splitting up, either, but the old woman was right. Not that she'd have said so out loud.

The old woman gave them a sharp nod. A dismissal, Mary thought. "Go down to the lab and get some equipment," the woman said. "Dr. Gordon just arrived, too, so let him heal that shoulder before you go."

Bradley bowed, swiveled, and headed for the door. Mary followed, and Eloise made to do the same.

"Eloise," the old woman said. "A moment, if you have one?"

Mary raised her eyebrows, but El just nodded as if she'd expected the summons. "Go ahead. I'll catch up."

5 / NATHAN

OTHER INVADERS MIGHT HAVE CHOSEN a symbolic spot for their home base. The White House, perhaps, or the National Mall. The United Nations. The Hague.

Now that Nathan had managed to sleep for a few hours, he could see that Sever had gone with a practical choice, if a surprising one. Nationals Park was a baseball stadium, which meant it was teeming with pockets and niches. Concession stands. Locker rooms. Dugouts. Hidden passages and high-vantage lookout points. There would be, Nathan assumed, routes for carrying supplies and hauling out garbage, plus secret exits for players.

The park even hulked over the banks of a river, like a Scottish castle ready to defend its people. Not an image he'd ever thought to place on a baseball park before, but it seemed almost painfully obvious now.

Under normal circumstances, Nathan would have been thrilled at the chance to get a peek into one of the seasonal suites at Nationals Park, let alone set foot in one. The room was like a private bar, with high-top chairs and a kitchenette, televisions, couches, and a wall-sized window facing the field. If there was a better view for a baseball game in more comfortable surroundings, he couldn't imagine it. The couches were comfortable enough to sleep on—he knew, as he'd spent the remaining hours of the night on one—even with Jenna Carpenter guarding the door.

At least Sever hadn't decided to keep his prisoners in the locker room. No doubt it smelled better up here. And there were temperature controls. It was hot as hell outside.

Jenna paced by the door, which unfortunately only led out to the hall that all the suites shared. A good choice for a prison, with double layers of security.

Good for Sever, of course. Bad for Nathan. Escape seemed a laughable idea; in the hours since he'd been escorted here, the pain hadn't abated. Besides, Sever was clearly ready to make statues out of anyone who displeased him. Still, Nathan couldn't help thinking about his options.

There weren't many.

Jenna was practically quivering with her need to move, her dark ponytail swinging behind her as she paced. She'd never much liked sitting still. Heat waves rippled the air around her, but she wasn't even breaking a sweat.

"You can sit down, if you want," Nathan said. "I won't try to escape."

He was lying on one of the leather-ish couches, hands propped behind his head. The couch was too short for him, so he dangled his legs off the end. He either looked very casual, or very ridiculous. With pain a constant—every breath was a stab to his ribs, every word an ache in his jaw—it took a concerted effort to keep his tone light.

Jenna kept moving. "As if you're the one I'm worried about."

"You're not on your own here. There's another layer of guards."

"Sure, because I *totally* trust them."

"Why wouldn't you?"

Jenna flicked a spark toward him. It fell short by several feet, sizzling into the carpet and burning out. "I'm not telling you things, so don't try."

She already had, but all right. "Sorry," Nathan said. "Bad habit. Always shooting for detective, yeah?"

Jenna glared at him. "The others might buy into that cop stuff, but you can't fool me. You're an IO now, through and through." She pointed a finger at him, though she kept her sparks to herself this time. "That's not a compliment. It's gross."

She said it like his time with LIO could simply erase years of previous training when in fact, they'd built upon one another. But fine—let her underestimate him while he regained his strength. Her contempt might well lead her to make a mistake, to reveal more information. To relax.

The door clicked open, and Diana Morton slipped into the room, bringing her poisonous vinegar smell with her. She was more than a head taller than Jenna and several decades older, her dark hair flecked with gray.

And yet when Jenna stopped pacing and stuck her hands on her hips, she was the one who looked like the teacher, staring down a misbehaving student. "You're supposed to knock."

Diana snorted. "Why? I have the key card."

"Mary could have the key card. Eloise could have the key card. If they can make a room full of holographic reporters, they can program a key card. You're supposed to *knock*."

Diana sized her up, disdain curling the corner of her mouth. "They'd have to get past Monster and me to use it."

"Yeah, because they've never gotten past you before."

Diana blinked at Jenna, unperturbed. Or at least, trying to seem calm. "I heard voices, so I came to check on you."

Jenna ignited her hand and waved it in Diana's face. "I think I can handle him. See the fire? I'm good."

Diana just smiled indulgently, though she had to be able to feel the heat. She looked like she might pat Jenna on the head. Which would've been a really good way to get killed. "Yes, I'm aware of your little party trick. Good job, dear. I came to make sure you weren't telling him any sensitive information."

She hardly needed to. Diana had told him plenty just by entering the room.

"She won't say a word," Nathan said. "It's very annoying."

Both women snapped their heads to look at him, as if they'd forgotten he was there. Which was ironic, given they'd been *discussing* him.

Diana just sniffed, scanned the suite as if checking for threats, then turned on her heel and drifted out with a distinct air of accomplishment in the tilt of her chin. Jenna glared after her, like she'd incinerate Diana if she could figure out how to do it through the door.

"That's rough," Nathan said. "She doesn't appreciate you, eh?"

Jenna flicked another spark his way. This one hit the armchair beside him. "Don't bother," she said. "I don't need your sympathy, and I'm not turning coat, so just sit over there and be quiet. If you can manage that."

"I find it difficult, but I'll try."

A knock sounded on the door, and Jenna smiled, smug. She opened the door a crack, and the smile shifted. Nathan watched it happen, the flicker of triumph changing suddenly to an open welcome. Her hands stilled, her back straightened, and she opened the door to admit not Diana, but Sever.

Sever had exchanged the cloak-and-tunic getup for jeans and a green polo shirt, which took a moment to absorb. He looked like he was here to invite Nathan for a round of golf. Or maybe make some calls about a stock trade.

Morik, who had followed Sever into the suite at a distance that managed to seem both respectful and hovering, hadn't made any changes to his wardrobe. He still had the same shoulder-length sausage curls and long burgundy robes.

Diana lingered behind Morik, sticking to the doorway, and Nathan tried to see past her, to get a location on Monster, catching a flash of his blue scales as the door slid closed. Who else was Monster guarding out there?

Sever paused halfway between the door and the seating area where Nathan was lounging. He looked to Jenna. "How is our guest?"

"He's annoying," Jenna said.

Sever breathed out a laugh, glancing at Nathan with something like amusement in his eyes. "Oh?"

Nathan wasn't equipped for this conversation. He couldn't decide whether to keep lounging or sit up, or even stand. He should have planned for this, but he hadn't really expected Sever to check in personally. It seemed out of place, beneath the notice of a being with godlike powers. Nathan would respect the touch, actually, had another leader bestowed such personal involvement.

But Sever was a godlike being with a track record of genocide and an obsession with world domination, and Nathan had seen firsthand how he dealt with opposition. Not to mention the stories that Sloane and her crew had carried from their faraway galaxy.

Of course, they'd originally shown up here to steal the Pearl Knife *for* Sever. But they hadn't known that.

Sever sat down in the chair across from Nathan's couch, making full use of the armrests and surveying Nathan with glittering, orange-specked eyes.

Nathan decided to keep lounging. And he decided to speak first. What was there to lose, at this point? "What does one do with a world, once they have it?" he asked. "Game of marbles?"

Sever touched a finger to his bottom lip. "Ah," he said. "I see what you mean, Jenna."

Still hovering in the doorway, Diana scowled. Jenna preened.

Sever focused on Nathan. He looked paler than he had at HQ, the only color on his face a pair of half-moon bruises under his eyes. They were so stark, it almost looked like someone had punched him. Even his lips were pale. Sever was tired, Nathan realized. Maybe even exhausted. That was good. But only if Nathan could figure out why.

Obviously, cracking open tons of rock could take a toll. But this was a man—alien—who'd destroyed entire worlds. If Nathan could drill down to the specific pain point or weakness, it might make all the difference.

It wasn't overblown to say, to feel, that he'd spent his life contemplating villainy after the way his mother had used him to blow up a building as a child. He'd spent his life finding ways to overcome it. And he'd do the same now.

"Been busy?" Nathan asked. "Blown up many secret hideouts in the last two days?"

Sever leaned back, still resting his elbows on the arms of the chair. "You cannot bait me. I only came to check on your wellbeing."

Nathan made himself smile. Friendly. "What, in case she comes? Don't want her to make any rash decisions because you've killed the man she loves?"

God, he hoped Mary wouldn't come. She *couldn't.*

Sever didn't move. "Love," he repeated, and Nathan couldn't read his tone. Was it a foreign idea to him? Was it just that he thought Nathan incapable of feeling it? Was he strug-gling to translate?

Or was he offended by the suggestion that Mary could love anyone but him?

Sever controlled his movements, his voice. But he almost controlled them too well. The more his body stilled, the more Nathan wondered what there was to hide.

Sever might not be human, but he was hardly infallible. And Nathan would uncover his weaknesses. Mary would come eventually. She'd come, or he'd escape and they'd attack Sever together. Either way, Nathan would be ready to help. He'd learn all he could. He'd find allies, if they existed.

Nathan swung his feet around the edge of the couch and leaned forward, ignoring the pain that surged through his torso as he forced himself to hold Sever's eerie gaze. It sent chills up his spine, but he maintained it anyway. "You know Mary isn't her. Right? They look alike. I get that. But look her up. She was raised in front of the cameras. She's not... She isn't your Adina."

Sever waited a beat before turning his head to look at Jenna. "True?"

Diana edged into the room. "She grew up under—"

"No," Sever interrupted, his voice quiet. "Jenna."

Jenna crossed her arms, tapping her fingertips on her elbows. Still moving. "It's true," she said. "Sorry."

"Never apologize for telling the truth," Sever said.

Diana opened her mouth, but Morik gave his head a single shake, and she closed it again.

Interesting.

Sever stood. It was strange to see him without his cloak. Strange to see him looking so... Earthly.

Nathan expected him to issue instructions, or a declaration. To respond to what Nathan had said. Instead, Sever simply turned and walked out of the suite, with Morik following in his wake.

Nathan pretended to watch them go. In truth, he was trying to see beyond them, to catch a glimpse of the suite across the hall. His effort was rewarded when the other door opened to admit Sever, a flicker of movement passing in the room beyond before it closed again. The other prisoner, or prisoners.

Whoever they were, Nathan would find them. And he'd make them his allies.

6 / DOLLY

Dolly wasn't sure why everyone else seemed so thrilled to sleep in the Nationals Park gift shop. It was rank with whatever chemicals they dowsed brand new clothing in, leaving her nose itching to sneeze, and the ubiquitous red decorations made it impossible to rest. It was like living in Wonderland, except they'd poured red paint over every stuffed animal, foam finger, and keychain, instead of the roses. It was like one big patriotic nightmare.

Worst of all, the shop looked directly out on the horror show of Sever's most recent atrocity. Dolly had escaped to the balcony that wound around the glassed-in second floor of the store, hoping to escape the relentless new-car smell of the place. But that just meant a closer look at the civilians Sever had frozen in place.

It was like looking at a war memorial, only the statues were all too real. They wore blue jeans and sundresses, suits without the jackets. They had hats and signs. They weren't the stone-gray statues of cemeteries and parks, nor the dark-metal monuments to soldiers and heroes.

They were people.

At Dolly's side, Diana leaned on the reinforced plastic wall that was there, Dolly assumed, to protect fans against falls and the park against lawsuits. Diana had a box of red-hot candies tucked in her waistband, like a weapon. One by one, she slid the candy pieces out of the box, placed them in her gloved palm and flicked them at the frozen crowd.

Most of her shots fell far short of her goal. If Dolly squinted, she could make out the oblong candies dotting the courtyard, red splinters against the tan concrete. She thought of asking Diana to switch to a different color—anything but red— but what was the point?

"Why you gotta do that?" Rocker leaned back against the gift-shop glass, arms folded over his chest. "Haven't they been through enough?"

His legs flickered as he practiced camouflaging against the reflective window, denim blue shifting to match the reflected clouds, then the outlines of crimson-clad mannequins on the other side, but never both at the same time. He'd always had trouble with windows and mirrors. Never stopped him from trying.

Diana lined up another shot. "Because it's fun, and there's no one else to torment."

"Just because Jenna's on your nerves doesn't mean you should take it out on them," Rocker said.

Diana flicked the candy out of her palm. This one sailed over the courtyard and dropped straight between the turnstiles, knocking a curly-haired man on the forehead before falling to the ground. It reminded Dolly of a pinball shot. "They don't know the difference."

Dolly wasn't so sure.

"Jenna Carpenter can kiss my ass," Diana continued. "But Sever's obviously a fan. How're we going to get out in front of this?"

She directed the last question to Dolly. As if Dolly knew.

She didn't want to be Sever's minion, but it wasn't the time to antagonize him, either. He was a tool, a means to an end.

This wasn't the old days, where they could preempt any bad behavior from Wave by seizing their powers or framing them for horrific crimes. This wasn't a news story gone awry, a coverup they could fix.

If only Dolly could get the Pearl Knife back, she could end Sever. She could be a hero again.

Dolly shook her head, looking out at the statuesque crowd. It was easy to imagine them cheering for her, falling to their knees to thank her for saving them. She could free them from their prisons. She could stand at the head of LIO again, at the head of the world.

And why not? She'd saved plenty of people in her day. The questionable routes she'd sometimes taken—her daughter might put that in stronger terms—didn't make her deeds less heroic.

Rocker growled in frustration as his long, gray-streaked hair shifted to Nationals red while his arms were mottled with the blue-and-white shades of the sky.

"Don't know why you bother," Diana said. "You should stick with what you've got."

"Excuse me for trying to better myself."

Dolly had her own powers now, whether the Knife had intended it or not. Perhaps she didn't need it. If she could seize other enhanced humans' powers, as she had when she'd wielded the blade, well... That might give her the upper hand.

It might even give her the ability to control Sever's powers. What a boon *that* would be.

Tentatively, Dolly reached out for Rocker's powers. She'd never been able to control Diana's—perhaps because the Knife hadn't bestowed them in the first place—but Rocker's hadn't posed a challenge.

Nothing happened. He was still standing there, completely

unaware of her fumbling as he tried to blend into the window. It made Dolly dizzy to look at him.

She tamped down a wave of disappointment. It had been a stretch, to expect that her abilities might match the Knife's one-for-one. Still, it was a shame. The ability to wrest someone else's powers away from them, to use them for her own, had always been the best part of wielding the Knife. The control it had given her, the power. She hungered for it.

If the Knife had cried into her mind when she did it, well, that had been an annoyance she'd been willing to bear.

"Better yourself," Diana scoffed. For a second, Dolly thought Diana meant her, but the Trap was rolling her eyes at Rocker.

"You're pathetic," Diana said. She lined up another candy shot. This time, instead of lobbing it toward the crowd, she swiveled and flicked it straight at Rocker's face.

Something tugged out of Dolly's gut, like a string pulled taught against her navel.

In the same second, the camouflager vanished.

One moment he was there, struggling to match the layered collage of reflections that lived in the window—and the next he was gone, his body neatly blended into the background. Either camouflaged, or completely invisible. It was too seamless to tell.

Diana actually gasped. Dolly wasn't sure she'd ever known the woman to show surprise, but she couldn't blame her.

"What did you do?" Diana breathed.

Rocker returned, like someone flipping a switch. "I got it," he said. "I finally got it."

"Unlikely," Diana said. She looked at Dolly.

Dolly pressed her palm to her belly. "I think I did that. I increased his powers."

Diana set a hand on her hip. "OK," she said. "Try it on me."

"The Knife could never control your poison."

"You're not the Knife. And you didn't control him. You just... enhanced his enhancements."

"Got a computer virus once from an email that promised to do that," Rocker said.

Diana rolled her eyes so hard, it had to have hurt. She nodded to Dolly. "Try it."

Dolly didn't know what, exactly, she was supposed to try. She *wasn't* the Knife, true; until this moment, that'd been the entire problem.

She'd reached for Rocker's powers, and hadn't found them.

Still, she shrugged and focused on Diana, conjuring a picture of her poison, the feel of it. She imagined that she could breathe the abilities in through Diana's crimson gloves, the vinegar scent, the oil-black texture. Imagining she could manipulate them as she had her husband's, long ago.

Diana gasped again and held up her hands. Black poison gushed through her gloves, dropping to sizzle on the pavement below. She whirled around, facing the courtyard, and thrust her hands over the wall to squeeze her fists.

Poison rushed between Diana's still-gloved hands, thick and malleable in a way Dolly had never seen it. Diana opened her palms and stretched her hands wide, and the poison churned into a waterfall that rushed down to coat the courtyard.

The taste of vinegar coated the inside of Dolly's throat, thick and acidic. "Can you stop it?"

Diana closed her eyes, and the waterfall stopped. "Better than I ever have."

"I can't believe that worked." Rocker sounded sulky, as if annoyed that his trick had been overshadowed.

The poison crawled across the courtyard, molasses-slow, and stopped about halfway to the turnstiles.

Diana grinned and reached for Dolly's shoulder, maybe to squeeze it in triumph, but Dolly held up a hand. "Better not."

Diana winked, rubbing her fingers together, her glee barely restrained. "Right. Right, of course."

To control Diana's powers would have been a boon. But to enhance Diana's powers, without being able to control them herself? The idea made Dolly's stomach turn.

Diana was still grinning, thrilled. Who wouldn't be? She lifted her now-black gloves, looked at them wonderingly. "Well, boss, I'd say this gives us the upper hand."

7 / ELOISE

ELOISE KEPT her gaze leveled at the Committee as Mary's footsteps retreated behind her. She'd memorized everything about the members when the League had arrived, her jangled brain latching onto names and faces as if good manners alone could save her people. In the end, it hadn't mattered. Wave had welcomed them with kindness.

Now, as then, Jian sat in the center of the semi-circle, flanked by Gem and Cole. The youngest and oldest of the group, Fran and Matthew, held up the row like bookends.

The door clicked shut, and still no one spoke. Eloise watched them. If this was a staring contest, she'd take them all down one by one. She'd faced tougher opponents.

The trouble was, they all looked at her as if they'd *also* stared down tougher opponents. Eloise could well believe that; she stood before them bruised and battered from the fight at HQ, eyes stinging from a night spent crying and cursing her mother, and the stars, and, yes, the Pearl Knife.

A bubble of regret chased the thought across her mind, as if the Knife wished to apologize. *Not your fault*, Eloise thought.

It didn't respond.

The silence stretched. As if the Committee had collectively

decided to wait for her to speak. They expected her to repri-
mand them for setting the rules, maybe, or demand a spot on
the Committee for herself. Part of her did want to wheedle
every last secret out of these people.

The decision to come to Wave had been more of an instinct
than anything else. Even now, she wasn't sure if the idea had
been hers or the Knife's—though the blade had definitely been
the one to find the path here.

And after everything that had happened, after living as
enemies for so long, Wave had taken her team in without an
instant of hesitation. Maybe—and this could be her diplomatic
streak talking—she could start by thanking them.

There'd be time to take them to task, later.

Eloise opened her mouth to speak, and Fran let out a sharp
laugh. Eloise would have thought it was triumph, except for the
obvious mirth in Fran's eyes.

Eloise wanted to ask what could possibly be funny, but the
woman was already on her feet, swinging her cane around as
she headed for Eloise. "Jian, be a dear and ask Agnes to meet us
down in cargo, will you? Mary and Bradley can find us there
when they're ready to leave."

Eloise grimaced. She and Agnes weren't on the best of
terms after the scientist had left LIO for Wave. Their interactions since then had been tense, at best. "I don't—"

"We need her," Fran interrupted. "Jian? Would you mind?"

Eloise expected the man to bristle at being asked to do a
favor, but he only chuckled. "Take it easy on her, at least."

On Agnes? Or on Eloise?

Fran looped her arm through Eloise's—like they were old
friends heading out for a stroll—and tugged her toward the
door. "Don't spoil my fun, Jian."

She didn't look like her fun was spoiled. She looked positively *merry*. If foxes could be merry.

Eloise supposed they could. Especially when they'd just captured a nice, fat hen.

Eloise knew little about Fran. She'd been there on the airfield when Sloane first told them about Sever, and she'd refused Wave's help in that fight. Though, to be fair, Eloise had also refused *LIO*'s help. She'd let her anger at Wave rule her decisions, and she'd left Mary and Nathan on their own. Maybe she and Fran had a few things in common, after all.

According to Steve, Fran had also shown up in Berlin to try and recruit him during his separation from the League. And that was all Eloise knew. The end of her knowledge. She couldn't help a twinge of curiosity as she matched Fran's step, out of the Committee's meeting hall and out to the elevator.

The Knife burbled in the back of Eloise's mind, like a brook babbling along. Maybe it was imitating the water. She couldn't say.

It had never sounded like this before. Never felt like this, either, tenuous and distant. It had stopped sparking after the battle at HQ, after it had chipped away at Sever's energy shield, but red-orange cracks still marred its surface.

It was injured. It was sick. And there was nothing she could do about it.

The elevator drifted to a stop, and Fran led the way into a large, open space. The ceilings were low, as she'd have expected on a ship, and there certainly wasn't any cargo.

Agnes was already waiting for them, sitting on the only piece of furniture in the space: a bolted-down table in the far corner. She had a clipboard in her hand and a questioning look on her face. Eloise wondered if Jian had warned her that Eloise was coming with Fran.

She wondered if Agnes would have agreed to come, if she'd known.

"What is this?" Eloise asked.

Fran gave her a sharp look. "Your training, of course. It's been woefully lacking up until this point, unless I'm mistaken."

Practically nonexistent, actually, though Eloise had no intention of letting Fran know that. How would her life be different, had Dolly decided to let go of her past, instead of embracing it? She could have guided Eloise. She could have taught her. Together, they might have figured out the secrets of the Knife.

Now, it felt like it was too late.

"You need a mentor," Fran continued, ignoring Eloise's silence. "I can't afford to push this one down the rank. You're too powerful. So, I'll train you myself."

Agnes slid down from the table and tucked her pen behind her ear. Eloise couldn't help but wonder if she'd known about this plan.

"I'm sorry," Eloise said. "Did you say *you'll* train *me*?"

Fran thumped her cane on the floor. "You heard me. Agnes can help. She'll study the Knife. Help us understand it, so we can heal it. And so we can get rid of its maker before he destroys the world."

Eloise licked her lips. Fran and her people had taken LIO in without argument, had cared for them, and Eloise didn't want to be rude. *Hey, thanks for your hospitality, but the Pearl Knife is kind of a big deal. I don't want to hurt you by mistake.* Fran wasn't a young woman, and while her presence might be imposing, Eloise didn't think she'd last long in a fight.

There wasn't a polite way to say that. Eloise cleared her throat. "I don't think—"

Fran flicked her wrist, and her cane split down the middle. Keeping one hand on the grounded half, she closed the fingers of her left hand around the top of the cane and squeezed.

A pulse of power thrummed out of the cane, pushing Eloise back like a physical hit. She stumbled back, her instincts landing her in a defensive stance as she tried to regain her balance. Legs wide, knees bent, arms half raised as the Knife struggled sluggishly out of its sheath to respond to the attack.

Too slow. She was way too slow. Fran raised her left hand, and the cane—the left half of it, anyway—rose with it, quivering. Either with effort, or like a racehorse ready to break into a run. Eloise tried to send the Knife toward it, but the blade swung wide, leaving her open as Fran continued her assault. She looked like a wizard, leaning on her cane-slash-staff with one hand while calling on the powers of the universe with the other.

The floating half of the cane spun. Fran's fingers danced behind it, and it swung around toward Eloise, whipping through the air with a sharp whistle. The Knife met it halfway, clashing against it with a shower of moon-white sparks.

The staff moved like it was tethered to Fran's fingertips, which gave it a tilted kind of movement. It was floating, yes—Eloise could see the tenuous connection that made Fran want to train her—but it was more like a baton than it was like the Pearl Knife. A party trick.

As Eloise was contemplating how to use that to her advantage, the staff-baton flinched up so it was parallel to the floor. It dipped past the Knife and came straight for Eloise.

Fran stepped forward, moving with fluid grace as she guided the baton. And that was all Eloise had time to register before the baton attacked.

She used a forearm to block, expected the thing to whack her. But when it hit her skin, the baton curled around her arm, holding her in place. Like the world's gentlest lasso.

She had a feeling it would grip much harder if it caught hold of a true enemy.

The Knife stuttered toward her, desperate to help, but Eloise silently urged it to keep its distance.

She pulled against the baton-snake, trying to find a weak point to let her slip out of its grip. But instead of tightening, the thing simply hardened into a coil of wood, spiraled around her arm. She tugged at it, but her arm was locked in midair.

Fran stood close, maybe two paces away, her thumb and forefinger touching.

Eloise nodded, conceding, and Fran released her fingers. The wood softened, rope-like, and slithered back to join the other side of her cane. The Knife breathed such a sigh of relief into Eloise's mind that it felt as if it should have been audible to everyone in the room.

The Knife had understood that they were sparring. It had understood, and yet... And yet, part of it had wanted to protect Eloise at all costs. She soothed it, thanking it for its restraint as much as for its loyalty. Baby steps.

"You use an artifact," Eloise said, breathing hard, her throat burning with the effort of keeping the Knife at bay.

"You have *powers*?" Agnes's voice was practically a squeak.

Eloise had completely forgotten that Agnes was in the room. Excellent. Because the one thing this display needed was a witness to gloat over Eloise's failure.

Although, to be fair, Agnes had never been the gloating type. Even now, she grabbed her pen and started to scribble on her clipboard, curls springing down to curtain her face.

Fran held the cane up for Eloise to see. It had the barest hint of a shimmer on one side, like a strip of mica set into the wood. "We call it magna-stone, which is about the stupidest name anyone could have come up with. But it's descriptive, I suppose."

"It has to stay close to you?" Agnes's pen was still scratching so fast that Eloise expected to see smoke rising from the paper.

"Within about two feet," Fran said.

"And your finger movements control it... how?" Agnes asked.

"It's not psychic, if that's what you're thinking." Fran glanced at the Knife, which had returned to rest at Eloise's hip. Eloise had never really thought of it as 'psychic' before, though she supposed it was as good a description as any for the way it communicated.

Fran lifted her left hand. Each finger had a small black dot just above the nail. As if someone had marked them lightly with a pen.

"Tattoos?" Agnes asked. Always a step ahead.

Fran nodded.

"And they're magnets, too?"

"I told you, the name is stupid," Fran said. "It's not a magnet."

Agnes just looked at her, the question plain on her face. *What is it, then?* Fran tilted her head, like her version of a shrug. "Eloise here isn't the only one with a mysterious artifact." She looked at Eloise, frowning. "And don't go thinking I don't need this cane. My arthritis doesn't care that I've got enhanced abilities."

"I wasn't thinking that," Eloise said. She wasn't thinking anything. She was mostly just gawking.

She'd met precious few people who used artifacts to give them enhanced abilities. The League had encountered one scientist, a couple years ago now, but his experiments had landed his company in deep water.

This... This was something else.

The Knife trickled a sad note into her mind that she didn't know how to interpret. It always sounded sad now.

"It's impressive," Eloise said finally. "Really, it is. But I don't know how you can use your background to train me. The Knife... it's different."

Fran held out her hand, palm up.

"You can't hold it," Agnes said. "No one can, except for El. Eloise."

"Hold it in your hand, then," Fran said to Eloise, sharply, as if she'd been the one to protest. "Your palm shielding mine. Come on now, I haven't got all day."

Eloise thought she just might, but she obeyed the command, anyway. She eased the Knife out of its sheath, place the blade in her open palm, and lay her hand over Fran's. The old woman's skin felt cool and dry against hers.

"There, now." Fran dipped her face toward the Knife. "That wasn't so hard, was it?"

And then, her face melted into a smile. Like she was looking at a kitten, rather than the most feared weapon in the world. Like she was about four seconds from wrapping it in a big hug. Which Eloise would definitely advise against.

"You are a darling, aren't you?" Fran said to the Knife. Definitely to the Knife. "Bit of mischief in there, but we can't fault you for scratching at the furniture, can we?"

Eloise couldn't help it. She exchanged a glance with Agnes, whose parted lips and crinkled brow mirrored Eloise's own confusion. For a second, they might have been back at HQ two years ago, pondering some operation together.

Then Agnes's expression iced over, and she looked away. As quickly as that, the moment passed, while Fran continued to coo at the Pearl Knife.

As for the Knife, it didn't beam confused thoughts at Eloise. No, its response was a warm trickle of honey, sweet and thick.

"It's... I think it likes you," Eloise said.

"Of course it likes me." Fran still spoke like she was gawking over a baby. "No one understands the poor dear. You want to help us understand, don't you?"

The Knife flickered, as if trying to reignite its moon-white glow. And for a second, it almost got there. But the cracks returned in force, shoving the light back with a fizzle of red fire. Eloise flinched, though it was the echo of the Knife's pain that stung; her own skin was untouched.

"Put the poor thing away to rest," Fran said, and Eloise complied. "It's hurt, and we need to find a way to heal it."

Eloise sheathed the Knife, gently. It burbled more gently now, soothed even despite its pain. "We need to heal it," she agreed. "But how?"

"I don't know yet," Fran said. "But I do know artifacts. We'll figure it out together."

Together. It was a nice thought. Still, she couldn't help the tendril of wary suspicion that threaded through her brain. Wave had taken them in so quickly, so easily, and now Fran wanted to train her—and to learn more about the most powerful artifact in the world.

Eloise wanted to trust her, to let her in. But doubt crawled into her chest and sat there, even with the Knife burbling happily in the background.

She wanted a mentor, and badly, but she couldn't afford to make a mistake that would put them all in jeopardy.

"Fine," Eloise said. "Thank you. Truly. But I'm sorry, I'm not fully ready to trust Wave yet."

Agnes hissed out a short breath. "Funny, since you came to *us* for help."

As if there'd been any other choice. Eloise opened her mouth, a retort ready on her tongue, but Fran held up a hand. "Fine, fine. You don't trust Wave, and we can't make you. Understood. Now if you're done wasting time with your speeches and caveats, let's get to work."

AGNES DIDN'T PRETEND to be less than fascinated by the Pearl Knife. Even after her years at LIO, the blade was a mystery. It'd always defied investigation.

Eloise's training session with Fran was nothing short of illuminating, and Agnes had found her eyes flitting back and forth between the two artifact-wielding women like she was watching a tennis match.

She wouldn't have minded some time in the lab with Fran's 'magna-stone,' either.

Yes, the whole situation made her stomach clench with anxiety. Working with Eloise. Trusting Eloise. And housing the League under Wave's roof. But she was a scientist first, and she couldn't ignore her interest in the Knife. She'd always been intrigued by it, even before she'd met Dolly and Eloise, and her time at LIO had only increased that—especially once Eloise had taken over and asked her to study it.

As best she could, anyway. All the sweet talking in the world would never convince the Pearl Knife to let someone other than Eloise touch it.

"Dad was able to hold it over for a few minutes, when he

transferred it to me," Eloise said. "He thought it was because Dolly used it to control his powers for so long."

They'd been working with the Knife for over an hour now, gently, stretching its muscles after its injury. Asking it to test its powers. Asking it questions that Eloise translated, as best she could. At least, Agnes wanted to believe she was telling them everything, though she answered with a confused head shake at least fifty percent of the time. Whether it was genuine, or whether Eloise wanted to hide the truth, Agnes couldn't say.

Most of all, they tried to figure out how they might be able to study it. Despite her proclamation about not trusting Wave, Eloise seemed to have settled into the exercises well enough. At least, she wasn't resisting Fran's suggestions.

"Maybe Dolly's control over Will did give him a connection with it," Fran said. "But Dolly abused poor Will in that manner for years. Longer than anyone else endured such a horror. With apologies to the Knife. It wasn't your fault, darling thing. But I'm not sure it would work for anyone else."

Wave had stepped in to save Will's life by helping him to fake his death. *He* trusted them, at least to an extent, and still Eloise refused to do the same. Agnes wasn't sure anyone had ever been more stubborn.

"Can we test it somehow?" Eloise asked.

"How?" Agnes couldn't filter the sharpness out of her voice. She wasn't sure she would have, even if she could. "By letting you take over our powers?"

Sure, because that didn't sound like a recipe for disaster at all. Dolly hadn't just controlled Will's powers. She'd also used the Knife to take over Wave members' abilities, and to frame them for heinous crimes.

Agnes didn't think Eloise would follow in her mother's footsteps. But she wasn't ready to trust her that far, either.

For her part, Eloise just stood there, hands on her hips, chin lifted. Like it was obvious that everyone should just trust her explicitly, no questions asked.

"Maybe," Fran said. Her favorite word today, apparently. "Let's break for today. You're still recovering, and the Knife needs to rest."

Eloise did look tired, and Agnes thought of the trauma she'd been through over the last few days with a twinge of guilt. Naturally she'd want to do everything she could to face an enemy powerful enough to rip LIO's headquarters to shreds.

It was hard to imagine HQ swallowed by Niagara Falls, even after the stream of news coverage that confirmed what had happened, along with startling aerial images of the falls' new shape. Sever had crushed one of the world's natural wonders, had bent it to fit his needs. She understood the weight of it, the lives that had been lost. And still, it was impossible to picture her old lab, her old room, washed away.

Agnes didn't mean to be unfair to Eloise. It was just... a lot to take in.

Still, when Eloise packed the Knife away and headed for the door, Agnes lingered. She didn't know how to broach the subject, how to raise her concerns, but Wave had done as much for her family as they'd done for Will. Her conscience refused to let her stay silent.

"You can go, too," Fran said. "Unless you've got something to say?"

Agnes narrowly stopped herself from toeing the edge of the sparring mat on the floor. She didn't need to give away her nerves. Still, she hugged her clipboard to her chest. Fran had done more for her than she could articulate. How was Agnes supposed to question her choices?

Fran raised her eyebrows, waiting. Agnes needed to say *something*, so she said, "You evacuated everyone from the island?"

Agnes had been working with some of Wave's operatives there, all of them former LIO prisoners. Quite a few had left by now, either to rejoin Wave's ranks or to retire in peace. A few remained, though. Or they had, until Sever's attacks.

Fran gave Agnes a sharp nod. "Wasn't safe anymore. Not with this Sever marauding around. They're all in the underwater base. Tam and Lucy, too."

Tam wouldn't be pleased about that. Lucy probably would. For an eight-year-old girl, it was like living in an aquarium. "Good," Agnes said. "That's good."

Fran nodded. Agnes didn't leave. The ship swayed under her, and she touched her fingertips to the bolted-down table to keep her balance. She'd forgotten they were on a ship at all, at least for a few hours. She barely noticed, most of the time.

"Is there something else?" Fran asked.

Agnes licked her lips. "It isn't a good idea."

The words spilled out, possibly ill-advised, but definitely unavoidable. If she didn't share her concerns, she'd regret it forever. No matter how many demi-god aliens descended to take over the world.

"What isn't a good idea?" Fran had to know, or guess, but she was going to make Agnes say it. All right. She could do that.

She took a deep breath. Let it out. Tried to sound reasonable, and not biased at all. "Training Eloise. She's dangerous. The Knife is even more dangerous. And hosting the League in the long term, it's not..."

"A good idea?"

Agnes clutched the clipboard, the edges of it digging into her fingers. "Their goals will never align with ours."

"You sound like Matthew."

"Maybe Matthew's right."

Agnes didn't understand the political maneuvers of the Committee yet—assuming she ever would. She didn't know if

Fran and Matthew were rivals, or friends, or both. Or neither. She didn't know *what* she was stepping into.

It didn't matter. Honesty did. If Fran was offended, then she'd just have to be offended.

But the old woman only smiled. It was a sad smile, one that deepened the wrinkles in her forehead just as much as the ones in her cheeks. "It seems to me that Wave and LIO have shared the same goals for some time now. I'll admit I was late to see it."

"What if you're wrong?"

Fran shifted her weight, leaning more heavily on her cane. "If I'm wrong, I think we can at least agree that we all want to get rid of this intergalactic infestation."

Infestation. Sure. And here Agnes had always been sure that visitors from another planet would be advanced enough that they'd want to share resources.

Turned out people were people, even when they were... well, aliens.

Fran was still watching her, waiting for a response. "Yes," Agnes said. "I do think the League wants to deal with Sever."

Fran thumped the cane once on the floor, then started for the elevator. "The way to do that, then, is to study the Pearl Knife. And you're our best chance at understanding it. You know that, yes?"

She did. She knew that. But she'd never been able to collect much data on it in the past, had never made sense of what she did collect. It was hard to believe she'd succeed now.

But Fran was counting on her. So was Eloise, though she'd never admit it.

Agnes had raised her concerns, and Fran had listened. Beyond that, there wasn't much she could do. Stifling a sigh, she nodded. "I'll do what I can."

9 / SEVER

Sever was familiar with the fatigue of punishing a world. He knew the week-long strain that came with crushing a moon to dust. He knew what it was to lie in the dark for a fortnight after wiping a planet out of existence, his head throbbing, his muscles stretched til they might snap from the strain of living.

Until Earth, Sever had never bothered to conquer worlds. He'd never seen the point. What fool wanted to manage that large a court? Worlds were full of countries and geographical divides, each with its own scaffolding, each with politics and bureaucracies and mind-numbing power struggles. To conquer a world was to claim it, and to claim it meant to take responsibility.

But Sever had allowed the Blade of Starlight to escape his grasp, and in doing so, he'd put this Earth in danger. He felt a sense of obligation toward these people.

He'd taken up residence in one of the suites at this strange, grassy colosseum. Not too far from the prisoners, though not in the same cluster, either. As he looked out at the game field, idly trying to understand the uses of the diamond-shaped patch of grass and the hill in the middle, he couldn't help feeling a bit impressed that they'd managed to build all of this with such primitive technologies.

Sever felt no disdain toward developing worlds. No, on the contrary, he often found they were impressively innovative. There was beauty in the gravity-bound dance of the trains, and in the roads that spiraled out from some invisible center to form nonsensical webs. Earth's cars sputtered rancid vapors, spoiling the air, but there was a provincial charm about the way the people still drove them around without a computerized escort.

And their art. Their art was so raw, so emotional. The music, in particular, made him glad Adina had chosen this place, of all places, to hide away. She must have loved the music here. Acoustic strings, plucked and drawn. Breath, so precious to Earthens, expelled from the lungs to make a flute sing. Voices, chanting melodic poetry in every language.

Oh, the Parse Galaxy had its versions these things, to be sure; but there was something about the unpolished harmonies and uneven rhythms that tugged at Sever's soul. It was difficult, he found, not to fall in love with the people who had created them.

These Earthens hadn't hidden Adina away from him, not intentionally. They hadn't risen up to fight him. They hadn't realized he existed at all, and they certainly hadn't known—still didn't know, if the incident at the colosseum's entrance proved anything—that the Blade of Starlight held them prisoner.

Sever was here to set things right. To conquer a world, instead of incinerating it. A new sensation, indeed.

An exhausting sensation, however. He thought the muscle-trembling fatigue of dismantling planets was bad, but this... This was a constant soreness at his temples, burrowing through his mind, into his bones. He'd thought the tiredness would abate after a few days, but it only seemed to dig deeper.

Was it the strain of holding the dome in place, or the rebellious humans outside the gates? Was it simply tiredness from cracking through layers of rock? Or was there something about this Earth, some material in the ground or molecule in the air, that made him weaker?

No matter. He'd grow stronger, over time. It was like developing a new skill, or strengthening a weak muscle.

"I had the kitchen prepare you a sear-weed tonic." Morik's voice was a businesslike clip, floating over from the suite behind Sever to snap him out of his reverie. "As best as they could manage. We brought the ingredients, of course, but the gravity here didn't allow us to mix it to the exact specifications. I've sampled it myself, however, and I believe you'll find it strengthening."

Sever enjoyed a last glance at the field before turning to face his advisor. Morik was bustling around the kitchen like an old grandmother, preparing ice to serve the drink cold. As Sever preferred.

"Sit, my lord," Morik said. "Drink."

Sever thought of protesting the order, but the notion was a childish one. To refuse the tonic on the grounds of his advisor's authoritarian tone would be illogical, and unwise. Sever crossed the room and sat on one of the tall chairs at the bar, nearly flipping his cloak out of the way before he remembered he wasn't wearing one. He'd be more acceptable here, he'd thought, more approachable, if he wore Earthen grab. Still, it was an adjustment. Everything felt so tight.

Morik hadn't made the same choice. He still wore his long robes, gray ones today, with silver lining at the hems. He pushed the tonic across the table and waited for Sever to drink.

The glass was garnished it with a purple leaf, which Sever would have liked to pluck out, but he had the strangest sensation that it would hurt his advisor's feelings if he did.

He left it in. Took a sip. The tonic was a good temperature, the sear-weed well cured. He'd have to thank the cooks for that later. "Rejuvenating," he said. "Thank you."

Morik nodded, the movement crisp and formal. Then he pressed his lips together, frowning slightly, like he wanted to say something.

"You have a report for me?" Sever asked.

Another nod, this one hesitant. "The prisoner's story aligns with what we've found about Mary O'Sullivan," Morik said. "We've been researching her, my lord. She was never in cryo sleep, as far as we can tell. In fact, this world has limited cryo capabilities, if any. In any case, Mary has been documented practically every month of her life since she was a very young child."

Sever had known Adina as a young woman, vivacious and whip-smart, full of life. He'd fallen in love with her, a mere mortal. He'd forged the Blade of Starlight for her so that she could gain powers and join his court.

And she'd thrown it all back in his face. Murdered his friends. Disappeared.

It'd all happened a century ago. Sever had searched for her, punished worlds he believed to have assisted her. Then, unable to locate her, he'd moved on. So why did the wounds still feel so fresh? It wasn't that he desired Mary; something about that felt wrong, as if the years had erected a wall between them. But if Adina had somehow survived in this form, she still needed to face justice.

"Mary might be Adina's twin," Sever said, though that did not explain her age. A clone, perhaps? But why? "And the Blade of Starlight is here. There must be a connection."

The Blade hadn't been stolen until long after Adina's crimes, though he'd never been able to pinpoint the exact date of its disappearance. The date was inconsequential; no matter when it had been stolen, the coincidence was too great to ignore.

He'd always believed that Adina must have had a hand in the robbery. But how? And how had she come to be here, on Earth? And who was Mary to her? To him?

Too many questions. Sever gripped the glass, clenched his teeth together. Too many questions, and too few answers.

Morik's gaze drifted to the glass, as though he feared Sever might break it by accident. "A relative, perhaps?"

A descendant. Yes, it could make sense. The simplest answer was so often the correct one. "Yes." He nodded, certainty replacing his frustration. "Trace it back. Find out who she was."

"And when we do?"

This was what he liked about Morik. No arguments. No protestations. No requests for instructions. Just the assumption that he'd succeed in the task he was given.

Sever took a long swallow of the tonic, willing it to fortify him for the road ahead. "First, we find Adina. In the histories, if not in the flesh. And then we find someone who remembers."

Now that she had a plan, a mission to bring her closer to rescuing Nathan, Mary wanted to resist every delay.

But a recently dislocated shoulder and a messed-up collarbone would definitely keep her from rescuing him, so instead of rushing off to storm Nationals Park, she allowed Bradley to lead her to the infirmary. He ushered her in, said something about collecting supplies, and skittered off down the hall before she had time to ask any questions.

The infirmary had a pair of exam tables, a bunch of bolted-down cabinets, and a single bed stashed in the corner. It smelled like rubbing alcohol, mixed with the ever-present salt of the sea. Rajni, the League's water-wielding recruit, was lying on the bed when Mary entered, knees to her stomach, arms crossed over her chest. There were strands of hair poking out of her long braid.

"Hey," Mary said, still hesitating in the doorway—Dr. Gordon wasn't there yet, and she half wanted to go looking for him. She couldn't afford to wait. But if she went looking, and he came back here, she'd lose even more time.

Rajni didn't respond. Mary stepped further into the room,

shutting the door behind her, and headed for the exam table closest to Rajni's bed. "You OK?"

The recruit nodded, but there were tears tracking down her cheeks. She was grieving her friend—she and Tally had been close—and Mary didn't think anything in the infirmary could help her. She wondered if the girl had eaten since they'd arrived here. Or slept.

She patted the girl on the arm, unsure of what to say—what words could comfort someone who'd lost a best friend?—and sat down on the exam table to wait for Dr. Gordon.

Unfortunately, the doctor's healing powers weren't the kind that worked instantaneously. Even when he finally bustled into the room, he didn't simply snap his fingers to weave her shoulder back together. He studied the x-rays the other Wave doctors had taken when she'd first arrived. He combed his fingers along her skin, assessed her pain level, and stopped frequently to listen to some unheard magical beacon in the air.

Or something. It was undoubtedly more scientific than that —Agnes would be able to explain it—but to Mary it just looked like the doctor was gazing into space for several minutes before getting back to his work.

Still, his powers were remarkable, and after a few excruciatingly slow hours, her shoulder and collarbone were pain free. It felt as if someone had lifted a heavy burden from her shoulders, one she hadn't quite realized she was carrying.

"I know you're headed out on a mission," the doctor said, glasses slipping to the end of his nose as he spoke, "but make sure to drink lots of water. And rest when you get back, for goodness' sake. Your body worked hard to heal itself so fast."

Mary thanked him, took the water bottle he shoved into her hands, and didn't argue, even though her body felt better than it had in days. She hesitated on the way out, casting a last glance toward Rajni, but there wasn't anything she could do to help the recruit. Dr. Gordon's expertise would have to be enough.

With the marathon healing session finished, Mary went to find Bradley—who was puzzling over every single piece of technology in Wave's extensive lab, no matter how minuscule. He should have had ample time to select what he needed while Dr. Gordon had stitched her back together. Instead, he was staring and frowning, picking up one gadget just to put it down and grab another. Over and over and over.

On a normal day, this process would have had her yanking out drawers and investigating every gadget, with as much interest as Bradley's. Probably more.

But there'd be time for playing with tech later, when she had Nathan back. He'd smile at her focus and lean on the table at the end of the room, doing his best to follow along with her excited explanations. He'd ask smart questions, and he'd tease her with that half smile she loved so much. The image squeezed her stomach so hard, she thought she might implode.

Today, the lab was only a delay that made her want to whack Bradley on the head with one of his boots. No matter how much she glared at him, he didn't bother to hurry as the engineers advised him at length about which meters and goggles and microwave readers might help him—and them—to better understand Sever's powers. And Mary's resistance of them.

That was the mission. She understood it. But she also wanted to get going already.

Finally, Bradley clipped and buckled and strapped his selections to his person—Mary was almost surprised when none of them went into the galoshes—and gave her a nod.

Mary restrained herself from making a comment about his meticulous shopping habits. The guy *was* helping her. No need to be a jerk.

"Is that what you're wearing?" Bradley asked, looking her up and down.

So much for withholding snide comments. She had on athletic pants and a soft black shirt, plus a tool belt she'd secured at her waist. Her hair was wrapped up in a tight bun.

Mary scowled at Bradley, anyway. "You had something else in mind?"

"You have to pretend you're there for a fight," Bradley said. "Like you're there to save the world, and not just your boyfriend."

"I'm aware of what the mission is, thanks."

Bradley curled his shoulder toward his ear. A twitch, or a shrug. Hard to say. "I'm just saying that it seems like *Coral* should be the one to do that."

"Which would be much easier if I actually had access to her stuff. But I don't."

"Oh." Bradley shrugged off his backpack and tossed it over to her. "I had these liberated from one of your safe houses."

Mary decided not to ask how he'd found one of her safe houses. Because inside the backpack, she found Coral's outfit, complete with her usual selection of tools: darts and stunners, and her grapple. She might have cried in relief, had relief not been impossible right now.

Mary looked at Bradley, who didn't look smug or teasing. He merely looked curious, like he planned to measure her reaction. "You could have just said 'I have Coral's stuff.'"

Bradley lifted a finger, and an eyebrow. "Never miss an opportunity to suss out an emotional block, Coral."

By the time Mary had changed into Coral's outfit, the sun was sinking toward the horizon, coating the ocean in a bloody film of red light. Eloise waited on the upper deck with Bradley, and it seemed to Mary that she stood a bit taller than she had earlier. She still looked tired, the corners of her eyes pinched, but there was hope in them now rather than raw despair. That was something, anyway.

"Red sky at night, sailor's delight," Bradley said, when Mary joined them.

"If you wait a few days, I can join you," Eloise said. "It's dangerous. Are you sure—"

"We'll be back in a jiff," Bradley interrupted, though Eloise had clearly been speaking to Mary. "Can't save the world without a little intel, now, can we?"

Eloise's mouth was set in a firm line. She knew it. "First portal is to the pitcher's mound, Mary. Then I'll let Bradley out in the concourse so he can watch."

"And measure," Bradley said.

With any luck, Sever would think they'd only opened the one portal. He'd feel its resonance, if Mary understood his connection to the Knife—Dolly might, too—but hopefully they could mask their intentions and outsmart him.

And if not, well, Mary was good at improvising.

"We rendezvous at the first-floor concession stand in one hour," Eloise said. "Don't miss the portal, or I won't know where to find you."

Bradley saluted, punctuating it with a grin that was almost charming. Mary hadn't figured the guy out yet. She wasn't sure she wanted to.

Eloise nodded. And then, she cut a hole through the universe.

It was strange, would always be strange, to be standing in one place—like the deck of an ocean liner—and look through a window to the other side of the world. From sunset-inflamed waves to the center of a darkened baseball field, a sea of empty seats looking on in shadowed silence.

Humid heat encased her as she stepped out onto the pitcher's mound, a shock after the cool ocean wind. The air felt heavy, thick, like it was an effort for her body just to draw it in and sort out the oxygen she needed. Sweat beaded immediately along her hairline, and her long sleeves felt like a major mistake. Yes, Coral's outfit was breathable, but that assumed there was something to breathe in the first place.

The stadium hummed around her, electricity and tentative city noises replacing the wash of the waves at sea. Mary had worked alone, once upon a time. With the League's backing, sure—well, most of the time—but happy to strike out on her own agenda when it suited her.

Now, she was used to allies. Eloise, the recruits, even Dawn Kimble and the enhanced humans they'd rescued from Philadelphia. And Nathan. Always Nathan.

She didn't want to be here alone.

The stadium lights flashed on, a blinding shatter of white that instantly made the park feel even warmer, though that was probably psychological. Mary squinted, shading her eyes against the light with one hand.

Sever stood at home plate, looking both casual and strange in blue jeans and a green polo shirt. Like if she pitched him a fastball, he might actually pick up a bat and try to hit it.

Human, only not. She couldn't see the sparks of orange in his eyes from this distance, but she remembered them well enough.

"Opposing teams," Mary said. "Symbolic."

Sever folded his hands together and dropped them to his waist. Did she unsettle him? She needed to get him to use his powers on her, or try, but he didn't seem the type to keep banging his head against a wall without any hope of breaking through.

"I don't know the game, myself," he said. "Perhaps you're here to teach me?"

Aware that Eloise's clock was ticking back on the yacht,

Mary flipped her stunner out of her belt and flicked it on, as though she was ready to fight. How did one take on a demi-god, anyway, and how authentic did she need to be here?

Sever actually frowned at the sight of the stunner, like a teacher with a misbehaving student. "I'm disappointed. I thought you'd come to talk."

"You kidnapped the man I love, so I feel like that's a nonstarter."

He opened his hands, held his palms out. Like an innocent bystander, like someone wrongly accused of heinous crimes. "Come, Mary. You know I won't harm him."

"Sure, because I trust a guy who crumbles entire planets when he's feeling cranky." It was difficult to keep her words light, hard to reach for even the barest level of humor. It was her defense, her shield, but this wasn't hyperbole anymore; it was a distinct possibility.

Mary licked her lips, glancing around. No doubt LIO's retirees were up there somewhere in the shadowed stands. Hopefully Bradley could avoid them.

If she looked carefully, would she catch sight of Nathan? This place was enormous; he could be anywhere.

She made herself drop her gaze to focus on Sever. She needed to pay attention. He'd called her Mary; maybe he was starting to catch on. "Does this mean you admit I'm not this Adina?"

He tilted his head, a dark lock of hair tumbling over his forehead. "I'm entertaining the possibility."

"Where's Nathan?" The words slipped out of her like they were someone else's, raw and desperate and not at all the controlled version of Coral she needed to be. Coral had been cool, aloof. Trusted by law enforcement... mostly. Feared, certainly. And admired.

The only independent operative without enhanced abilities, at least back then, but just as powerful in her own way.

That version of Coral hadn't been in play for a year. Maybe more. And Mary had done more to strip away that identity than Jenna, Wave, and the retirees combined.

"One-track mind," Sever said, black hair drifting when he shook his head, as if it answered to a different law of physics. "He's comfortable. Only the best accommodations, I assure you."

She couldn't stop herself from scanning the stands behind him, and the concourse beyond, trying to work out whether he'd just given her a clue—or a distraction. She could practically feel Bradley willing her to focus, to provoke Sever into using his powers on her.

Could she resist *all* his powers, or just that freezing trick? And could she trust Bradley to get her out of here if she ended up in a bind?

Maybe it would have been better to wait until El could've come along, after all.

Too late now. Mary aimed her stunner at Sever like she meant to shoot, at the same time withdrawing her dart gun from her sleeve. Had to make it look real, and all that. Besides, there was a possibility—a slight one—that she *could* take him down, that she could save Nathan and avenge Tally and get them all out of this before anyone else got hurt.

Stranger things had happened.

The thought flashed across her mind, then died as Sever sidestepped the dart with ease. As though the laws of time, as well as physics, didn't apply to him.

When he moved, he left an image of himself behind.

Mary blinked, and the image flickered back to Sever. And then there were a hundred of him, a thousand. One for every base, a row in the dugout, a thousand in the seats. When she risked a glance behind her, a dozen of him crewed the outfield.

"I thought you didn't understand the game," Mary said, dizzy, as the second-base Sever took off as if to steal third.

"I believe I'm beginning to."

When he spoke, they all spoke. The voices echoed around her, choking her ears, making her want to clap her hands over them.

"Your powers don't work on me," Mary said, though this one clearly did.

The Severs laughed.

Let them. Mary gritted her teeth and strode for home plate. When she got there, she thrust her stunner into the first vision. It saw her coming—if it had working eyes of its own—but did nothing to stop her; when the electrodes hit it, the vision dissolved, taking the rest with it.

The real Sever stood up in the stands—how he'd gotten there so quickly, she didn't know—with ghosts of his visions flickering around him like wisps of smoke. She didn't know if Bradley, or the retirees, or anyone else could still see them all. She only knew that she could focus on the real one.

Mary leapt over the rail and bounded up the steps, dodging past the row of seats behind home plate. The most expensive seats in the place, except for the VIP boxes.

The VIP boxes. Those *would* be the best accommodations. Had Sever given her a real hint about Nathan's whereabouts, though? Or was he misleading her? Even without using his powers on her, he could trap her here easily enough.

She still had forty minutes before El's rescue portal. It was impossible to tell if he was still trying to freeze her—or worse—but she'd defeated the visions. That should have given Bradley plenty of information to bring back to the yacht.

So Mary decided to change the plan.

Instead of attacking Sever where he stood, she released her grapple hook, shot it over Sever's head, and rappelled up to the next level.

She'd have felt a lot better about that choice if she hadn't been able to hear him laughing.

When she pulled herself up over the rail, she found herself in a narrow bank of seats with a row of VIP suites behind them. But when Mary looked up, she could see rows of tinted windows gleaming above her at every level below the press box. If Nathan was really in one of those rooms, how was she supposed to find him?

She took a guess that he'd be higher, that the narrow balconies above would be better for keeping a prisoner. She was grasping at straws, desperate, but she ignored the thrumming doubt that urged her to find Bradley and get out of here. She hooked her grapple on the railing above, trying not to feel unsettled by the fact that Sever wasn't bothering to pursue her.

Mary's grapple line lifted her halfway to the next level before it jammed, lurching to stop so abruptly that she nearly lost her grip. She clung to the handle and shook the line, trying to work the wire back into motion while dangling five feet off the ground. Not a murderous distance, unless she landed very wrong—which she wouldn't—but not a pleasant one either, especially given the concrete steps below.

Not to mention the vengeful alien demi-god.

Mary gave up and started to climb the wire, wishing she'd added gloves to Coral's outfit after the outing of her identity. The heat made her palms sweat, forcing her to grip the wire with extra strength to keep from slipping.

It might've been smarter to drop. To cut the loss of the grapple, easily replaced, and rendezvous with Bradley.

But now that she was here, the thought that Nathan could be just a few feet away, and that she could leave this place without him—it was too unbearable. So Mary kept climbing, hand over hand, until her fingers wrapped around the upper rail.

As soon as they did, a pair of crimson-gloved hands closed over her knuckles. Familiar, wretched pain shot through her fingertips, like she'd dowsed them in hot oil.

And then the Trap's face appeared from over the rail. "Nice to see you, Mary," she said. "Why don't you join us?"

11 / NATHAN

Nathan hadn't wanted her to come. He hadn't wanted her to come, and yet... And yet he couldn't help rejoicing, relief coursing through his veins and filling his lungs with so much fresh air that he hadn't quite realized the extent of the tension in his chest—or its cause. Mary was alive, and she was here.

And it was inevitable, really, that she'd not only come, but had shown up in the middle of the field to taunt Sever from the pitcher's mound. Nathan couldn't hear what Mary was saying to the alien, whose figure was gloriously lit by the stadium lights. But from the window of the VIP suite, he could certainly see them both. Prime seats, indeed.

The sight of her made him ache.

He didn't see Eloise, or Ire, or any of the others, but Sever must think they were here; he'd called Jenna out of Nathan's suite, though Monster was still pacing outside the doors, left alone to guard the prisoners in the nearby suites. If Sever feared Mary had enough backup to mount a rescue, then surely she *had* backup. Surely she wouldn't come alone.

If rescue was here, as he had to hope, then it was here sooner than Nathan had anticipated. But the League knew better than to take action without a plan. For all her impulsiveness, *Mary* knew better.

Nathan didn't want to consider what this might be if it wasn't a rescue, so he had to get to the other prisoners, whoever they were. He needed to make sure they made it out of here, too.

Even with his mind made up, his body felt sluggish. Slow to respond. It didn't help that he wanted to keep his eyes on Mary, that some panicky node in his brain was screaming irrationally for him to watch. As if he could protect her simply by bearing witness.

Nathan forced himself to turn away from the window, and away from Mary, to look around at the suite. He'd checked the bathroom this morning, searching for an easy route through the ceiling or vent to the next suite over. No luck. And there hadn't been a chance to examine the rest of the space, not with Jenna watching.

Now, free of Jenna's gaze, Nathan investigated the kitchen. He tugged the refrigerator a few inches away from the wall to see if the appliances connected in some mysteriously helpful way.

They didn't, that he could see. But then, he wasn't an electrician.

He checked under the sink. He opened every cabinet, every drawer, but no secret passageways jumped out at him.

If he were Mary, he'd probably find a way to use the televisions. Connect to the other prisoners with Bluetooth, turn on their screens, send them a message.

If he were Ire, he'd just bust through the window. But Nathan didn't have super strength, and besides, if he didn't end up leaving here today, he'd want to pretend he hadn't found a way out of the room.

If Eloise were here, she'd use the Knife to cut a secret hole through it. Agnes Jenson could probably just disappear the glass altogether.

But Nathan was the guy who'd tailed Coral because he'd paid attention, who'd discovered her identity. He'd been keeping up with the League for a year now, and there had to be more he could do.

Not enhanced abilities, maybe. But abilities nonetheless. He just needed to think, to observe.

Nathan stepped up to the window, resting his elbow on the bar. A nice place to watch baseball. An unnerving way to watch this play. Mary was so close, it made his stomach clench. How could he help?

He touched the glass, as if he could reach out and help Mary from here, and his fingertips landed on a rough spot on the window. He looked down.

There was a hole in the door, about at shoulder level. The shapes of two holes, actually though they'd been sealed shut with glass—or, more likely, plastic. It took a moment of rubbing his thumb over the raised section to realize that this had once been a door, with a handle attached to the holes.

Now, blue-backed seats edged the windows from rail to rail. But once upon a time, there'd been an exit here. Maybe a balcony for suite members, maybe an extended seating section. Instead of replacing the door, they'd simply repurposed it.

Nathan examined the crease where this panel of the window met the next one. Instead of smooth frames, there were hinges.

On the field, Sever multiplied, and Nathan paused, staring out at the multitude of polo-shirted aliens that now populated the diamond. And the stands. He blinked, but they remained, each appearing to move independently of the others. It had to be an illusion, a manipulation, and yet he couldn't stop himself from taking a step back. One Sever was more than enough trouble. Hundreds? *Thousands*, maybe? He recoiled at the very thought of it, his brain rebelling against the images. But no matter how he rubbed his eyes, they remained.

Mary threw herself across the field and launched a stunner into the closest Sever, but it didn't make any difference that Nathan could see.

The Severs all watched her move, and he wondered if she could see them all, or if this ability, too, failed to affect her.

Mary charged into the stands, moving out of Nathan's view.

Nathan paused, watching Sever—the Severs—for a moment. Why resort to illusions when he could control people with a flick of his fingers? Mary had resisted his powers before, yes, but he must still have a way to use them, to throw stadium seats at her or whip the dust into her eyes. In comparison to the bone-cracking horror show he'd put on at the restaurant—never mind the Niagara Falls-cracking show at HQ—the illusions seemed... unimpressive.

Nathan wasn't sure what it meant. Maybe Sever was hesitant to hurt Mary. Or maybe, just maybe, he was weaker than he'd been.

Nathan didn't know, so he filed the observation away. There wasn't time to figure it out now; Mary was coming. He needed to get out of here, to find the others. To help her. He turned his attention back to the window that had once been used as a door.

Sever might know about it. His people might have rigged it with alarms, or with poisonous gas. But Nathan didn't think so. He didn't think they'd been here much longer than a day, and he'd almost missed it himself. It was his safest bet. He gave the window an experimental push; it didn't budge.

But of course the door would be difficult to open. It would be secured to the other side of the frame. He was thinking too slowly. He shook his head, but the constant pain seemed to have settled over his mind, clouding his thoughts.

A closer investigation showed that the door was indeed sealed with rubbery material, probably to weather-proof the gap. It might be soldered together underneath the rubber, and then he'd be back to square one, but there was only one way to find out.

Nathan cast a glance over his shoulder before kneeling in the corner. He started to pick at the weather proofing with his nail. Not easy to pull apart, but a quick trip to the kitchen put a metal spoon in his hands. A knife might have been better, but they'd removed those, and he didn't need a sharp point to remove the strip. Once he teased up the end, it was easy enough to peel away.

Nothing was soldered in place. There was a slip of a gap between the glass and the wall, perhaps an eighth of an inch thick, and a black coating of weather proofing stuffed into the other side. He cleared it away and gave the door an experimental nudge.

It moved.

With a last furtive glance at the suite's main door—Monster could burst in any moment, though Nathan hadn't been making any noise to speak of—Nathan wedged the door open.

It didn't open far before it hit the back of the stadium seat in front of it. But it opened just enough for him to squeeze through the door and out into the open air.

The hot, humid air. But still, it was *free* air. Nathan dropped to a crouch behind the seat, hoping Sever—and any allies he had out here—was too distracted to notice. He waited, breathing as silently as he could, but no one came to yank him to his feet, and none of his bones cracked in half. So far, so good.

He could hear Mary's grapple working, the zip of the wire.

He couldn't see her anymore, couldn't tell if she was on his level, or somewhere above him. Hopefully, Monster was still guarding the common entrance to all the suites—which meant that Nathan needed to move left to find the prisoners who shared the area.

Still gripping the spoon, he started to crawl, the concrete warm and a little sticky under his fingers. The air smelled like sweet flowers and river water, and—ever so faintly—popcorn.

Nathan shuffled behind the seats, feeling like a kid misbehaving in church as he kept his head down and tried not to bump the seatbacks. He could almost see the wave of motion that would create, the attention it would draw.

Somehow, miraculously, he made it to the next suite over. With the windows tinted near black, he couldn't see inside, couldn't tell if the other prisoners were still guarded inside the room. Or if this was even their suite. They might be in the next one, or the one after that. They might not exist at all.

Only they did. He was sure of it. Who would Sever have brought here? Another League member? Someone from Wave?

Sounds of fighting echoed from above, and Nathan risked tapping on the window.

There was a pause—a long one, too long—and he considered climbing the rafters and going up to help Mary. She had to be fighting Sever's allies, unless it was her backup—she *had* to have backup—but his job was to help Sever's other prisoners. His job was to be ready.

Finally, a tentative knock responded to Nathan's, a flutter of a sound that he might have missed had he not had his fingers on the glass.

It could be Monster, or Jenna. It could be Diana.

Nathan dug his trusty spoon into the weatherproofing strip and edged up the corner, then pulled it up carefully. It took some tugging to get it to detach at the top without having to stand and reach up, but whoever the prisoner was, they seemed to have caught on, because another set of fingers started to assist him from the other side.

It felt like forever, to the soundtrack of a distant fight clanging and thumping above him. Every second he pursued the other prisoners was a moment he wasn't helping the woman he loved. His fear for her was like a living thing, writhing and screaming for him to abandon his quest.

But his faith in her had to be stronger. In his current state—injured, foggy—he could help her most by securing Sever's other prisoners.

Time seemed to stretch as he stripped the weatherproofing away, but it was only a few seconds before the door cracked open, allowing him to slide inside and close the door on the sounds of Mary's fight.

The man on the other side of the door had closely cut hair and deep wrinkles etched across his forehead, but his severe expression lightened when he saw Nathan. "I know you," he said. "You're with the League."

Nathan nodded, and the man stepped aside to let him all the way into the room.

When he saw the other prisoners, he understood the man's protective stance, and the need for a guard outside the door. The severe man was a bodyguard. Secret Service, most likely.

The older, gray-haired man in the chair rose when his bodyguard stepped aside. Trusting, apparently, that the military-looking man had his best interests in mind. And, Nathan supposed, that any threat would come through the door that Sever controlled.

Nathan nodded to the President of the United States, though he couldn't help the confusion of angry feelings that crowded into his head. This man was partially responsible for the situation they were in, with his anti-enhancement policies and his endorsement of the EAEA.

President Caldwell nodded back, looking almost as hesitant as Nathan felt. Vice President Grafton stood behind him, hands balled into fists as if ready to fight if she must. "I thought you were a prisoner, too," Caldwell said. "Are you here to rescue us?"

12 / DOLLY

DOLLY DIDN'T KNOW how Mary had managed to press through Sever's crowd of illusions. It made her dizzy to watch them, so many versions of him piling on top of one another. She looked down on the scene from the open-air press box, just a collection of empty desks in whitewashed cubicles, and she watched Mary's progress nervously. She could taste the Knife's recent closeness on the air, sweet and biting. Like sugar-coated static on her tongue.

Sever preferred for Dolly to stay hidden, as she was the only person here with the ability to create portals. And Dolly certainly had no wish to face Mary, who was sprinting up the center of the stands with her grapple clutched in one hand.

She had no wish to deal with Sever's clones, either. Were they solid? Would they stay? Or were they like holograms, or optical illusions? They certainly looked like funhouse versions of the alien, with their rainbow of polo shirts, many of them wearing bright red Nats caps. Was that Sever's sense of humor, or his weak grasp on Earth fashions?

Not for the first time, Dolly wondered if Sever's earthly form was a true representation. His real form could be a giant, three-stories tall, or a tentacled alien. For all she knew, he might be a dragon.

Down in the stands, Mary shot her grapple and rocketed up, only to meet Diana.

It was too bad, really, that Mary was so predictable. Dolly hated to use her as a test, but she needed to explore the limits of her new abilities. Closing her eyes, she squared her shoulders and reached for Diana's poison.

13 / MARY

As far as Mary had seen, Diana Morton could never do things the easy way.

Instead of simply letting Mary's stinging fingers lose their grip, Diana seized her by the wrists and hauled her up to the narrow walkway above. The narrow strip of concrete ran between a set of tinted windows and the rail Mary had been hanging onto. No seats here, just unimpeded views for the VIPs.

Pain radiated up her arms from her hands as Diana dropped her, but she caught hold of the railing instead of crumpling to the ground. Her suit protected the rest of her, for now, and she could handle a few blisters on her hands. As long as Diana didn't smack her in the face, she'd be good for long enough to escape.

Still, she'd much rather have fallen to the level below. Dealing with a broken bone would be so much better than dealing with the Trap.

Diana cracked her knuckles. "I don't know how many times I need to put you in your place."

"Funny," Mary said, "I was just thinking the same thing."

Diana lunged for her, and Mary used the rail to swing her

legs up and over the Trap's head. Inertia carried Diana forward, and Mary's heels landed on her back, sending her sprawling across the concrete.

Diana was back on her feet in mere seconds, her chin dotted with beads of blood. She held up her hands like a boxer, ready for the next round.

Mary didn't run from fights. But Diana reveled in them.

Mary rushed her, feinting with her right arm as though she meant to throw Diana over the rail. Instead, she surged close enough to knee Diana in the hip, throwing her into the tinted glass behind them. Which didn't even crack. Did they make the stuff bullet-proof or something? She could imagine Nathan standing on the other side, palms pressed against the window. Mere inches away.

Diana bounced back, landing solidly on her feet without so much as a stumble. "You can't beat me, Mary. I'm not the enhanced human I was."

"Oh yeah? You seem like the same washed-up has-been I've always known."

Usually, an insult like that would turn Diana's face red with rage. Instead, she smiled, a long, sour stretch of her pale lips. "That's where you're wrong. I've been reborn."

Mary had no idea what that was supposed to mean. "What, are you saying Sever souped-up your powers? Because again, not seeing much difference."

Diana grinned. "Someone did."

There wasn't time to work out the woman's cryptic ramblings. Diana strode toward Mary, hands held wide—like a sorceress, calling on her dark magic—and poison streamed from her fingertips in thick black waves. Not in the usual water-gun-obeying-the-laws-of-physics kind of way, but in arching droplets that looked as if they'd been caught by a slow-motion camera. Little spiraling missiles, they defied gravity to push up against the atmosphere. They looked too heavy to fly, yet they managed it. How?

And they were thicker, much thicker. The rancid vinegar scent felt close to overwhelming her, like the fumes might kill her before the poison even touched her skin. It was the same, but new: the Trap's power unleashed in unthinkable horror.

Mary couldn't fight this. Not by herself.

If she was going to help Nathan, she needed to survive. And she needed to stay free.

As the first drop of poison sizzled against her the back of her hand, she stumbled back, looking for the closest escape.

14 / ELOISE

ELOISE PACED on the yacht's deck for the full hour, trying to breathe deeply, trying not to imagine what Mary was dealing with at the baseball park. Eloise shouldn't have allowed her to go in alone, with only Bradley for backup, but the fact was that they needed the information Mary'd gone to gather. Without it, they couldn't possibly risk all their resources in a full-on attack.

If Mary didn't come back... But Eloise couldn't allow herself to follow that train of thought. If Mary didn't come back, it might well mean Sever's victory.

Finally, the timer buzzed in her pocket, and Eloise slashed the fastest portal she'd ever slashed before. The Knife itself pulled her hand along eagerly, as if it, too, were desperate for answers.

The air parted, and Bradley came running through the portal.

Eloise's heart seized. She hadn't spent much time with Bradley, it was true. But in the time she had, she'd never seen him run like that, a mad dash, his eyes wide and wild.

"Where's Mary?" she asked. It wasn't possible to keep the breathless panic out of her voice. She didn't even try.

Bradley crouched, breathing hard, and began divesting

himself of all the gadgets he'd brought along with him, arranging them in neat lines on the deck. But for all his attempted normalcy, his hands were shaking. "Trying to save Nathan Pearce, of course."

Eloise cursed. Of course. Yes, of course she was. "Where?"

"On top of the VIP boxes. It's very dramatic."

"Which VIP boxes? There must be rows of them."

Bradley splayed a hand across his chest, obviously still working to catch his breath. "Apologies, I was running too hard to see more details." He actually sounded sorry, too. A puzzling man.

Praying the Knife could handle one more mission before resting for the night, Eloise opened another portal.

MARY TRIED to ignore the drops of hot poison that pattered against her back, Coral's suit the only thing protecting her against a rainfall of painful death. Already, she could feel them sizzling through the tough fabric, working their way toward her skin. And after Bradley had gone to all that trouble to get her the suit, too. Just one more grudge to hold against Diana.

Unable to work out a decent escape without her grapple, Mary worked her dart gun free of her belt. If only Diana had decided to meet her on the next level down, she'd have been able to duck behind one of the seats. For about thirty seconds, until the poison melted it into a puddle.

At least Diana's love of the dramatic was slowing her down. She just *had* to attack Mary with an elaborate waterfall of poison, showing off with a gushing lacework of oily fluid that writhed out of her arms in a shining wave. From what Mary could tell, she could let loose a monsoon at any moment. And melt Mary into a puddle of nothing.

Fortunately, the Trap liked to toy with her victims.

Mary took a shot with the dart gun, and Diana snapped her fingers, collecting the dart in a petroleum-black sphere of poison. So much for knocking her out. She definitely had *not* been able to do that before.

On the level below, a silver portal split the air. One of El's; Mary must have missed the deadline, and now El was searching for her, trying to find the right place to cut her an escape hatch.

The edge of the portal expanded, but Mary had to look away as Diana's footsteps scraped toward her. Another volley of poison came for her, a rancid rainstorm, and Mary spun, ducking as the poison spattered against her back, splashing up to sear the back of her neck.

Pain lanced across her spine, sending a kaleidoscope of red and gray spots spinning across her vision. She tried to step forward, to stand and face her enemy, but she lurched instead, losing her balance. She steadied herself with a hand to the pavement, breathing deep. Diana's poison was everywhere, the air thick with acidic rot.

"Your problem, Mary, is that you never quite think things through." Diana stood tall, her smirk taking up half her face. "Look at you. You came here by yourself, didn't you? You thought you could win. Is this really where it ends? How anti-climactic."

Still half crouched, Mary staggered for the rail, doing her best to pretend that she'd lost control of her body. Not so far from the truth, really. At the last moment, she wrapped her stinging hands around the metal and swung herself over.

Just as the portal zipped out of sight, leaving her dangling, her hands smarting painfully.

Diana laughed, gleeful. "You can't stop yourself from fighting. It's so beautifully predictable."

She appeared above the rail as the air split once again, this time right beneath Mary's feet. It was satisfying, really, to see Diana's eyes widen in shock as the portal opened in midair.

Trusting El, Mary let go of the rail and let herself fall.

Gravity pulled her through the door in the sky and then twisted, sending her sprawling horizontally across the deck of the yacht. Her stomach turned, confused by the shifted vantage point.

The portal zipped shut, leaving Diana and her speeches far behind. The scent lingered, though, the poison eating through Mary's clothes, her skin, and she peeled the fabric away with stinging hands, leaving her in a tank top and leggings.

Eloise knelt beside Mary, the Pearl Knife in her hand. The cracks in the Knife's surface were back, pulsing an orange-red glow. Mary somehow felt like it was breathing hard, panting from the effort. She had the strange desire to pat it, to thank it for a job well done. But she was already in enough pain. No need to add the Knife's bite to her injuries.

"I didn't know you could do that," Mary said, flicking her ragged suit to the deck. "Open a portal in the other direction."

Eloise gave her a wry smile and offered her a hand to help her to stand. "Neither did I."

Lucky. Mary cringed at the pressure on her fingers, but she got up, anyway. "Hey, at least you can trust me to challenge you. Push you to new heights."

Eloise was just looking at her, brow creased, so she attempted a smile. And failed, miserably. She'd left Nathan behind, locked up somewhere in that stadium. She'd *lost*.

But she needed to get to the infirmary. This time, she wouldn't argue about any delays. She only hoped Dr. Gordon had a way to counteract Diana's poison. Before she could take a step in that direction, however, she noticed Bradley. He was sitting cross-legged on the deck, a pile of discarded tech by his knee, and she needed to know what he'd found before she could submit herself to Dr. Gordon—and probably bed rest, too.

For all his obsession with equipment and measurements,

Bradley seemed entirely distracted by a single strip of metal. A familiar one, to Mary at least, but not one he'd found in any Wave lab.

Bradley held the strip up to the light, turned it over in his hand.

"What is that?" Eloise asked.

"It looks like Sloane's tech," Mary said. She'd had a chance to look it over when they'd been working, briefly, with Sloane and her friends. The non-evil aliens from Sever's galaxy. "Hers flipped out into a kind of a tablet. Who does this belong to?"

"Sever's right-hand alien," Bradley said. "Morik, I think?"

Mary doubted there was a single relevant fact that drifted past Bradley's attention. She said, "Yes, Morik. Was that your actual mission, or did you get your measurements?"

"Well, both," Bradley said. "I got the data I needed immediately. Thank you for the extra time, incidentally. I was counting on it."

Mary narrowed her eyes. She didn't like the idea that Bradley had anticipated her deviance from their mission. Especially since she hadn't intended to do it until she was actually there. "I'm telling the Committee about this."

"By all means. It was their idea."

Of course it was.

Eloise sighed. "Well, they did say they wanted intel. I suppose this counts."

"Yes," Bradley said, "but how do we use it?"

Mary plucked the strip out of Bradley's hand, ignoring his squawk of protest. "I'm not sure. But once the Knife recovers enough to create one more portal, I know who we can ask."

It took a concerted effort for Sever not to shake off Morik's ministrations as he stepped out of the blazing lamplight of the game field. Stumbled, really, back into the shaded walkway these people had made of poured stone as a path to their game seating. Morik appeared at his side like a phantom, and Sever wanted to push him away. Would have, perhaps, if not for the spinning in his gut.

Morik held him lightly by the arm, urged him to sip a fresh batch of sear-weed tonic out of a straw. He helped Sever to a set of steps, urging him to sit. Why were there no chairs back here? It was more like a space station than an entertainment venue.

"They were mere illusions," Sever said. Illusions Mary had been able to see past. A question for later, when his head ceased its spinning. "They shouldn't drain so much of my power."

They shouldn't drain *any* of his power. He should have been perfectly capable of participating in the battle, of helping his new allies to fight off a single attacker before she disappeared through a portal.

And of reminding his allies how strong he was, too, in case their thoughts turned to mutiny. It was a constant worry, with new allies. An itch at the back of his mind. Were they true friends? Or did they plan to deceive him?

"It's the shield upkeep." Morik's tone was crisp, forthright. Like a nurse overseeing a worried patient. Or a parent, trying to hide their own concern. "It's draining you."

"I'm inclined to agree." Sever rested his elbow on his knees, his head in his hands. He could not allow any of the newcomers to see him this way.

Not that he was without his own army, of course. Morik had brought a team of soldiers and scientists, the best in Sever's court, but the newcomers—though valuable—were unproven. They fought between themselves, an irritation, yet Sever had seen fit to stoke that disharmony. They were too worried about one another to turn against him. Especially with his powers draining him so quickly.

If creating mere illusions caused him so much distress, it was clear that he needed a way to increase his power. Mary had come and gone by herself, apparently, and he wasn't a fool enough to think she'd done that without reason.

Oh, she wanted to save her lover; that was clear enough. But that this League had launched anything less than a full attack upon him was an indication they'd been after something else. Information, perhaps. A test of some kind.

Whether they'd succeeded in their goal, he couldn't say. He only knew that when it came time to face the group together, he would need to operate at full strength.

"The Blade carries a sliver of my power," Sever said. "If I retrieve it, it may help restore my health."

Morik licked his lips. "The Blade of Starlight is evil. I thought you meant to destroy it."

This was what Sever appreciated about Morik. He was no sniveling companion, inclined to nod along with every whim. He spoke his mind, yet was courteous about it. An advisor in truth. As irritable as he was, Sever had to appreciate Morik's presence here. His loyalty.

Morik knew who Sever was, what he was, and yet he had never wavered.

Sever had hidden his identity once, and only one. And it had ended in disaster.

When he remembered the night he'd gifted the Blade of Starlight to his love, his Adina, he always thought first of the sky. The sunset had burned hot across the plains of Modinthin's northern hemisphere, an aurora of reds and purples. Adina had come to him in a blue silk dress, her feet bare, her green eyes alight.

And then he'd presented her with the Blade of Starlight, and he'd watched understanding dawn across her face. A sudden realization of who he was, and what he'd done.

She was supposed to become his queen. Instead, she'd made herself his enemy.

Never again would he hide his true nature.

And yet... And yet even now, he fought to contain it. To sculpt it into something that would inspire not fear, but awe. Respect. Even love.

Foolish. It was foolish. And yet, so it was.

Morik was watching him, awaiting his response, concern plain in his pursed lips, his too-wide eyes.

"I do mean to destroy the Blade," Sever said, trying to sound comforting, though it was difficult when he could hardly keep his sear-weed tonic in his stomach. "I do. But it may have its uses, before this is over."

It could carry the well of power he needed to overcome this mysterious weakness.

Sever took a breath, slow and expansive, and let it out. Then he brushed off his pants and stood, hardly wavering at all. "Did you trace the portal's source when it came through?"

He'd asked his people to track any portal that arrived here, by whatever means. As always, the resonance of it had thrummed through him, yet Morik had people to pinpoint it more exactly, instruments to isolate its location.

Morik bobbed his head. "Yes, my lord. We sent flash drones through, and they signaled us."

Always prepared, Morik. Always ready. "Good," Sever said. "As soon as Dolly can lock onto the location, I want you to send a team. But tell her to stay on this side. We don't need her getting captured."

He knew that the League defectors were split now, that some had gone with his soldiers to study Adina's history while the rest remained here. He still needed guards here at the colosseum, but he must still have enough resources to bring the Blade in.

"It may take a few minutes of study," Morik said. "They appear to be in the middle of the Pacific Ocean."

That meant nothing to Sever, though presumably Morik had been analyzing the maps in depth. Sever clasped his advisor on the shoulder, reminding himself that he appreciated the man's transparency. But that, ultimately, Sever's will still needed doing. "Bring me the Blade."

ELOISE WASN'T sure who Mary wanted to dial with a portal. She only knew that the exhaustion echoing from the Pearl Knife would have gone marrow-deep, had it been her own. She was tired, too, but the Knife—the Knife was sick. Yet she could feel its eagerness to help, even as its song lurched toward slumber. Or whatever version of slumber the Knife employed.

All the trauma, the testing, the portals. The Knife needed a rest, and preferably a long one. They all did.

Mary was still grasping the scrap of metal Bradley had stolen from Sever's right-hand alien. She opened her mouth—to explain how she meant to decipher it, Eloise assumed—but before she could speak, an eye-searing strip of light gouged the air behind her.

There was nothing Eloise could do to stop Dolly's portal from yawning open. Nothing she could do to protect Wave's headquarters. This yacht had survived a long time, possibly even for decades, by hiding in the vastness of the Pacific. Now, after one League operation, it was exposed.

Bradley scooped his instruments into his arms and made a beeline for the ship's interior as sirens screamed to life, the portal already spotted. The Knife roared in Eloise's head, like a distant waterfall. It was sorrow, and anger, and the kind of fatigue that had pushed to its final limit.

Rest, Eloise thought. *I'll handle this.*

Two armored soldiers leapt through the still-expanding portal, followed by two more. And then Jenna Carpenter, unarmored, her dark hair hanging loose around her face, her fingertips ablaze; Diana Morton, rubbing her own toxic fingers together; and Donny and Brenda, the golden-haired twins who read each other's minds to coordinate an almost unbeatable fighting team.

No Rocker, Monster, or Carlisle. No Ranger. No Goldi. And no Dolly, though she had to be nearby; no one else could open a portal.

Wave operatives poured out of the interior of the ship, and Eloise had a second to wonder where they'd been for the past two days before the deck exploded into a full-on battle. Steve rocketed up from belowdecks, Ire and her father a few steps behind.

Still half-dressed after shucking her damaged suit, Mary launched herself at Diana, apparently eager to continue their fight anyway. Jenna's eyes gleamed like she was ready to set the whole ship alight.

Eloise expected that Dolly would come through eventually, to give her friends an escape route if nothing else. But as chaos erupted, the portal began to ease shut, like a wound attempting to heal. Would she and Sever leave their companions here, in the middle of the sea? They couldn't expect that to end well.

And suddenly Agnes was at Eloise's side, staring at the doorway in the air with a furrow between her eyebrows that suggested it had insulted her personally. And maybe it had.

For a second, Eloise thought Agnes might actually be able to stop the portal. Grab onto its molecules, rip it apart. Something. But the sides just kept collapsing toward one another.

"What are you doing?" Eloise asked. "Staring it to death?"

Agnes ignored her. A beat later, Dolly soared through the portal, wrists locked together, legs kicking in protest. She lifted her feet just in time to avoid hitting the laser-sharp edge of the still-closing portal.

"I didn't know you could do that," Eloise said.

Agnes was still staring at the portal in concentration, or anger, or both. "I manipulate molecules, El. It's not hard."

Eloise thrust her hand out toward the battle, toward Mary and Diana, and all the others. "Then why not just freeze them all, like Sever? Stop the fighting?"

Agnes cast her a look that might as well have been rolled eyes. "If I were that powerful, I'd have stopped him already."

"Either it's not hard, or it is," Eloise snapped.

"The two things aren't mutually exclusive. What I can do isn't hard, but there's still a limit."

Seemed like splitting hairs, really. Agnes was actually shouting to be heard over the melee, while Dolly's feet hit the deck in front of them. Agnes released her feet, or appeared to, and she stumbled half a step before finding her balance.

Eloise had faced her mother since Dolly'd escaped from HQ, several times. But to see her again, just a few days after the damage she'd wrought... Half of her felt rooted to the deck, but it was only because that half wanted to stop her from rushing Dolly and throwing her into the ocean.

"Nice trick," Dolly spat. "But kidnapping me won't keep us here."

Agnes ticked up an eyebrow. "Oh? And how well can you make a portal with your hands bound?"

Dolly looked to Eloise. "Went crying to Wave for help, did you? I can't say I'm surprised. You never could work things out on your own."

The twins barged toward them then, splitting Eloise and

Agnes from Dolly and saving her from the need to respond. She ducked out from under Brenda's rabid attack, nearly tumbling straight into Donny. Her fingertips tingled, aching to bring her own budding powers into the fight, but she stuck with her fists, cracking one straight into Brenda's nose.

Steve and Ire were off to the left, fighting off the soldiers together, and she spotted Jian at the rail with his hands raised to bring a curtain of water crashing over Jenna's attempts to set things on fire.

A great idea, since they'd nearly left their portalist behind. Set fire to the boat you're standing on, sure. It would have been good to have Rajni here, too, but Eloise didn't see LIO's water-wielding recruit anywhere.

The Knife sputtered into Eloise's mind, like a warning, and she turned to see Dolly lifting her arms, her hands freed. Agnes was locked in a fight with a bloody-nosed Brenda, her concentration split.

Dolly burned a portal line into the air, and Eloise raised a hand, answering its resonance. When she felt the vibration, thick and loud, she slashed her own line through Dolly's to make an X.

A piercing tone screeched through Eloise's mind, like sustained feedback, and Dolly clapped her hands over her ears. The battle continued all around them, the fighters oblivious to the noise of the portal lines cancelling each other out.

The Knife shuddered—inside her head, or physically, or both—as Eloise fought to stay on her feet. She was aware of Agnes battling the twins at her back, of Mary and Diana trading barbs as they fought. Angry red stripes ran down Mary's bare arms, and Eloise didn't know how long she'd be able to keep the fight going. They needed to get out of here.

But Eloise only had eyes for her mother. It was still hard to recognize this straight-backed woman, her gaze clear, her power impossible to ignore. Before, the Knife's proximity had made her ill; maybe the blade wasn't capable of it now, wasn't capable of anything. Perhaps she was too powerful. Or just too far away. She made a point of keeping her distance, practically cowering ten yards away by the rail.

"Wave, Eloise," Dolly said, her voice cutting through the noise on deck with sharp judgment. She'd locked onto a weakness, a question mark in Eloise's leadership, and wasn't going to let it drop. "I'm disappointed."

"*You're* disappointed?" Eloise's own voice sounded just short of hysterical, and it made her feel like a child again, like she was throwing a fit over a forbidden candy bar. "You destroyed HQ. You forced us out of our home. Where else were we supposed to go?"

It felt like they were talking to each other inside a snow globe, protected from a fight that increased in urgency as mother and daughter stared each other down.

A flicker of shadow passed across Dolly's brow and was gone. A blink, and Eloise might have missed it. "I've only done what I needed to."

She might have passed the responsibility off on Sever, might have pointed out that he'd been the one to grind HQ to dust. But Dolly had partnered with him, *still* partnered with him. She had no rightful claim to innocence, and she obviously knew better than to try.

"I would ask you to join us," Dolly said, her tone full of regret, "but I suspect that would be a fool's errand."

Damn right, it would. Eloise wanted to know on what grounds Dolly would ask, what arguments she'd make, but it didn't matter.

Heat blasted across the deck as double plumes of fire jetted into the sky, and for a moment Eloise thought a missile was landing. But it was Jenna, taking off from the deck, fire rocketing out of her palms. Her movements seemed erratic, nothing like Dad's smooth control; her boundless energy made her look like a darting hummingbird.

"Oh, good," Dolly murmured, deep lines cutting across her forehead. "She learned to fly."

Eloise nearly laughed. She'd been thinking the same thing. And in the same tone, too. "Trouble in dystopia?" she asked.

Dolly's frown deepened. She looked like she might actually respond, might tell Eloise all her troubles.

Eloise wished she would. She'd use every one of them against her mother, without hesitation.

Jenna landed on one of the upper decks, chin tilted up, a regal smile on her face. Like a queen taking her rightful place before her people. Fire streamed out of her hands in dangerous tendrils, and Eloise could well imagine one of the sparks taking hold, engulfing the entire ship. They were out in the middle of the ocean; powers or not, people would die if the yacht sank.

From the frozen concern on Dolly's face, she might have been thinking the same thing. Whether they'd planned this out in advance, or whether Jenna was going rogue—a talent of hers —Eloise couldn't guess.

When Dolly wrenched her eyes out of the sky, her gaze landed on the Knife at Eloise's hip. And Eloise knew, without a shadow of a doubt, that if Dolly could get her hands on the blade again she'd seize control over it once more. Or she'd try. Of course, she'd have to find a way past its barriers first. Could she?

Before Eloise could make sense of this, Agnes was grabbing hold of her hand and rearranging the air to lift them both up toward Jenna.

"The fight is down there," Eloise said, the words sharp on her tongue, though mostly out of surprise.

Agnes rolled her eyes. "I'm aware."

"And I can fly by myself." Pockets of fighting still clashed below—Mary landing kicks, Steve and Ire tackling another soldier, Jian washing enemies off their feet—but Eloise rose up out of the battle, over it, straining to catch Dolly's eye, to understand what it meant. The Knife's proximity did hurt her mother; even now, Eloise could see the relief smoothing out her cheeks, and the corners of her eyes, as she and the Knife moved farther away.

So it could still cause her pain. So how did she hope to become its mistress again?

Jenna raised her arms as if to fight them off as they floated toward the deck, her face a mask of fury. But Agnes's fingers tightened around Eloise's, just barely, and Jenna's fire blinked out as Agnes's powers smothered the flames.

Agnes's abilities, Eloise thought, might well be some of the most powerful ones in existence. Not that Eloise planned to tell her that.

Jenna screamed in rage, throwing herself at Agnes as she and Eloise landed on the upper deck. A long bank of windows ran along the balcony here, the room inside crammed with important-looking instruments. Eloise might be new here, but she was fairly certain this was a room she didn't want Jenna to access. Control, maybe, or navigation. Engineering.

Agnes threw a shield up around herself and Eloise, reversing Jenna's momentum. Jenna went sprawling back across the balcony, arms flailing as she tried to grab the rail for purchase.

Eloise started toward Jenna, intending to keep her on the defensive. But an eardrum-tearing alarm blared to life just above her head, so loud she could feel it reverberating down her spine. Jenna doubled over, and Eloise flinched, clapping her hands over her ears.

As she watched, craning her neck to peer above the equipment room, the dome above it cracked open like an egg, spilling out a series of transparent panels.

The panels clicked together so rapidly that, by the time Eloise had a chance to take a breath—and to realize this wasn't a result of Sever unleashing his powers on Wave's hideout—a clear dome had enclosed the entire yacht from rail to rail.

Before Eloise could ask what the hell was going on, the ship began to descend.

For years, Wave had been hiding safely on a hulking cruise ship in the middle of the Pacific—probably sneaking across several oceans, over the years—and making use of at least one remote tropical island. Not to mention the underwater base she'd lived on, where a network of vehicles and submarines brought people in and out like a miniature Grand Central Station.

So Agnes was only a little surprised when the cruise-ship-sized yacht took on the properties of a submarine and began its underwater plunge. The ship was dropping fast, water already lapping at the dome from several feet above the deck it protected. The deck which, just a few seconds ago, had been several meters above the water line.

When she looked up, the sky still shone clear and blue. Not yet obscured by water.

As far as Agnes could tell, Wave took the symbolism in their name a little too seriously.

The ship's descent set off a flurry of motion on the deck below. Though she couldn't hear the shouting, it was easy enough to see Dolly's cornea-burning portal, opening to usher her people to safety. Sever's allies—his soldiers, and the original

LIO members—all abandoned their fights to leap through the gate. And whether out of surprise or relief, the current LIO and Wave operatives let them go.

All but Jenna. Standing above her retreating colleagues, she used the balcony railing to haul herself to her feet, bottom lip curled away from her teeth in an expression of pure disgust. Whether for LIO, or Wave, or her own allies, Agnes wasn't sure.

"Cool trick," Jenna said. "I know a better one."

While Agnes watched, Jenna set the air on fire.

One moment, Agnes had a firm grip on the girl's powers, a fire-suffocating shield closed tightly around her fingertips. And in the next, Jenna was scorching through the barrier with unbridled energy.

Heat pulse out of her fingers, and Jenna flashed a triumphant smile before raising her hands and blasting a jet of fire at the roof of the dome.

Agnes had no doubt that this dome could withstand bullets. And yet under Jenna's onslaught, the transparent material wavered and caved in.

The water level had now risen above the balcony where they stood, leaving only the cap of the dome above the waves. They had minutes, maybe, before the submarine would drop below the surface, before water began to pour in through the gap in the ceiling.

Agnes wasn't an engineer, but she knew it took time to pump air back into the chambers of a submarine. And to lift a ship of this size... Now that it was sinking, she'd have bet good money that it would take time to raise. Far too much time.

Jenna had always been strong, but this... This was more power than Agnes could have anticipated.

"I won't be your prisoner again," Jenna said. "I'll end this whole thing before it starts."

Eloise said, "I doubt Sever will be happy it if you kill Mary."

Jenna scoffed. "What does it matter? I'm about to drown. A noble sacrifice."

"You don't think Dolly and the others will come back for you?"

Jenna spat on the deck. "I know they won't."

Agnes wasn't sure why Jenna would bother to stay on the ship, then, when she could fly away. Maybe she couldn't fly far, and she knew it. Maybe she intended to inflict as much damage as she could, to ensure a fiery death instead of a watery one.

Agnes wasn't going to let that happen. She grabbed Eloise's hand, half expecting her powers to abandon her. But Jenna hadn't removed her abilities; she'd only enhanced her own, somehow. The molecules answered Agnes's call, lifting her up over Jenna's head, with Eloise at her side, and up through the still-steaming hole Jenna had blasted into the dome. Agnes breathed in the smell of scorched plastic as they ascended, careful not to brush against the molten edges.

Agnes set them down on top of the dome and knelt beside it, reaching for the molecules in the fortified plastic, trying to understand the puzzle of their existence, to knit them back together into the right shape.

"What's the point?" Eloise asked, watching as the melted folds of the dome straightened and smoothed back up into the shape of the dome under Agnes's careful attention. "She'll just burn another hole."

Agnes focused on the plastic—some glass mixed in? Something metallic? She couldn't put her finger on it—which was the one thing in this situation she could actually control. Jenna was still staring up at them from the upper deck, eyes shielded. As if she were waiting for Agnes to finish her fixes so she could obliterate them.

Or maybe she was waiting for the waves to close in over her head. Once that happened, Agnes wouldn't be able to work fast enough to keep the water out. She might buy them some time, but that was it. Already, she was kneeling in an inch of water, the sea pooling on the submarine's dome. Now two.

Still on her feet, Eloise pointed down. "Guess Jenna's wrong about some things."

Agnes finished her patching and followed Eloise's gaze through the dome, the view now wavery through the water. At Jenna's back, Dolly opened another portal and stepped through just long enough pull the girl away. Presumably to the baseball park where they were keeping Nathan.

Interesting. Jenna hadn't expected them to return for her. Had they done it of their own volition, or because of Sever? And were there other cracks in the alliance?

"Now what?" Eloise pointed at the ankle-deep water, wrenching Agnes back to the present.

Agnes rolled her eyes. "Why do you think I brought you up here?"

"To unnecessarily and self-righteously save me from the dangers of Jenna?"

"No." It was impossible to keep the snap out of her tone. Eloise always had an accusation. Always had a reason to mistrust. "Because you can make your own portal, without the Pearl Knife."

Eloise actually raised her eyebrows in surprise, though whether it was because she'd forgotten she could do it—Agnes had to allow that it was understandable, given everything that had happened in the past two days—or because she didn't think Agnes would remember or value it.

Either way, Eloise finally managed to do something without digging her heels in. With a nod, she sliced a finger into the ether and ushered them back to the safety of the ship.

DOLLY WOULD HAVE LIKED to leave Jenna behind on Wave's yacht. That thing—their secret to staying hidden all these years, so simple that she was embarrassed to have missed it—had been about to plunge into the depths of the ocean. Jenna might have drowned.

Then again, she might not. She could fly now, somewhat. And anyway, Sever would be most displeased with Dolly if the girl had perished down there.

As soon as Jenna stumbled through the portal and into the Nats gift shop after the others, she sent a volley of sparks spitting through the air at Diana, who stumbled backwards. A rack of jerseys between them burst into flame, and Donny calmly yanked the fire extinguisher off the wall to coat them in thick white foam.

"You blew it." Jenna was spitting, rage coursing off her body in waves of blistering heat. "You're so focused on revenge and making people pay for shit they did a year ago, you can't focus on actually winning a fight."

Diana recovered enough to shoot poison back at Jenna, who dodged the bullet-like drops easily. "You're one to talk," Diana said. "Do you care more about cheeky one-liners, or causing actual damage?"

Jenna screamed and threw herself at Diana, hands blazing. Dolly wished she could suck all their powers away and throw them into separate rooms to cool off. Literally, in Jenna's case. Or maybe she'd put them in the same room. Why not?

But she couldn't control them. Not until she got her hands on the Pearl Knife.

"Shut them up," she said to Monster, who'd been waiting here when they arrived. Done with his prisoner shift, probably. She didn't really care. She slipped outside before he could respond, ignoring the crash and shatter of glass that followed her out the door.

Hopefully, they wouldn't burn the place to the ground.

Dolly took the half-spiral of stairs up to the small balcony where she'd stood with Diana and Rocker the other day. She leaned her forearms on the plastic wall, looking out at the still-frozen crowd. They were shadows, no more than a lump of silhouettes, yet she imagined she could hear them whispering. Accusing.

Dolly wasn't surprised when Sever rounded the corner at her back, sneakers squeaking on the concrete as he walked toward her. She swallowed and turned back to the rail, wondering if she'd known all along that he'd come. Wondering if, subconsciously, she'd snuck out here to wait for him.

Sever propped his arms on the rail by her side, mirroring Dolly's posture. It might have been friendly, companionable, except that it wasn't. She didn't know how she knew; he wasn't frowning or pursing his lips, even when a crash from inside the gift shop shook the wall behind them.

She couldn't control her people.

"I'm sorry," Dolly said.

Sever tilted his head. Raised an eyebrow. "For?"

"Today went badly. We lost."

A long silence. Not true silence, not with Jenna and Diana still pummeling each other inside—possibly Monster too, now—but Sever just looked at her, searching her face. "You're meant to stay out of the action," he said finally. "I have many powers, but if I lose you, I lose the ability to create portals."

She wasn't sure whether to be relieved that he found her so useful, or concerned that he seemed to be discussing her like he would a favorite hammer or wrench.

"Agnes Jenson," Dolly said. "She pulled me through."

"And her powers are superior to your own?"

No. Yes. It was hard to say. "They're... different."

She could tell him about the newfound abilities that let her increase her allies' powers. Even Diana's, whose abilities had always eluded her grasp. But she could almost hear his answer in her head: *you have this power, and you lost anyway.* How would she explain that?

Maybe it was preferable to hold a few truths back. To play her cards close.

"Your daughter," Sever said. "Is she a weakness?"

Dolly blinked. She hadn't been thinking of Eloise when she'd been dragged through the portal to join the fight, nor when she'd remained to help. She'd been thinking of the Pearl Knife—of avoiding it, and of holding it in her hand again. The push and pull of fear and desire.

But she couldn't say that.

"Mistakes happen," Sever said, like the most reasonable tyrant in the world, "but I need to know now. Can you do what you must?"

He sounded so measured, so controlled. Almost kindly.

Her gaze wandered back to the crowd of statues, hulking motionless out there in the darkness. If she touched their skin, would it feel like stone? Cold, like death's rictus? Or would it be soft and warm?

She wasn't sure which would be worse.

"I can do what needs to be done," she said.

She didn't need to tell him what that was: the Knife. She needed the Knife, at all costs. And she needed a new plan, a way to get close to it. Everything rested on it. The fate of the *world* rested on it. Eloise was doing her best, but she was inexperienced. She was naive, too, insisting on taking the high road at every single turn and running to Wave like a needy child.

No, the world needed Dolly. And it needed her at full strength.

Sever nodded, straightening away from the wall. "Good. And Dolly?"

Her heart stammered, panicked that he'd somehow read her thoughts, her intentions against him. "Yes?"

"Get your people under control. It's unseemly." He nodded toward the gift shop, then adjusted his already-straight collar, tipped her a shallow bow, and glided back toward the park.

Wave's underwater hideout reminded Mary of home. Oh, it was much cushier than LIO HQ had ever been, with artwork-lined walls and soft carpeting instead of the shiny titanium look Dolly had favored. But the hallways wound in a carefully mapped grid, and it seemed like every doorway had a screen to guard the door, just like HQ.

Mary would have expected Wave's relentlessly soft aesthetic—the carpeting, the curtains, the tapestries—to make the hideout moldy, or damp and heavy with recycled air. Instead, it smelled fresh and pleasant, almost as if they were pumping extra oxygen in here. Tinged with mint, maybe. And of course, it had all the required amenities of a quality secret hideout; a garage, several laboratories, and a long hallway of living quarters.

Impressed though she was, Mary did avoid the occasional viewpoints that dotted the outer rim of the dome. Lanterns could only illuminate a fraction of the murky depths outside, and though she'd never been claustrophobic, she wasn't quite ready to be reminded of the miles of ocean piled on top of this bunker.

She'd barely escaped the disaster at HQ. If Sever could

crack the thick rocky shell between Niagara Falls and LIO HQ, he could probably drill a whirlpool down to Wave's dome.

But the place had comfortable beds, and once she'd seen Dr. Gordon for poison extraction and submitted to his pleas for rest—at least for long enough to be useful again after the trip to the baseball stadium and the battle on the deck of the yacht—she met up with Bradley and Eloise in Conference Room C.

Yes, Wave's underwater compound had a conference room. In fact, judging by its moniker, the place had at least three.

Eloise and Bradley were waiting when Mary arrived, Bradley examining the stolen strip of metal under a magnifying glass while Eloise watched. Mary could imagine her attempting —and failing at—small talk with the man before giving up and lapsing into silence. Just a guess.

For some reason, Rajni was also sitting at the table. She had her head in her hands and was staring miserably into space. She clearly didn't want to be here, though Mary wasn't sure she wanted to be anywhere else at the moment, either.

"Fran wants me in training in half an hour," Eloise said, by way of greeting.

"Good morning to you, too." It was probably close to midday, but whatever. Mary took a seat on the edge of the table beside Bradley, rather than taking a chair. "Fran will wait. That tablet could be the key to rescuing Nathan."

"Not to mention the key to renewable resources, potentially endless ones, and brand-new types of metal alloys," Bradley said, still studying the strip. "Oh, and stopping a genocidal demi-god from killing us all. But by all means, let's make sure we save that one person."

He said it lightly, like he was too absorbed to give it much thought, yet Mary had the distinct impression that he meant it.

Her head throbbed, her throat expanding with a painful bubble of grief that wanted her to crawl under the table and sob. Of course, that grief was at war with the fire in her ribcage that wanted to slam Bradley's head against the table.

Yes, she cared about the tech, the potential. And yes, she wanted to save everyone. She *always* wanted to save everyone. But she could want that while also wanting to saved Nathan.

She leaned back, bracing her palm against the edge of the table and crossing her legs. "Your empathy astounds me."

He lowered the strip of metal enough to meet her eyes. "Oh? Your lack of it disturbs me. You abandoned the mission at Nationals Park, without thought to the consequences. And now here we are, our position exposed, our partnership out in the open."

As if Mary didn't know that the appearance of portals on the field had put them all at risk. She didn't need Bradley Archer to tell her how she'd messed up. "You said you knew I'd go after Nathan."

"That doesn't make it less contemptuous."

"You were eager enough to use it to manipulate the situation. You could have stopped me."

Eloise's eyebrows rose so high that Mary thought they might actually fly away. OK, so Bradley probably couldn't have stopped Mary from doing exactly what she wished. The point was, he hadn't wanted to.

"It doesn't matter what we do." Rajni's voice was thick and quiet, with a raspy edge to her tone. "He's going to kill us all, anyway."

"You can go rest," Mary said, but Eloise raised a hand, cutting her off.

"Dr. Gordon sent Rajni to help," she said. "He doesn't want her to be alone."

Mary nodded, her throat dry. She understood, and she didn't. Nathan was alive. Her friends were, too. But Rajni's best friend was gone. The least they could do was let the girl be with her grief.

Ignoring the exchange, Bradley set the metal strip on the table and slid it over to Mary, apparently finished with his lecture for now. "Who are we calling?"

Mary picked up the strip of metal. She'd seen one just like it, one that'd morphed into a fully functioning tablet-like technology. There would be information in here, lots of it. She just didn't know where to find the secret button that'd let her access it.

Mary looked to Eloise. "Can the Knife cut a portal to another galaxy? I mean, I know it *can*, because it's done it before. But is it well enough to try that again?"

Eloise frowned. "To reach your alien friends? I... I think so. But Alex said she was turning off the wormhole generator, so it won't have the resonance to follow."

"It's been to the ship," Bradley said. "Maybe it wouldn't need the resonance."

"Weird thing about spaceships," Mary said, "is that they *move*."

Usually, the Knife could reach to places it hadn't been: Nationals Park, for example. Another galaxy though? That was a big ask.

Eloise licked her lips, her gaze moving across the table as if she were reading. Mary thought, though, that she was listening. Allowing the Knife to respond.

"It doesn't need to lock to a specific coordinate," Eloise said. Translated? Hard to tell. "That makes sense. When I cut a portal without the Knife, I have to form a complete picture in my mind and then reach for it. The more accurate it is, the better. I can do it from a picture, but it's better if I've been there."

Eloise ran a thumb over the surface of the table. "The Knife does the same thing, only it has... I think it has more options, more senses to pull from. Like the resonance. But it remembers the ship, so it can talk to it."

"Great," Mary said. "Let's do this."

Eloise slid the Pearl Knife out of its sheath, shutting her eyes as she held it out in front of her. Mary could remember a time when El's knuckles would have been white as she gripped the hilt, her jaw ticking as if gritting her teeth would exert the control she needed.

Now, though, Eloise's mouth was relaxed, her eyelashes fluttering only slightly as the Knife pulled *her* hand down toward the table, cutting a moon-white slash into the air.

The slash split, opening a window into the same laboratory Mary had visited several months ago, when she'd fallen through another portal and onto a spaceship.

"This is the world's weirdest conference call," Mary said.

Bradley snorted a laugh. Rajni lay her head down on the table.

Mary had worried that the lab might be empty. But, perhaps predictably, Alex sat in a chair across the room, her red curls tied in a messy knot on top of her head. More unpredictably, she was eating a snack from a bag that seemed to be staining her fingers an unnerving shade of green, and she had her bunny-slippered feet propped up on the counter.

Mary had trouble reconciling this lounging woman with the exacting scientist she'd met a few months ago.

When she saw the portal, Alex squeaked and dropped her feet, stumbling toward it. "What are you *doing*?" she said. "Do you want to implode the universe? Close that wormhole. Close it!"

Sloane's face appeared next to Alex's. "It's just a little window," she said. "Like a mail slot. Or a fly-through window."

Mary really wanted to visit a galaxy that had fly-through windows. Did they serve fries?

"Universe," Alex said. "*Implode.*"

Sloane shrugged. "Hasn't yet."

"This is my lab," Alex muttered.

"Hilda doesn't want me on the pilot's deck when she's flying away from bad guys, so it's your turn to babysit me." Sloane looked back through the portal, hooking a thumb over her shoulder to point at Alex. "Sorry. She's a little upset since her life's work kind of went poof."

Mary wondered how Alex had figured out that the wormholes were so unstable. Maybe it had something to do with the resonance between the Knife and Alex's machine. Feedback of some kind? She'd have liked to sit down with Alex, to talk over the details. It wasn't her area of expertise, but it was fascinating.

Maybe someday, when the Earth and Nathan were safe, she'd get a chance to do that. Assuming Alex allowed them to open one more portal. She'd love to spend a week, or twelve, working in Alex's lab, learning about her tech and sharing ideas. Somehow, it helped to picture that future. And Nathan there at her side.

Eloise leaned in to look through the window. "Are all portals risky? Or just the galaxy-hopping ones?"

Alex crossed her arms. "I don't know, but I'd rather not find out."

Given how much they'd been using portals on Earth lately, Mary hoped they were safe. Though she'd seen the way Eloise's line had clashed against Dolly's back on the yacht, felt the thrum of power in her gut. There might be something to it.

Mary cleared her throat. "We'll get to the point, then." She passed Morik's strip of tablet through the window to Sloane. "Our friend here stole this from Morik, but we don't know how to activate it."

"Stealing from Morik? Bold." Sloane dug a fingernail into a crack in the corner of the metal, a slot that was nearly invisible. She swiped it across and twisted, and the tablet unfolded. She closed it the same way and demonstrated the opening again.

"It's all in Common Parse," Sloane said. "Let me see, my audio translator knows English... It activates automatically, but I bet it can do writing, too."

She flicked through settings while Alex wrung her hands in the background. Mary thought the scientist might actually snatch the tablet, throw it back through the portal, and shut down the wormhole for good. In her place, Mary might do exactly the same thing.

"There," Sloane said. "You can now read in English. I'll warn you, Morik's a weirdo and you'll probably find some disturbing things."

"As long as they're helpful things," Mary said.

Sloane gave her a quick tour of the tablet and had her practice opening and closing it.

"Thanks for risking the universe for us," Mary said.

Alex unfolded her arms, clasped her fingers together, then seemed to change her mind as she stuck her hands on her hips. "You can charge it on Earth," she said. "But you'll have to make an adaptor. And use the strongest power source you have."

"Will do," Mary said. "Sever's guys still chasing you?"

"Oh, they gave up a while ago." Sloane's tone was light, but her smile didn't quite touch her eyes. "New bad guys to deal with now."

"Try to stay out of trouble," Mary said. "Thanks. For everything. If we can help, just let us know."

"Not imploding the universe would help," Alex said.

"Right. We'll remember that."

Eloise closed the portal, and Bradley snatched the tablet

from Mary's fingers. She opened her mouth, but Eloise gave her a pleading look, so she settled for a scowl instead.

If Bradley saw it, he didn't let on. "Correspondence, a lot of it." He tapped at the sort-of screen, slowly and more clumsily than Sloane had, but well enough. "Here. Assignments. This is strange."

A pause. Mary drummed her fingertips on the table, wondering if there were a way to hook this thing up to a big screen so they could go through everything together.

"Well?" Mary prompted, when she couldn't stand it anymore.

"Oklahoma," Bradley said. "There's a concentration of Sever's people there. Small town... nothing notable that I can see."

A memory tugged at Mary's stomach, and she leaned over Bradley's shoulder to get a better look at the screen. "My grandmother was born in Oklahoma," she said.

She still couldn't believe, couldn't quite fathom, that she somehow stood at the center of this whole situation. Sever seemed to know she wasn't Adina. And yet, he was still chasing the connection. It had to be a mistake.

"That's it, then," Bradley said. "Next stop, Oklahoma."

As if it were that simple. But then, maybe it was.

If he started singing the song, though, Mary would punch him for real.

Eloise was still holding the Knife, looking thoughtfully at the data. "Good. I want you to take Rajni this time."

The recruit didn't look at all prepared to participate in a mission. Her forehead was resting on her folded arms, her desperation plain.

"What's the point?" Rajni asked, her voice muffled. "I can't use my powers. They're broken."

She couldn't use her powers, or didn't want to? It was hard

to say. Mary certainly understood the crushing weight of grief. She'd help Rajni, if she could. If Dr. G wanted her on a mission, on a mission she'd go. "We could use another set of hands," she said.

Rajni just shrugged. Mary decided that meant she wouldn't fight it.

Bradley pushed his chair away from the table and handed her the tablet. "All righty. Let me just get my cowboy hat, and then we'll be off."

HQ's walls contracted around Eloise, the hallways so tight she could barely squeeze through sideways. Water dripped through punctures in the ceiling, rock gaping through tears in the walls. She was searching for someone—*who?*—but when she opened her mouth, she couldn't make her voice work, couldn't shout to them. Grinding boulders rumbled to every side, shaking dust into her hair. Alarms called in the distance, their gentle vibrations crescendoing into an insistent buzz.

When Eloise opened her eyes, the telecom box beside her door was shrieking at her, an orange light blinking in the bottom corner. She staggered out of bed, disoriented by the small room and the soft carpets. They felt wrong, after the shifting danger of the dream.

And Wave had telecoms in each room. Something she'd never considered installing at HQ. She pressed the blinking button to accept the call.

"About time." Fran's voice echoed out of the box, a tinny accusation. Did the woman ever sleep? Eloise's cranky, sleep-deprived brain supplied an image of the old woman dangling upside down in a cave, cuddling her super-powered cane.

She rubbed her eyes. "We just fought back-to-back battles,

then made an intergalactic conference call." Eloise wasn't even sure how much time had passed, or whether she was waking up from actual sleep or just a nap. Her head swam with fatigue, and a fair bit of overwhelm. "What do you want from me?"

"Oh, nothing much," Fran shot back. "Just for you to save the world. If your schedule isn't too busy, that is. Meet me in the training room. Five minutes."

Training room. Indeed, every secret hideout needed one. "Ten."

"Four. Get moving."

Eloise cursed, threw on the gray training gear Wave had provided for her, and stormed out of her room. She didn't think Fran would refuse to train her if she showed up late, but she surely had intricate ideas for other punishments.

Mentorship was definitely overrated.

"How am I even supposed to find the training room?" she grumbled, picking a direction and storming down the hall. "I don't see any directories."

"It's behind you."

Eloise whipped around to see Agnes waiting for her, arms crossed, eyebrows furrowed. She'd probably been up since dawn—if dawn existed in Little Mermaid land—coming up with radical solutions to all the world's problems.

After fighting alongside Agnes on the yacht, Eloise might have expected the scientist to warm to her. A new camaraderie, perhaps. A new understanding.

But no. Agnes was staring at Eloise as if she'd intentionally smeared the microscope lenses with chocolate, or washed her precious lab beakers with sand. Her eyes were narrowed, and Eloise thought she might be one snide remark away from tapping her foot.

Eloise decided to go for innocent nonchalance. She opened

her fists and tried for a smile, though it felt tight. "So you're coming to training today, too?"

"Don't sound so disappointed."

Eloise pressed her tongue to the roof of her mouth, willing herself not to say something she'd regret. "I'm not disappointed. I'm just making conversation. Where are we headed?"

Agnes pointed to the closed door beside Eloise's room.

"I guess Fran decided I should sleep by the training room."

"I guess Fran decided someone needs to keep an eye on you," Agnes said, acidic, as if returning fire. Eloise didn't know what she'd said wrong. She wasn't sure she wanted to.

The door opened, and Fran stuck her head into the hall. "Fran decided if you two don't stop bickering and get in here in ten seconds, she's going to open a window and see if you can swim."

Agnes stuck her nose in the air and glided into the room. Eloise rolled her eyes, then followed.

Targets of various sizes and materials lined the far side of the room, which had one mirrored wall and a barre, as if it had once been a dance studio. It was more compact than the space on the yacht, but it still had punching bags and mats on the floor. Familiar. Unfamiliar.

"Let me say good morning to the darling Knife," Fran said.

The Pearl Knife cooed in Eloise's mind, clearly happy to be in the same room with Fran again. Eloise withdrew it from its sheath, placing it flat across her palm and trying not to let her thoughts drift to grumpy comments on it being a traitor. Fran leaned close and asked it how it had slept, if it had slept.

The Knife babbled to Eloise, like water skipping over stones in a shallow brook. As far as she could tell, though, Fran couldn't hear its responses.

Fran straightened and thumped her cane. It squished into the mat, which somehow didn't lessen the threatening impact of the gesture. "Targets today," she said. "Let's see what material the Knife likes."

"It can cut anything," Eloise said.

Fran glowered at her. "I didn't say what it *can cut*. I know it *can cut* anything, can't you, darling? No, I said we'll see what it *likes*. Pay attention."

"I don't know what that means," Eloise said.

"Clearly. So, we'll find out."

Foam, plastic, aluminum, steel, copper, cloth, glass. Even stone. Fran had targets to test them all—though Eloise noted she had yet to produce diamonds—and she didn't test them by rote; she had Eloise practice different maneuvers each time, sending the Knife in different directions, asking it to take its own paths.

How would it respond to a moving opponent made of stone? Could it slice through an aquarium full of water—which Fran *did* produce—or portal inside it?

Each time, she had Eloise report how the Knife sounded. Which made sense, except that there were only so many different ways to describe the sound of water. Gurgling. Babbling. Rushing, in the case of the aquarium, which she had to admit was interesting—only she couldn't say *why* it sounded different. Or why it had abandoned the melodies, the harmonies, and the occasional images it had once communicated with.

While Eloise struggled to interpret and Agnes took furious notes, Fran treated the Knife like the best puppy in the world. She cooed at it, praised it, and instructed Eloise to pat it regularly. If they'd known what kind of treats it liked, Eloise had no doubt Fran would be stuffing it full.

Eloise, on the other hand, felt like she just might be living in the doghouse. Fran only had scowls and sharp instructions for her.

"All right, Agnes," Fran said eventually. "Put the clipboard down and join us."

Agnes looked up, startled. "Join you?"

"We need you to manipulate some molecules. Come. Take charge of that target, and face off against Eloise."

Agnes's eyes widened, as if she'd rather face off against Sever himself. But she set the clipboard down in the corner, shook out her hands, and joined them in the middle of the room.

Fran waved for them to begin, and Agnes flicked her fingers at the ceiling, raising one of the targets off the ground. She didn't need the gestures, but Eloise knew she liked them, knew they made her feel more tethered to the molecules she could manipulate. Or coax. Eloise wasn't sure what the difference was.

Eloise released the Knife, and it soared obediently toward the target. She could feel fatigue leaking through its eagerness to help, like a drip slowly emptying a vat of water.

Agnes squeezed a fist, and the target vanished. The Knife sped toward the spot where it had been, moving so quickly that it hit the wall, embedding half the blade in cork and drywall.

"Interesting," Fran said. "You moved the target?"

Agnes nodded.

Eloise stomped over to the Knife and withdrew it from the wall. Loosened paint chipping away as she dislodged it. "That was unnecessary," she said.

Fran opened her mouth, but Agnes spoke first. "Because we shouldn't challenge the Knife? See what confuses it? We're not just training, Eloise. We're testing."

Eloise could feel her cheeks going hot, her hands shaking. She could feel the rage rising, sending her vision tilting, along with her reason. "It's not a lab rat. It's a sentient being."

"Rats are sentient."

"You know what I mean. It's been traumatized. We don't need to torment it."

She could hear herself, hear the gaps in her own arguments. She could also hear the Pearl Knife, bubbling anxiously. Not because of the target, she thought, but because of the argument. But she couldn't stop, couldn't backpedal. She couldn't articulate why she felt betrayed, only that she did.

"The Knife needs to be its best self, traumatized or not," Agnes said. "We can get it there."

"The Knife needs us to take care of it, not cheat to defeat it."

Agnes scoffed. "Leave it to you to argue that I cheated just because you can't do what I can. If you think Sever will hold back in favor of fairness, you'll lose. As soon as you have to face him, he'll kill you."

"Don't sound so hopeful."

Agnes threw her hands in the air. "You're impossible."

Eloise opened her mouth to argue back, but Fran thumped her cane against the ceiling. Apparently, the floor hadn't been loud enough to stop their fighting.

"We have enough enemies without you two making enemies of each other," Fran said. "I'm going to make you get along, whether you like it or not."

Agnes huffed a laugh. Eloise had to stop herself from doing the same.

Fran pointed her cane at Agnes. "You are going to give Eloise a tour of the facility. And you," she pointed the cane at Eloise, "are going to listen to what she tells you. Don't come back here until you can tolerate each other's company. You don't have to be friends, but you do need to remember you're on the same side."

"We used to be," Eloise said.

"No, we never really were," Agnes shot back. "You've never

listened to anyone else's ideas, ever. Or acknowledged that LIO committed far worse crimes than Wave ever did."

"Not under my watch."

"And the prisoners you kept under your feet for months? They don't count?"

Still gripping her cane, Fran threw her hands up. "New plan. Come back when you've worked out a solution, together. When you can understand how to communicate with the Knife. I'm not your mother, and we don't have time for this."

She paused, reached toward the Knife for a brief instant. "Sorry to leave you with them, doll, but it has to be done."

The Pearl Knife made a hushing sound in Eloise's mind, like waves foaming over a beach. Agreement, she thought. She frowned, but it held its ground.

As soon as Fran was gone, Agnes stomped over to the corner, picked up her clipboard, and stormed out of the room without saying a word to Eloise.

Sever never reinstated the guard inside Nathan's room after Mary's attack on the ballpark. He'd have expected the alien to double security, triple it, but instead he rotated the guards at the entrance to all the suites on this level. Monster, Jenna, Diana, and Dolly all came and went. There was no one else.

Nathan didn't know if the others were guarding rest of the ballpark, or if Sever had sent them out on other nefarious missions. He could only hope that they'd been stretched thin, with too much of the world to control and too few resources to do it with. But that certainly wasn't a guarantee.

He'd connected briefly with President Caldwell and Vice President Grafton during Mary's attack, before slipping back to his own cell. He hadn't expected to like either of them, but the first words out of the VP's mouth had been an apology for the executive order that she'd had nothing to do with.

Aside from that, the meeting had been brief. Nathan wasn't clear on what had happened during the fight; only that Mary was gone, and he was still here. But he'd made progress. He'd made his connection. And, as far as he knew, he'd maintained his secret passage out of his prison.

Now, he was back in his cell. But after a night and a day of telling himself that he was biding his time—and perhaps more importantly, allowing his body to heal as much as it could—he itched to find something useful to do. He could attempt an escape, but it seemed like he should do some spying instead. This was LIO's chance to get knowledge from the inside.

Mary was alive. He had to believe the rest of them were, too. But if he ran away now, the League would never get anyone else behind enemy lines. Besides, he'd have to leave the president, and he couldn't do that.

The guards seemed to want Nathan to think they checked in on him at random, but when he noted the timing of their visits, he discovered an obvious pattern. While Jenna was apt to truly check in at any time—she obviously found guarding a door extremely boring—the others kept to a pretty exacting schedule.

The guard would deliver a meal, wait half an hour, then return to take the tray. They'd then check on him again after fifteen minutes, as though to remind him that they were watching and could—would—enter at any time. After that, it was a regular rotation of fifteen minutes, then thirty, then forty-five, and back to fifteen.

Until the next meal delivery, when the pattern would start again.

As soon as Nathan realized he could set his watch by the check-ins, he made a plan.

On the second evening after Mary's attack, Nathan caught a glimpse of Sever out on the baseball diamond, taking a leisurely stroll with Morik—just as Jenna ended her guard shift. The two men moved slowly around the field, and though Sever didn't lean on his advisor, Nathan had a feeling that Morik was there for physical support.

It took a concerted effort to wait until Monster had

completed his thirty-minute check-in. Of all the guards, Monster was perhaps the most meticulous about adhering to the routine.

As soon as the door shut behind him, Nathan stripped the weather-proofing off of the secret door and slipped out into the stadium.

The evening air was thick and stiflingly hot as he made his way down the rows, careful to stay out of sight. Just as he was weighing a quick sprint and a leap into the dugout, Sever and Morik strolled toward the stands, climbed up, and headed back into the darkness of the concourse.

Luck. Pure luck, that Nathan hadn't had to risk an open sprint. Staying low, he edged along the shadows—Mary's style —and crept forward until he could see the line of abandoned concessions stands and souvenir shops that made the place feel like a ghost town.

When Morik's voice drifted toward him, he realized the aliens had taken a seat on the stairs leading up to his right. They were just above Nathan's head, allowing him to stay hidden in the triangular sliver of shadow below. One more careless step forward, and he'd have given himself away.

"...regular doses of the tonic," Morik was saying. "Especially when the weather here is like a jungle. Without the benefit of trees."

Nathan had had plenty of bosses over the years who might have objected to his tone—it fell just short of scolding—but Sever didn't respond in anger. He merely said, "I like the heat. It reminds me of Cal Cornum."

Morik tsked. "As long as your power continues to flag, we must do all we can to keep you healthy."

It took a concerted effort not to lean in closer. So Nathan had been right; Sever *was* struggling with his powers.

"The illusions ought not to have taxed me so, it's true." A

pause. A breath of wind. Nathan could only hope these two didn't have some kind of enhanced sense of smell—he'd certainly been sweating as he made his way across the stadium.

And the physical strain was getting to him, too. It took more of an effort than it should to keep his breathing quiet, to keep himself steady on his feet. His ribs ached with the strain of standing straight.

He felt off balance. Wrong, in a way, or slower than usual. He'd certainly handled enough trauma when helping victims as a police officer to recognize the state in himself.

And now that he was here, his brain helpfully started listing off the number of ways he could be discovered—and the danger in his injuries. Not to mention the lagging response times they could impose. Sever might have guards, either his soldiers or the ex-LIO people, patrolling the concourse. Monster might break his pattern and check in early. He might fall ill and call the next guard, which would start the process all over again.

Too many variables. Hands shaking slightly, Nathan checked his watch. If Monster stuck to the plan, Nathan should have twenty-five minutes. Plenty of time.

If. Too many ifs. But this kind of information was worth having. If he got caught in the process of obtaining it, he'd figure it out. He had to believe he was still a valuable enough prisoner to keep alive.

Nathan stayed where he was.

"I believe it's something particular to the Earth that stunts my powers," Sever said.

What, like how Superman got his strength from the yellow sun, only the opposite? Did he dare to hope?

"The illusions left me far too ill, but I do feel better," Sever continued. "I'm getting used it, perhaps. And if I can capture the Blade of Starlight, it can help me regain my full powers."

"Set the Earth right, and then destroy the Blade," Morik said.

"Yes." But Sever sounded distant, uncertain. He'd seemed so intent on destroying the Knife before, so certain it was evil. Now that he thought he might need it for himself, he sounded like he might break his word. Interesting.

Nathan wasn't entirely sure Sever's reasoning made sense. It seemed to him that Sever's powers actually drained much, much faster when the Knife came around. Sever thought it would help him regain them—but could it be the opposite?

The Knife had drained Dolly's powers for years, even made her ill. Sever must know that. But now, it might not even be weakening Sever intentionally. Nathan had seen the resonance of the Knife's portals, of Dolly's and even Eloise's portals. Its powers were complex, and often inscrutable.

What about the resonance of the enhanced abilities that the Knife had—purposely or inadvertently—bestowed on the people of Earth?

Sever might think the Knife was his key to regaining his strength. But there was a possibility—albeit a small one—that the blade might be his undoing.

A shuffling sound called Nathan's attention back to Sever and Morik, and he dove deeper into the shadows just in time to hear their footsteps descend the steps. He flattened his back against the wall, praying they didn't intend to return to the field.

"I should visit the prisoners," Sever said. "I haven't inspected personally in days."

"Very good. I'll go with you."

Nathan didn't wait to hear Sever's response. With a silent curse, he ducked out of the concourse and back into the stands. He narrowly resisted the urge to run, which would put him out in the open. Instead, he dropped to crawl behind the seats, knees protesting as he scraped them against the concrete. He bumped his shoulders on the backs of the plastic chairs, but he kept moving, ignoring the pain that bloomed between his ribs.

He threw himself across the perilous aisles, just short of careless. On the last one, his jeans caught on one of the screws that held them in place, and he had to wrench the fabric free.

He didn't stop until he'd scrambled up to his level, eased through the door—closing it carefully behind him—and dropped onto the couch, fighting to calm his breath.

Voices mumbled outside the door, and it was less than a minute before Sever swept into the room with Morik right behind him. Despite the conversation Nathan had just heard, Sever seemed the opposite of fragile; his skin practically glowed with health.

"Nathan," he said, settling in the chair across from the couch like a shrink about to start a loaded conversation. "How are you feeling?"

"Bit caged." The room was air conditioned and perfectly comfortable, yet sweat was pouring down his neck. Sever would notice that, *had* to notice that.

The alien inclined his head. "Perhaps a walk tomorrow. I'm sure we could arrange an escort."

As long as it wasn't Jenna. "That'd be good. Thanks," Nathan said.

Sever watched him for a long moment, expression completely unreadable. Nathan looked back, trying to scan for signs of Sever's illness without revealing his purpose. But other than the paleness and the dark circles under his eyes, Nathan couldn't make out what might be wrong. Or how he might leverage it.

If Sever was searching Nathan's face for something, it was unclear whether or not he found it. His expression, mild and almost pleasant—eyebrows raised a touch, lashes half lidding his eyes—didn't shift. "Morik," he said, "see that they lower the temperature here. Our friend is clearly too warm."

Nathan let out a breath. "Northern blood," he said. "Can't be helped."

A smile, just a thin tip of the lips. Tired? False? It was hard to say. "I won't have it said that I don't treat my visitors with respect."

Oh, no. Never that. Only entire planets and moons. Only good people, like Tally, who just happened to get in his way.

Sever moved to stand, then paused, his gaze caught on Nathan's leg. When Nathan glanced down, the tear in his jeans seemed huge, his scraped skin painfully obvious. It might as well have had searchlights beaming out of it.

Nathan's brain struggled for an excuse, a place in this polished room where he could have torn his clothing and injured his knee. Anything to say. Anything at all.

Before he could, Sever rose and nodded. "Sleep well," he said.

And then he was gone, the tear dismissed or forgotten—or filed away for future reference.

DOLLY UNDERSTOOD why Sever had chosen a ballpark as his fortress. The place had fences, layers, doors. It had tiered levels and underground passageways.

It also had more shadows than it had people to watch them.

Still, they kept a routine watch schedule. It was, she felt, as much for appearances—and to keep the retirees busy—as for anything else. Her assignment was to patrol the middle of the concourse, past silent concession stands and empty bathrooms. It was a job she'd have given to un-enhanced team members at LIO. Guards. Nobodies.

It was not a job she'd have assigned to the only person capable of cutting portals.

Perhaps this was her punishment for losing the fight with Wave and LIO, or for getting dragged into it to begin with. Perhaps it was a warning.

Or perhaps Sever really was that shorthanded. Dolly brooded while she paced, trying to piece it all together. Trying to think hard enough to figure out his weaknesses, or an opening for her to make her move.

This place hampered her thinking process. It was too quiet, and she jumped at every shadow, every flicker of light. The concourse was a glorified parking garage, ribbons of concrete wound around a central spool. Not the kind of place that should intimidate her. It certainly wouldn't have done so, before Sever.

Yet the concession stands stood abandoned, the bars empty, their darkened TV screens catching ghostly threads of light as she passed. Every time it made her jump, she had to restrain herself from throwing a chair at the screen and shattering it into a million pieces. Why would anyone attend a ballgame just to watch it from a bar? It was absurd.

Dolly hated the whole place.

Still, she did her job. She passed under the hanging banners, resisting the temptation to slash them apart with a portal line out of spite. She paused at each entrance to the stands, and she scanned the field for movement. There was never anything interesting to see.

Tonight, Sever and Morik were strolling around the baseball diamond like it was a court garden. They weren't interesting, however; they made her want to clench her fists, made her wish she could bring herself to slash a portal through both of *them,* just murder them where they stood. Take care of this whole situation, once and for all.

If she were at all confident that would work, she'd do it. Or so she told herself.

In the meantime, she patrolled. Once, she looked out to see Goldi, peering out from across the way and down one level. Goldi checked the field from her side, her metallic-gold hair tied back in a purple headband. They exchanged a wave, then moved on.

Goldi, patrolling. Sever would have Diana cleaning the toilets next.

After half an hour of this nonsense, Dolly paused at the entrance on the far end of the concourse to lean between against the concrete wall that led out to the stands. She wasn't tired, exactly, but she felt she'd earned a rest just the same. If Sever could stroll, Dolly could pause.

She'd been to a ballgame, once or twice. In her youth. She looked out at the diamond, trying to remember if she and Will had ever attended one together. It was hard to picture sitting beside him in the stands, eating hot dogs and drinking over-priced beer. What team would they have rooted for?

They'd had fun, when they'd first been married. They might never have been to a ballgame, but they'd certainly gone to parties. Plays. She remembered dancing with him, his smile as he whirled her around. That had been before, long before it had all gone wrong.

Sometimes, she missed him so much that it felt like a deep wound, one that would never heal.

Something glinted in the center stands, underneath the press box and down to the right. A brief flash of light, no more than a blink. Dolly glanced at Sever and Morik, but they were facing the outfield, heads bent together in conversation.

Dolly squinted, searching for the source of the light and expecting to see Goldi checking the field again.

But no. It was one of the VIP suite windows. As she watched, it slowly opened, catching the distant glare of a street-light as it moved.

And then, a shadowy figure slipped out into the night.

Nathan Pearce. It was difficult to narrow in on the precise box—she'd only accessed it from the interior door; she hadn't known there *was* an exterior one—but she couldn't imagine stodgy President Caldwell sneaking out of his suite.

She could sound the alarm. She probably ought to. If Nathan escaped, Sever would hold it against Dolly's people, whether he knew she'd witnessed it or not.

But she still needed a plan, a way to use her position to get the Knife back, and something was niggling at her mind—the seed of an idea.

Dolly ducked back into the concourse and hurried past several entrances, then drifted back out into the stadium, careful to stay among the shadows. If she hadn't been watching so carefully, she never would have noticed the occasional shudder of a seat, the flutter of movement between them.

Sever and Morik moved out of the field and back into the concourse, entering the level above Dolly's current one. They didn't so much as glance toward the seats.

Nathan was good, but Dolly was better. Or she was luckier, anyway. It so often amounted to the same thing.

Sever had taken Nathan as a hostage, hoping to keep Mary in line. She'd already been lured here, unable to resist trying to save him. But perhaps... Perhaps there was a way to use him further, to bait the League into attacking on Sever's—and Dolly's—territory.

They'd have home advantage. And if they forced the League to act before they were ready, Dolly would have every chance at seizing the Knife back from Eloise and using it to defeat Sever.

Dolly watched as Nathan slipped out of the stands, following Sever and Morik into the darkness of the concourse. Not an escape attempt then, clearly. No, he was sneaking around out here to collect information, which meant he intended to act. But how? And when?

It didn't matter. If she was going to manipulate Sever, whose eye was sharp and ruthless, she'd have to do it carefully. Bide her time, and wait until Nathan made his move. Then, Dolly would move the pieces on her game board, ever so slightly, with ever so much subtlety, so that no one would even know she was even playing until it was too late.

AFTER THE RETIREES managed to track El's portal resonance to the yacht—not to mention Alex's dire freak-out about imploding the universe—Mary and Bradley had decided to head for Oklahoma the old-fashioned way: through a super-fast underwater tunnel that would spit them out on the coast. After which they'd jet over to Tulsa.

Totally old-fashioned.

As soon as they'd loaded up their gear, Bradley had draped himself across the back seat of the boxy vehicle and shut his eyes, leaving the front seats for Mary and Rajni. The vehicle was the size of a car, but it hummed like an airport transport carrying passengers between terminals, a persistent whine in the background as it jetted through the underwater passage.

The tunnel walls rushed by too quickly for Mary to make out the material or any details about the design. Everything was frustratingly dark.

She was dying to get some time in under the hood of this thing.

Rajni was sitting next to Mary, staring out the window even though there was nothing to see. Or at her reflection, or at nothing. It was hard to tell.

"If this is too much," Mary said, "you can stay on the plane when we get to Tulsa. No one will blame you."

Rajni blinked, so slowly that Mary actually thought she might keep her eyes closed. "What's the difference? I can be sad in the bunker or sad on the plane, or sad helping you watch this mystery house. I don't really care."

Mary had never really been good with this part of the job. She could remember sitting next to a terrified Jenna Carpenter —or so she'd thought at the time—and thinking the same thing. Even then, when they'd only had one conversation, she'd wished Nathan were there to face the task of comforting instead of her.

But Nathan wasn't here, and she sure as hell wasn't going to wake Bradley. Whatever he'd say, it wouldn't help.

Mary didn't know if she could help, either. But she could tell the truth. It was all she had.

"I failed Tally, you know," she said.

Rajni sat up and turned away from the window, as if startled out of her misery. She wasn't crying, but her eyes were rimmed in red, like she'd run out of tears. "What? How?"

At least with Jenna, Mary had been driving. A wheel to hold, a road to watch. Now, she could only look into Rajni's dark eyes. She made herself unclench her hands. "Tally was like me. She went her own way, and she wanted action over waiting. All the mistakes she made? I used to make the same ones. Not long ago, either."

Rajni's expression didn't change. She just sat there, looking at Mary. Waiting for her to say more.

OK, well, there was more to say. Might as well spit it out. "I saw that in her, and I should have mentored her. I should have taught her what I'd learned, but I didn't. I just yelled at her when she screwed up. And then she died to save me."

She'd thrown herself between Mary and Sever, and he'd

batted her out of the way like a toy. The worst part was, it hadn't been necessary. Tally had acted before thinking, before listening to Mary as she tried to warn the recruit that Sever wouldn't hurt her.

Or maybe Tally simply hadn't been willing to take that chance. Either way, she was a hero. Would always be a hero, in Mary's memory.

Rajni turned to look out the windshield. Not that there was anything to see out there, either. At least she didn't lean against the window again, or close her eyes. Felt like progress. "She admired you."

Mary couldn't help it. She snorted. "That seems highly unlikely."

Tally had been on Mary's patrol team when the League had worried about EAEA spies, and they'd only ever butted heads. Yeah, they'd come to an understanding, but not until the end. Much too late.

Rajni shrugged. "She did."

"You knew her best." Mary paused, not wanting to push. "You'd know, I think, if she'd want you to stay back. Or if she'd want you to try. To figure out what's up with your powers. Help us finish this fight."

Rajni pressed her fingertips into her thighs, hard enough to make little divots. Her nails were ragged, like she'd been biting them. "My powers are there. I just... It feels wrong to use them, with her gone."

Mary didn't understand what it was like to have powers, not really. But she understood the pain in Rajni's eyes. "Grief is such an asshole," Mary said. "Do what you can, when you can, OK?"

Rajni nodded and leaned back in her seat. Mary wasn't sure if she'd be OK, couldn't promise everything would work out. She couldn't bring Tally back; she couldn't make that right.

But she could keep an eye on Tally's best friend. And together, they'd take out her killer.

25 / AGNES

AFTER THE BLOWUP WITH ELOISE, Agnes took refuge in the infirmary. Mostly because it happened to be the first open door she happened upon, which made it the first place she could sneak into without running into Eloise. Or Fran.

Agnes needed a break from Eloise—she wished it could be a permanent one—and she definitely wasn't ready to face Fran. She shut the door behind her and let out a breath of relief, though she doubted either woman would follow her.

When she turned, expecting to find Dr. Gordon—or, preferably, an empty room where she could collect her thoughts—she found herself face-to-face with Ire. He was standing by an open drawer, eyebrows raised, his red hair sticking up in every direction, and Agnes realized they hadn't really had a chance to speak since LIO's arrival.

She probably should have sought him out. They'd been friends, once, good ones. He'd been the only person at LIO, other than Eloise, who'd known that Tam and Lucy existed.

And now she was staring at him. With her mouth open. Excellent.

"Needed a bandage," he said, holding up his hand as if to answer an unasked question—though she'd been so focused on her own reaction that she hadn't thought to wonder why he was in here. A deep cut ran across the back of his hand, all the way from the pinky knuckle to the base of the wrist. It was puffy and red around the edges.

"No one looked at that yesterday?" Agnes asked.

"They did. But it's from the Trap."

Agnes winced. It wasn't pleasant to imagine Diana's poison leaking into a wound. That might require Dr. Gordon's assistance.

Agnes waved for Ire to sit on the exam table. She hadn't spent much time in here, but she could find him some bandages. She checked another drawer, then moved to the cabinets. With her surprise at finding Ire here abating, her thoughts pulled her right back to the fight with Eloise.

If she'd had her wits about her, Agnes would have responded to El by listing the League's long, long list of crimes. Especially the ones against Wave. She'd reminded Eloise that it was under her watch that innocent Wave operatives had been imprisoned at HQ, yes, but there were more details. More nuances.

Of course if she'd had her wits about her, she'd never have agreed to help in the first place. The world was in actual danger, and Eloise couldn't forget her grudges, couldn't compromise long enough to save it. The whole thing made Agnes want to scream and break things, but not in here.

In El's room, maybe. Agnes grabbed a roll of bandages and some disinfectant out of a cabinet and slammed the door shut.

"You're pissed," Ire said. "Am I not supposed to be in here?"

Even with the bandages in her hand, Agnes had nearly forgotten he was here. She shook her head, trying to smooth her face back to a pleasant expression. Or at least, not a rage-filled one. "No, no, you're fine. I'm mad at Eloise."

"Oh, gotcha." Ire leaned back, using his good hand for support while he rested his injured one on his knee. "Back to old times already?"

Agnes blinked. "What?"

"It's like old times. When we were all together at HQ."

Agnes motioned for him to flatten his hand, then sprayed disinfectant over the wound. He didn't even flinch. He'd always had a high threshold for pain, though she'd never quite gotten around to studying whether it was related to his powers or just part of who he was.

"No," she said, "El and I used to be friends. We got along fine at HQ. But she's changed. Now she's..." Agnes groped for the right word. "Infuriating?"

Ire sat up, rubbing his ear with his free hand. "Friends? I guess. I mean, we got along. But she was more like our boss, remember?"

Agnes frowned. Had she been? Yes, she'd been in charge, and the League certainly hadn't operated as diplomatically as Wave seemed to. Even with the Committee at the head, Fran had made a point of letting all their operatives vote on decisions that directly impacted them.

When she didn't respond, Ire said, "We wanted to educate enhanced humans, remember? Find them and make a place for them to get a handle on their powers, decide what they wanted. Not just to fight."

We. Yes, that had been Ire's dream as much as it'd been hers. It wasn't that she'd forgotten her friendship with Ire, not exactly—she'd thought of him often during her time at Wave, missed his companionship in the lab—just that the nuances seemed to have faded.

But he was right. She'd butted heads with Eloise over that idea. El hadn't wanted to devote their scant resources to it, while Agnes and Ire had argued that it should be a priority.

And then Agnes had left. Wave had used its mind-control serum on Ire, and she'd let them do it. And then she'd left him behind, without so much as an explanation.

Agnes draped the edge of the bandage across Ire's hand, directing him to hold the end with his thumb while she wrapped. "How is it you're not as mad at me as she is?"

He shrugged, a shudder of his mountainous shoulders. Other people were always surprised at how well he moved around spaces like the lab, full as they were with fragile equipment. Agnes knew he took care to practice, to observe his environment. He didn't like to hurt people, and he knew how easily he could break things.

"I was mad," he said. "I was hurt. But in the end, you did what you thought was right, like always. And it turns out you weren't wrong. Wave's a decent group, even if their past is as bad as LIO's."

Agnes bristled. "I don't think—"

"They manipulated a teenaged kid into blowing up a building." His voice was gentle, but firm. "A teenaged kid who's now our grownup friend, and needs our help. How can we help him if we're at each other's throats all the time?"

Nathan. Agnes didn't know him well at all, but he was important to Mary. And he'd been the one to release the Wave prisoners from LIO.

More to the point, Ire was right about Wave. She didn't want to admit it, but even if she could set the mind-control serum aside as a necessary evil—and she didn't like to set *any* evil aside as necessary—she couldn't justify terrorism under any circumstances.

Wave had used Nathan to exert their own justice. Was it really so different from Dolly using Will to exert hers?

Agnes paused her bandage wrapping to look into her

friend's face. "You have a point. And for what it's worth, I'm sorry. We... we were friends."

Best friends, maybe. Always had each other's backs, until she'd turned against him. Or so he must have seen it.

Ire twisted his lips, an almost-smile. "We still are friends."

Agnes sighed. If Ire could be forgiving, maybe she needed to make more of an effort, too. "So, if Fran says I should give Eloise a tour... and try to get along with her..."

Ire shrugged again. "Up to you. But she's doing her best. And she did start that recruiting program."

"Did I hear you're in charge of it?"

He inclined his head, a real smile touching the corner of his mouth now. "They're good kids."

If Eloise was allowing Ire to run a program like that, to teach recruits even if they didn't want to be fighters, maybe she really could change. And maybe Agnes could, too.

She placed a piece of tape carefully at the end of the bandage to secure it. "Make sure Dr. Gordon sees that later, in case the poison's hanging on."

When he winked, it really *did* feel like old times. "Sure thing, doc. Good luck with Eloise."

Agnes nodded, her stomach twisting with nerves. She had a feeling she was going to need all the luck she could get.

THE MORE ELOISE saw of Wave's ocean-trench hideout, the more convinced she became that she'd never do anything the way they did, or really understand the way they operated. The place was more luxury resort than operative headquarters, where they seemed far more concerned about the ice cream sundae bar in the cafeteria than they were about creating a waypoint for decisive action.

Wave was adept at hiding, after all. They weren't so good at taking the offensive.

Eloise had been unable to mask her surprise when Agnes had appeared at her door, several hours after Fran's ultimatum. She'd stowed her clipboard away somewhere, and had changed into soft gray pants, tucking her spiral curls back behind a purple headband. She looked, for all the world, as if she'd been expected.

Now, she was giving Eloise the full tour of the underwater complex. And Steve, who Eloise had dragged out of his own room so he could accompany her. Definitely not as a buffer. Just as... moral support.

Eloise assumed Fran must be holding Agnes's clipboard hostage, though Agnes didn't show any more frustration at the assignment. Eloise didn't see how she could be reveling in the opportunity, either. Agnes didn't mention the blowup, though, so Eloise kept her mouth shut as Agnes paraded them through rooms and labs as politely as a tour guide showing off a historical house.

Even without the tension from their fight, Eloise didn't particularly want the tour. She wanted to get back to training and studying the Knife, before Sever found a way to track them here.

She doubted this complex could rise above the surface to escape. Though she supposed she shouldn't doubt Wave's proficiency in that arena.

"This is the lab I worked in before Fran reassigned me to the island," Agnes said, leading them into a large room. "It gets the best of everything Wave has."

It looked like every other lab Eloise had ever seen. LIO, CLEAR, Wave. They were all the same. Tables, microscopes, test tubes, and cabinets on the walls full of equipment that no one was supposed to touch, until they'd earned at least one Ph.D.

"What makes it better than the stuff on the yacht?" Steve strolled along the row of cabinets, peering into each one. They hadn't discussed what had happened between them at HQ, that kiss—that *kiss*—they'd shared in the moments before the walls caved in around them. Not that there'd exactly been time to focus on romance.

Still, he'd been there at her side on the yacht. She'd cried into his shoulder. And her stomach still flipped excited butterflies when she saw him, the same way it had when they'd been kids together. It was silly, with everything that was happening, but she supposed she could allow herself a sliver of joy.

Agnes watched Steve, eyebrows pinched, as if she was ready to slap his hand if he tried to touch anything. "This lab is just more extensive. Not a great idea to store your most precious equipment on a moving ship."

Steve grinned, and Eloise was grateful for his friendliness, his ease. And his willingness to come on this tour. Maybe he *was* a good buffer. A little bit. "Especially one that makes sudden dives," he said.

Agnes actually smiled back, though she didn't stop watching him. Not that she'd be able to stop him, if he decided to start super-speedily juggling beakers. "Wave's always full of surprises," she said.

"Did they choose their name because of all the water stuff, or vice versa?" Steve asked. "Yachts, islands, under-ocean bunkers. It's all rather on the nose."

Agnes laughed. A genuine, warm sound that Eloise realized she'd missed. "No idea," she said. "But I'd love to know." As if she'd wondered the exact same thing. Well, maybe she had.

It made Eloise want to reminisce, to think about the way things had been when they'd all worked together. The early days of her leadership hadn't been easy, but they'd been able to rely on each other.

Or maybe she remembered the whole time incorrectly. Maybe sentimentalism was twisting the truth of the past into idealistic nonsense. She wasn't sure how she could ever know.

The Knife shuffled in the back of her mind, a hushed murmur. Like a sleepy sigh, or a yawn.

"How deep are we?" Eloise asked, before she'd quite realized she meant to join the conversation. Her voice sounded too cheerful in her ears. Stretched, or fake, like an echo. Did she not know how to just be *normal* anymore?

Maybe she'd never *been* normal.

"I'm not sure," Agnes said. "I just know they've got networks of tunnels leading here. With little railed cars."

Impressive. Eloise didn't want to admit it, but it was. She

glanced around the lab, taking in all the equipment—most of which had uses she didn't understand at all. "Is there anything in here that can help us study the Knife?"

Agnes shook her head. "It's all back in my cabin. Come on, I'll take you there."

Agnes's 'cabin' was more like a comfortable escape in the woods than a ship's quarters. The main area had a kitchen, a round dining table, and a cluster of overstuffed couches, and it smelled like cocoa and apples. There was even a piano in the corner, with a guitar on a stand beside it. A hallway led back to what Eloise had to assume were bedrooms.

"Lovely place," Steve said as Agnes herded them into seats around the table and bustled into cabinets for tea.

"Are you regretting your choice not to join Wave?" Eloise asked, settling into her chair.

Steve propped an arm around her shoulders. "I'm here now, and I'm here with you. Not sure there's a better combo."

In the past, Eloise would have tried to keep him out of this. Not for his own good or anything like that, but for hers. She'd have argued that the distraction would keep her from focusing on what mattered, and slow her down in her quest to learn what she needed to know about the Knife.

Now, though, she was glad he was here. The whole idea of the League, even from its dubious foundations, had been about strength in numbers. They could help each other. That was the point. Somewhere along the line, that idea had been corrupted. But it'd started out well.

Agnes deposited a teapot and cups onto the table, somehow juggling a jar of honey at the same time. "Let me hop into the back and pull out my equipment."

"Why isn't all your equipment in the lab?" Eloise asked. "Do they have closing hours or something?"

Agnes had always been a round-the-clock kind of worker,

especially when she got engaged in an important project. But the scientist just shook her head, curls drifting around her as she moved. "No one really trusted me when I first showed up here. Except Bradley, I guess. Anyway, their stares were distracting. So sometimes I worked in here."

She said it almost too matter-of-factly, like she didn't want Eloise to hear the pain behind the story. It was there, though.

Eloise supposed the League would have responded similarly. She herself had forbidden Nathan to contact his Wave friends when LIO had needed an assist. They'd only come to Wave because there'd been no other choice. And as ungrateful as it seemed, Eloise still wasn't entirely certain it'd been the right one.

And yet, she felt a sliver of indignation on Agnes's behalf. Eloise might not agree with her choices, but she did mean well.

Agnes disappeared down the hall, and Eloise reached for the tea—and paused when she caught sight of a small girl standing in the hallway entrance, watching her. The girl had light brown skin and big brown eyes—Agnes's eyes. Eloise thought she was about eight or nine, though she couldn't remember exactly. She should. She should remember those things.

Eloise tapped Steve on the shoulder, and he followed her gaze.

"You must be Lucy," Eloise said. She'd known of Agnes's family long before the scientist had defected for Wave, and had kept them a secret at Agnes's request. Her wife and daughter had to be protected at all costs.

Here, it seemed, Wave brought entire families into the fold.

Lucy pinched her lips together, knuckles paling as she gripped the door frame. "Are you the Pearl Knife?"

Her voice was quiet, like a small flute, but steady. Like she wanted to run away, but wanted the answer even more.

"I am," Eloise said.

"Why are you here?" *Was* that fear? Or was it anger? Eloise didn't have much experience with kids. She couldn't tell. Either way, the girl wasn't excited to see her. That much was plain.

Steve cleared his throat, but Eloise gave her head a shake. The girl was looking at her, and Eloise had a feeling she wouldn't be deflected by his charm. "Your mom's helping me out with a problem. Wave is helping me, too."

"Why would they help *you*?"

The words came out with much more vitriol than Eloise would have expected from a little girl. Eloise opened her mouth to answer—as best she could—but Lucy went on.

"You hurt our friends," she said. "Dr. Gordon, and Gigi, and everyone who lived on the island. They didn't do any crimes, and you pretended they did."

"They knew about crimes," Eloise said. Like using a thir-teen-year-old Nathan to blow up a building in London to 'pre-vent terrorism.' "Some of them."

Lucy let go of the door frame and crossed her arms over her chest. Whether or not Dr. Gordon and the others had known about those crimes, what Dolly had done was still inex-cusable.

"That wasn't Eloise," Steve said. "It was her mother."

"She has the same name."

"It's a generational thing," Steve said.

The little girl's scowl made her look so much like Agnes, it would have been funny—if she hadn't been so very serious. Eloise had a feeling she was just getting started with her accu-sations. "You kept them in prison," she said.

"But we let them go," Steve said.

For her part, Eloise couldn't begin to formulate a defense, or even the barest explanation. *Nathan* had let them go. Not Eloise. Not the League as a whole, and certainly not Eloise.

Lucy's scowl didn't loosen. "Did Mary O'Sullivan's parents know about crimes when you crashed their plane?"

Eloise's heart dropped into her stomach, pain and nausea mixing. She swallowed.

Steve said, "Eloise's *mother* made a bad choice. She took over Will's powers. You know Will?"

Lucy nodded.

"She did a bad thing to him. She hurt him."

Lucy looked at Eloise, unmoved. "Did Mary's parents know about crimes?"

All she knew was that they'd been affiliated with Wave, and that Dolly had punished them for it. She'd intentionally rescued Mary, too, not out of compassion for a little girl—of about Lucy's age, incidentally—but because she'd known that Mary would inherit vast resources that could help fund the League.

Eloise could only shake her head. "I don't know. I don't... I don't think so."

"Are you going to take over my mom's powers?" Eloise hadn't seen the tears collecting in Lucy's eyes, but now a pair of them dropped down her cheeks. The girl sniffed and ignored them, even as they caught on the corners of her mouth.

"No." Eloise's voice was a husk. "No, I'm... No."

Agnes appeared behind Lucy, set a hand on the girl's shoulder and gave it a squeeze. "Go to Mama," she said, gentle. "See if she'd like some tea."

Lucy retreated, but Eloise could hear the echo of her sniffling down the hall. She wanted to say that Wave had brainwashed the girl, that spending nearly a year among them had just poisoned her against LIO.

But what had Lucy said that wasn't true? The League's mistakes—and, in some cases, *Eloise's* mistakes—were hardly less horrifying than Wave's. The League *had* framed Dr.

Gordon and the other Wave operatives. In some cases, Dolly had used their own powers to do it, like she'd done to Dad.

And Eloise had been the one to keep those same operatives in her own prison, dosed with power-suppressing serum, until Nathan confirmed that their trials had been a sham. He'd been the one to let them go.

In Lucy's eyes, that made Eloise as much a villain as her mother. And the worst part was that she just might be right.

27 / MARY

THE ONLY TASK more boring than a stakeout was an assignment to stake out someone *else*'s stakeout.

And doing it in the late afternoon heat of Oklahoma made it even worse. Mary didn't know why she kept ending up in hot places, why the bad guys couldn't choose a temperate spot to carry out whatever villainous plans were next on their agenda. As she watched the rotation of Sever's guards—each trying to look casual while they paced down an otherwise quiet residential sidewalk—she mentally planned a trip to Antarctica.

Nathan would probably like that. They'd never discussed it, but he was definitely the kind of person who could appreciate icebergs and penguins.

As long as she kept thinking forward, she could keep her brain from panicking about the present.

In the meantime, Sever's people were clearly better at shooting space guns and bashing heads than at casually stalking. There were two of them staking out the neighborhood, that she'd seen. They'd dressed in plain, Earth-acceptable clothing—though the blue and white Dallas Cowboys jersey on one of them might lead to more problems than solutions, in Kansas City territory—but they moved along the sidewalks at obviously timed intervals, scowling and scanning, their posture ramrod-straight.

They'd have fit in better at Buckingham Palace, and the changing of the guard.

Well, except for the football jersey.

And if those things weren't enough to draw interest from the neighbors, the too-muscled arms that bulged out of their shirts definitely would. They weren't even bothering to mask themselves by pushing baby carriages, or perhaps walking an eerily believable robot dog up and down the block.

In Mary's mind, advanced alien civilizations definitely had robot dogs.

The woman whose house they were watching was named Beatrice Carter. She was a seventy-something former nurse. A civilian. Mary didn't know for sure who she was, or why Sever's people would be watching her. She could only guess the woman must have some connection to her grandmother. Could Beatrice have known her?

As evening descended—taking its sweet time—Bradley crawled out from behind the house at her back and came to crouch beside Mary. She'd been lying flat out in the grass behind the hedge, which separated the yard from the street. The family who lived in the house had been moved to a safe hiding spot for the day.

And she'd been doing just fine on her own. "You're supposed to stay in the car," Mary whispered.

"Rajni's keeping watch from the car."

Mary rolled her eyes at Bradley, wondering what Wave's Committee would do if Bradley came back with a black eye. Maybe she could blame it on a bad guy. It'd be Bradley's word against hers. "Not because we need a view from that angle, because we're not supposed to move around. We're supposed to sit. And wait."

She hated everything about it. But that was how stakeouts went.

"I'm familiar with the concept." He rolled up his sleeves, his galoshes squeaking as he shifted his weight.

"Why do you have to wear those things?" Mary asked, keeping her voice low. "They do not scream 'subtle.'"

Bradley blinked at her. "Trust me, you'd rather I wore them than not. Besides, I put on the black ones today. Perfect for subterfuge."

One of Sever's not-so-inconspicuous guards paused, glancing around warily. At the sound of their voices, or the galoshes squeaking, Mary didn't know. Bradley was distracting her.

The guard moved on, and Bradley nodded toward the house across the way. "I say we sneak in through the garage."

"No offense," Mary said, though she hoped he'd take some, "but sneaking around is my area of expertise. So let's just wait until nightfall. And when it comes, let's listen to my instructions. No manipulations, no side quests. OK?"

Mary had been watching the house all day. It was a single-floor brick home with a two-car garage and a few stubby trees in the yard. Not much cover for daytime sneaking.

But there was also a stubby stone fence that led, if the draping morning glories were any indication, to a back garden. As long as Sever's guys were intent on staying 'inconspicuous,' they might not have anyone watching the garden, which would make it the perfect entry point.

She'd have to confirm that first, of course, but she'd already routed the ideal path for scouting, around the other side of the house and along the roof. Under the cover of night, which was still a few hours away.

The Dallas Cowboys guard passed the second guard, nodded as though they were neighbors saying hello—these guys *really* didn't know how to do the spy thing—and moved deeper into the neighborhood. The new guard paused on the corner and took his phone out of his pocket, like he wanted to check a bus route. Even though there wasn't a bus stop here.

There was, however, a fire hydrant. And as the guard slipped his phone back into his pocket, a stream of water burst out of the hydrant and knocked the guard off his feet.

"Huh," Bradley said. "Looks like Rajni found her powers."

Apparently so. The girl had abandoned the van and was already running for the house. She vaulted over the fence and disappeared into the back garden. Which Mary definitely had not vetted for safety. Didn't *anyone* listen to instructions?

Mary swore and jumped up, leaping over the hedge and hoping that the only two guards they'd seen today were, in fact, the only two guards.

The hydrant-hit guard was passed out on the sidewalk, but breathing. Thankfully. Mary didn't like that he worked for Sever, but she didn't go in for murder.

She grabbed the unconscious guard's shoulders and dragged him toward the wall. Bradley picked up his feet without being asked, though he did glance smugly at his galoshes as they dragged the guard through the thickening mud and toward the back garden.

With Bradley's help, Mary hoisted the guard over the wall and dropped him into a bed of marigolds, then hopped over the wall and dropped to a crouch in front of a wide-eyed Rajni.

"What was that?" Mary said.

"You wanted me to use my powers," Rajni said. "I used my powers." She looked dazed, like she didn't quite believe it herself.

Mary took a deep breath, let it out slowly. She couldn't get pissed. She couldn't yell. She had to do better with Rajni than she had with Tally.

"We had a plan," Mary said.

Rajni rubbed her hands together, and Mary hoped she wasn't about to get blasted in the face with water. "We needed a new one."

Mary sat back on her heels, risking a glance over the wall. "Unfortunately, your plan will bring the other guard running, assuming there's only one. And probably the fire department to fix the hydrant."

"A distraction, maybe," Bradley said.

Mary forced her teeth apart. Grinding them to dust wouldn't help anyone. It was done; they had to work with what they had.

She looked past Rajni and out across the yard, doing a quick survey of the area. Sever didn't have any guards back here, at least not that she could see. But there might be cameras. Drones. These were aliens; for all she knew, the marigolds could be spying. "We didn't need a distraction."

Rajni flipped her braid over her shoulder, which might have looked casual if she hadn't paired the movement with a nervous flick of her tongue against her bottom lip. "Sorry," she said. "I'm sorry. But at least, I mean, I got us inside."

Mary picked up the guard's shoulders and nodded to Bradley, who picked up the feet. The longer they kept Sever's people searching for him, the better. "OK. We're here now. There's a back door across the patio. Let's move."

Hoping Rajni would follow, but half-expecting her to crack a water main, Mary guided Bradley across the perilously open stretch of yard. In another time, Mary might have thought this garden was a fairy garden, with little stones and orbs arranged just so through the tiger lilies.

Now, she just felt bad for stepping on the tulips.

Mary and Bradley dragged the still-unconscious guard across the patio, where Mary dropped the guy so she could jimmy the lock. It cracked quickly, and she shoved the door open.

And found herself staring down the barrel of a shotgun.

The woman holding it was definitely Beatrice Carter. Mary recognized her from the photos they'd pulled before they arrived.

Beatrice had wide shoulders and tight white curls on top of her head, a shimmer of blue-green eyeshadow dusted across her lids. And she looked pissed.

Mary raised her hands, trusting Bradley to do the same.

Beatrice lowered the gun. "You." She set the rifle on the washing machine to her left with a clatter. With a quick glance around the yard, she opened the door. "It's about time you showed up."

AGNES WATCHED Lucy retreat down the hall at a half run, as if she'd spent all her courage confronting Eloise. The girl was a spitfire, no denying that. But she'd also been hurt by Agnes's involvement with the League, and with Wave. She'd been picking up half conversations and whispers for months now, and Agnes hadn't realized just how much she'd put together.

It was confusing enough for an adult mind, let alone an eight-year-old.

When Agnes turned back to the table, Eloise hardly looked less upset than Lucy. She looked bereft, the corners of her mouth twitching down as she stared at the space Lucy had just vacated.

Agnes left the hall and set her equipment on the table, taking a seat across from Eloise.

Eloise touched her finger to the corner of her eye, like she was checking for tears, then sat up straight and looked Agnes in the eye. "All right. Where do we start?"

And for the first time—maybe because of her conversation with Ire, or because of the grief painted across El's face—Agnes saw where she'd left El when she'd chosen to abandon the League for Wave. Eloise had always taken everything onto her own shoulders. The point of the League was to carry the burden together, but Eloise had always tried to be everything to everyone. To make every right decision. To manage the weight, no matter how much piled on, without asking for help.

No wonder she and Mary butted heads so much, or used to. They were two sides of a very lonely coin.

It wasn't that Agnes would make a different decision now. She believed in Wave's trajectory, in their dedication to the future, and their mission of using enhanced abilities to make the world a better place.

But Eloise wasn't her mother. Maybe it was time Agnes accepted that.

It was a wonder that Eloise had come to Wave at all, instead of trying to dig a new HQ by herself. With a shovel, if she had to.

Eloise was looking at her with eyebrows raised, though she still clasped Steve's hand. Like she knew she needed to jump into the work, like the world depended on her and her alone.

Add to all that a suite of powers based on an artifact that spoke only to her? No wonder she felt so isolated.

Agnes took a deep breath. Let it out. "I'm sorry about Lucy. I kept her out of this life for a long time, and for good reason. It's been unavoidable but... she's working through some things."

"Aren't we all," Steve murmured.

"It's good for you to meet her," Agnes said. "For her to sort out who you are, and who Dolly is."

Lucy wasn't the only one who needed to do that. Agnes obviously did. Eloise might still need to do it, too, to an extent.

Steve might be the only one in the room who'd gotten it straight.

Agnes opened her equipment case and began arranging a set of circular plates inside it, connecting each to a monitor. "I was testing resonances before they reassigned me to the island.

I'd been checking different materials to see if they could detect enhancements from forensic evidence. Pick up on frequencies in fingernails, blood, feathers. That kind of thing."

Eloise leaned in, examining the plates. "You want me to put the Knife on those?"

Agnes nodded. "Don't worry. It just sends a small current to the screen here, and we can measure the energy output. The plates are made of common materials. Glass, copper, limestone, etc. Nothing harmful."

Tam padded into the room as Agnes worked, humming, and Agnes glanced over her shoulder. Her wife had on a long-sleeved dress and gray leggings, her auburn curls loose around her heart-shaped face. Agnes never knew how she didn't get a chill walking around barefoot down here.

"Is Lucy OK?" Agnes asked. Tam could be known to launch into lectures of her own, though she tended to hoard those for Bradley Archer. If she was upset about Lucy, though, she wouldn't hold back.

Tam fluttered her fingers. "Oh, she's fine. She fell asleep in a blink. Still tired from the trip, I think." Tam reached over Agnes's shoulder and plucked a teacup out of the stack. "Mind if I play a bit? I'll keep it quiet."

Agnes glanced at Eloise. "Tam's a musician."

Eloise gave Tam a smile that was both warm and a bit tenuous. As if she, too, expected another tirade from Agnes's family. "I'd love to hear you," she said.

Tam poured herself some tea and drifted to the piano while Agnes finished connecting cords. She switched the monitor on, and Eloise withdrew the Knife.

"Limestone first," Agnes said, pointing. "It's meant to catch the resonance, at least in theory. Just a measurement."

She tried to direct her words to the Knife as much as to Eloise, the way Fran had done. The blade was sentient, after all, and could react to what they said. They just needed to find a way to understand it.

Tam began to play a few scales in the background to warm up her fingers, the notes soft and comforting. The background of so many of Agnes's warmest memories.

"If anything hurts," Agnes added, still speaking to the Knife, "tell Eloise. We'll shut it off."

It felt strange to speak to an inanimate—well, seemingly inanimate—object, even given Agnes's vast experience in the realm of enhanced abilities. But Eloise nodded and set the Knife carefully down on the limestone circle. The poor thing was still showing its cracks, only faintly, but Agnes had spent hours in its presence. She could almost feel the difference in it, the wound beneath the surface. It felt like a name on the tip of her tongue, a word she'd forgotten—but one she'd remember, with sudden clarity, in the middle of the night.

Agnes turned the machine on. Eloise leaned forward.

Nothing registered. Agnes dialed up the sensors. Nothing. She turned on a low vibration, meant to set off a resonance. It worked in a few more physical attributes, but she didn't expect it to work here. It was part of the study she'd designed, though, and she couldn't know until she tried it.

Still, no spikes registered on the machine.

"Don't worry," Agnes said. "That's why we have twenty different plates."

They might need to find twenty more, with the Knife. They might need to plunge it into water. Or jello, for that matter. But every study had to start somewhere.

They tested the glass, the copper, the aluminum, all with Tam's soundtrack of Beethoven in the background. Beethoven shifted to Brahms, then Lennon and McCartney, and the monitor registered nothing. Not so much as a whisper.

When they'd run through all the materials, Agnes had

Eloise place the Knife back on the table. "We know the Knife gives off some kind of vibration when it creates a portal," she said. "Can you ask it to create a small one now? Just to the kitchen, somewhere easy."

"Should I put it on a plate first?"

"No, let's see what we can observe when it's on the table. Especially what you observe."

Eloise shrugged, like she didn't expect much, and shifted the blade to the tabletop. It was just simple wood. Nothing fancy. Probably just a sheet of cheap cork with a fake wood finish, despite Wave's luxurious preferences.

When Eloise let go of the Knife, it flicked a sketch of a line into the air, a portal too small to admit more than a fingernail.

Agnes leaned forward, staring at the Knife so hard it took an actual effort not to let her nose touch it. "Do you hear anything?" she asked.

"I always hear something," Eloise said.

Another way she was alone.

Agnes opened her mouth to ask El to move the Knife to the limestone plate. But in the background, Tam's music shifted, and Agnes paused as her wife's fingers moving farther up the keyboard to the high notes. Lucy liked to call that the 'fairy realm,' because of the tinkling sounds. Tam had even named one of her own compositions after it.

This music sounded like fairy-realm stuff, like one of Tam's pieces. Only there was a beat behind it, too, a thrumming sort of babble that Agnes hadn't heard her play before.

And then Tam said, "I can hear it."

Agnes looked up. Her wife's eyes were closed, her shoulders swaying just slightly as she played. It didn't seem possible, and yet... Somehow, it also seemed right. Inevitable, even. "What is it saying?"

Tam laughed. "It's *singing*. It's true that it's some kind of language, but I don't know if you'd ever get words."

Maybe not words. But music was mathematical, wasn't it? Beautiful math, yes, but still math. A precise kind of magic.

Eloise was staring openly at Tam, her dark eyes like wide, startled pools. .

"It sounds like a waterfall." Tam was still playing, but little dissonances dropped among the fairy-realm tinkles now, like stones skipping across the surface of a still pond. "But there are interruptions in the flow. It might be a heartbeat. It might be a wound."

Agnes glanced at Eloise. She nodded, still staring, her lips softly parted. Like she couldn't believe what she was hearing. Steve squeezed her hand.

Agnes ripped the monitor cords out of the limestone plate and shoved them against the table. Her hand might interfere, so she shoved her clipboard on top of the cords and willed them to stay.

Static burst across the monitor and out of the speakers, and Agnes dialed the audio down so she could hear the music. The spikes on the screen matched the soft beat of the notes, but when she asked Tam to pause, they kept spiking. Kept registering.

When Tam started playing again, the spikes leaped back into action. As if the Knife really was harmonizing with Tam's music. And as she played, as the rest of them listened in silence, Agnes imagined she could hear it, too: the soft pull of an almost-sound that her wife's sensitive ears—and maybe her heart—had caught right away.

When the Knife closed the portal, the spikes calmed, but they continued. Like waves on the beach after a storm.

"OK," Agnes said, still fiddling with the dials. "I think we have a language. If we keep at it, and if Tam can maybe teach the Knife some Earth music and learn about its harmonies, I think we'll all be able to understand it. On some level."

When Eloise didn't respond, Agnes looked up.

Eloise had buried her face in her hands, and her shoulders shook. Steve was rubbing small circles on her back, but Agnes couldn't tell if she was crying or laughing until she dropped her hands and wiped her eyes, beaming in a way that Agnes had never seen before. Her eyes were sparkling with tearful joy.

Eloise had been carrying this burden for so long. And now, she wouldn't have to carry it alone.

Leaving the unconscious guard sprawled on the laundry-room floor, Mary followed Beatrice Carter down a short hall and into a big, open living room. The floors were hard tile, covered at intervals with throw rugs, and the TV was so far from the couches that Mary wondered if Beatrice ever watched it. There was an open fireplace surrounded by a gray-stone shelf, with a variety of concrete statues arranged around it: a Chinese Boxer, a Buddha, a Tolkienesque dragon, and several cone-hatted gnomes.

Beatrice trundled over to a bookcase near the front door, limping slightly, and waved for them to sit down on the couch as she withdrew a green photo album. It was stuffed with extra pages, its binding close to bursting, rogue slips of paper sticking out at random angles.

When Beatrice thumped the book down on the coffee table, Mary understood why she'd gone to retrieve it. On the cover, she'd pasted a full-color photo of the Pearl Knife.

"I've tracked it since it first showed up in public." Beatrice tapped the picture three times with her index finger, then settled onto the end of the couch. "It inspired me to choose a career where I could help people, so I worked as a nurse. Then as a volunteer, after retirement. At least, until these knuckle-heads set up a perimeter around my house."

Beatrice frowned, rubbing her palms on her pants. "They think they're discreet, but this town's the size of a peanut! I know *everyone*. And I'm gonna notice if you show up in my back yard and melt into a tree."

Mary blinked. *She* hadn't noticed that. "Rocker's here?"

"Was yesterday."

And might well have watched their every move as they'd dragged the guard through the back door. Excellent. "This," she said, "is why we surveil the entry points *before* entering."

"He's a dirty turncoat," Beatrice said. "They all are. How can those ex-heroes side with this... this monster?"

"Never much like heroes." Bradley paged through the scrapbook slowly, pausing to scan each photo, each article. Beatrice had cut them out of newspapers and magazines for years and years, labeling each meticulously. The seventies, the eighties, the nineties. As the scrapbook moved toward the present, there were also printed articles from online magazines and blogs. Mary caught Dawn Kimble's name on more than one OperativeWatch post.

But despite the impressive research—and it truly was, with multiple articles sourced from around the world, some of them even translated—Mary doubted that Beatrice's Pearl-Knife knowledge would have drawn Sever's people here. Not by itself.

"Do you know why they're here?" Mary asked.

Beatrice scoffed. "Of course I know. I've expected you for years. Only I thought you might knock at the front door, 'stead of breaking in the back."

She looked at Mary expectantly. When Mary didn't say anything, she leaned back. "Wait. You *don't* know why they're here?"

Mary shook her head. "We followed them."

Beatrice folded her fingers and put them in her lap, her fingers shaking almost imperceptibly. Whether from age, or from nerves, Mary wasn't sure. "Well, I knew your great-great-grandma, for starters. And I was there when her daughter showed up with Bonnie Reyna. She helped her, in case you didn't know. I was ten, just a kid, but I was there."

She paused, as if this might be enough information. Mary's thoughts felt foggy, like maybe the heat had half melted her brain. "Bonnie Reyna. A relative of Eloise's?"

Beatrice pursed her lips. "*Her* great-grandma." When she got no response, she sighed, exasperated. "The one who brought the Pearl Knife to Earth?"

Rajni gasped quietly. Other than that, the room was silent. Mary could practically hear her own heartbeat. She could feel it in her fingertips. In the background, a clock ticked rhythmically.

"What," Beatrice said, "Eloise never told you?"

Mary shook her head, numb. "I'm not sure she knows." Dolly hadn't exactly been forthcoming on most things. Though Mary wasn't even sure that *Dolly* knew who'd brought the Pearl Knife to Earth. She'd only ever heard the story that Dolly's mother had kept the Knife in a safe, and that she'd passed it on to Dolly after her death.

Could this woman really have been here all along, sitting on the knowledge about the Knife's origins?

Beatrice settled deeper into the couch. Lips still pursed, she lifted a pair of glasses with hot pink frames, which hung around her neck from a matching cord. "Well then. I'll tell you the story."

Bradley leaned forward, steepling his fingers in front of him. "If you're willing," he said, "I can show it."

Mary wasn't sure how many shocking revelations she could

handle before her brain would decide it was all too much. She looked at Bradley. "What?"

He gave her a little smile. "Oh, I can read thoughts. And project them."

He said it like it was the most natural thing in the world, like nothing could be more expected. Oh, the sky is blue. Oh, the ocean has fish. Oh, Bradley Archer can *read minds.*

Mary hadn't encountered anyone with the ability to read thoughts. Not even a rumor of such a thing. Not even a whisper. And the one who could do it was Bradley Archer?

Rajni inched away from him, just a bit. Mary doubted that would help.

"Are you reading my thoughts now?" Mary asked.

"I told you," he said, "that you wanted me to keep the boots on. But with her permission, I can help Beatrice to share her story. If, ma'am, you happen to have a wading pool?"

———

Mary thought she was used to the varying quirks of enhanced abilities. Each one came with its own set of requirements, its own limitations. Rajni couldn't call water out of a parched desert, for example, any more than El could force the Knife to chop some kale for dinner.

Although, the Knife certainly *could* chop some kale, if it felt inclined. It would seem... out of character. If such a term could apply to a blade.

Even with most of her life spent around enhanced abilities, it was strange beyond measure to see Bradley Archer sitting with his bare feet plunged into a plastic storage box. Beatrice had dumped a pile of musty sweaters out of the thing before filling it with six inches of water.

"So this is the reason for the galoshes," Mary said. The

boots sat beside the makeshift pool, a towel propped on top of them, as though ready for him to step right back in when he was finished. Mary imagined Bradley's closet as a rainbow of boots, galoshes for every occasion.

"Affirmative," Bradley said.

She'd always assumed it was... Well, one of Bradley's eccentricities. He let people believe that, didn't he? In the end, he only let the world see what they wanted to.

Fair, though, wasn't it? Mary was used to enhanced abilities, all kinds of them, and *she'd* been shocked. Rajni had inched away from him, even though he'd made it clear he couldn't use his powers with the boots on. Mind reading obviously freaked people out. Tough to make friends that way.

Great. The last thing she wanted was to start feeling bad for the guy.

"Now, Beatrice," Bradley said, his feet in the pool, his tone steady and kind, "if you don't mind accessing that memory. I'll just tap in and project it."

Mary blinked, and the room shrank. There was no vertigo, no brain-tilting rush. Just a snap of change, and they were in a cozy living room. The walls were close and covered in bookshelves. Nathan would have liked that. There was a chair in the corner with blue flowered upholstery, and a white-shaded lamp with a thick layer of dust around the edge.

"Right," Mary said. "I can see how you'd want to rein that in."

She was looking at the room from the doorway, from behind the head of a small girl with light brown hair. As Mary watched, the girl hefted two paper bags filled with groceries through the small space.

"That's me," Now-Beatrice breathed. Mary couldn't see her, or Bradley, or Rajni. They were invisible, not part of the memory. Mary wondered if they could all see the memory that way. Probably.

"Why can I see her—me—from the outside?" Beatrice asked.

"Part of it." Bradley's voice sounded distant. Not quite strained, but not quite easy, either.

The girl moved into the room, and the perspective shifted with her as she hurried the groceries into the kitchen, where the floor was checkered in white and daisy-yellow tiles, with matching curtains hanging above the sink. The curtains looked worn, a bit frayed at the edges. The refrigerator was turquoise, with round corners. Mary wasn't great with her time periods, but she thought it looked like the 1950s.

At the kitchen table, an older woman sat paging through a newspaper. When little Beatrice entered, a few steps ahead of the vision—it felt like a camera, moving with the scene, but wasn't—the woman's entire face lit into a smile.

"Adina." Now-Beatrice said it along with little Beatrice, her whisper a distant echo from her seat on the couch.

Mary couldn't quite guess at Adina's age. Her back was slightly bent, like she'd been dealing with some pain, and she'd tied her thick white hair back with a strip of black cloth.

Adina. Sever's supposed love.

"Her eyes," Rajni said.

Mary looked at them. Green. Exactly the shade of her own.

"She'd been ill." Now-Beatrice's voice drifted through the vision, a bit clearer than Rajni's or even Bradley's. Her voice belonged here. "I'd been helping her."

Little Beatrice bustled into the room, clearly a caretaker even at ten. "I got the last package of the tea you like," she said. "It was all the way back on the shelf."

"My hero." Adina's voice was clear and quiet, and Mary found herself unable to look away from her great-great grandmother's face. She'd only ever met her own maternal grand-mother once, as a very small child, and she remembered little more than a round face and a halo of white hair. As white as Adina's.

Little Beatrice continued to unpack the groceries, chatting as she worked. She knew her way around the kitchen; she'd done this before.

A knock sounded on the front door, quick and loud, and Adina rose slowly from her seat. "Probably the mailman," she said. "I ordered a new vacuum from Sears Robuck. They're supposed to be like magic."

"Mom says those don't work," Beatrice said.

Adina headed for the door, slow but steady on her feet. "Always worth trying the newest innovation."

A thrill of recognition resonated in Mary's chest, her own love of tech shining in her great-great grandmother's eyes. Maybe some interests could pass through generations.

When Adina gasped from the living room, little Eleanor dropped her groceries and sprang out of the kitchen, dragging Mary's vantage along with her.

Two women stood on the front steps. One of them was tall, her golden curls bobbed at the chin. The other had brown skin and long ebony hair that she'd secured at the nape of her neck.

Mary's great-grandmother, standing beside Eloise's. Both women wore black hip-length jackets, maroon pants, and belts so loaded with equipment that they probably needed extra-strength buckles.

Not your typical 1950s getup.

Adina held a shaking hand over her mouth, tears leaking freely down her cheeks as the blonde woman took her other hand and gently led her inside. Her friend—Eloise's great-grandmother—shut the door behind them, slid the lock into place, and then moved to the window and closed the curtains.

"Hey," Little Beatrice said, the girl already radiating the stern presence of a veteran nurse. "You can't just come in here."

She planted her fists on her hips, like she might just remove the intruders herself.

"It's OK," Adina said through her sobs, allowing her daughter—it had to be her daughter—to lead her to the chair in the corner. "It's OK. Celeste... Celeste. She's my daughter."

Now-Beatrice let out a husky laugh. "I wondered where she'd been. But I was afraid to question her."

Celeste knelt beside the still-crying Adina.

Bonnie moved away from the window, apparently satisfied that their entrance hadn't been noted. She stood before Adina and Celeste, her dark eyes sparkling.

And then she reached into her belt, to unsheathe a moon-white blade.

Adina stood with a quickness that Mary wouldn't have thought her capable of it. "You fools." Her voice quaked. "You *fools*. You bring that thing here?"

Celeste opened her mouth. "No one else knows—"

"Not here to me," Adina interrupted. "Here to this *planet*. Do you know what he'll do, if he discovers it? You must get rid of it. Shoot it into orbit. Shoot it into the sun. Just get it away from this soil."

Bonnie and Celeste exchanged a glance, as if this was a conversation they'd already had. "It's bonded to me," Bonnie said. "I can't just kill it."

Adina turned. Faced Bonnie, who still held the Pearl Knife flat in her hand, and Celeste, who stood beside her friend with grief trembling across her features.

The old woman reached toward the Knife, allowing her hand to hover just above it. She curved her finger, just slightly, toward Bonnie's palm.

The Knife glowed blue, and Adina snapped her finger back.

"It doesn't want you near it." Bonnie's voice was both apologetic and protective at the same time. Did *she* know how to interpret what the Knife told her?

"And why should it?" Adina said softly. "I abandoned it, after all."

Silence. The Knife had been intended for Adina, but she'd rejected it. She'd rejected its maker. It belonged to Bonnie, now.

"We need your help," Celeste said.

Adina turned to look at her daughter, and her profile hardened. "You need to be gone from here. If Sever comes looking for that, he'll seek me out first. Every second you spend with me puts you in danger. And the rest of the world, too."

Mary could relate to that.

"He doesn't even know it's gone," Bonnie said.

Adina held up a hand. "Every. Second."

Celeste looked at her mother for a long, long moment. Then she stepped forward and folded the older woman into a hug, her own eyes glittering with tears.

The vision began to fade, and Mary kept her gaze locked on Celeste's until the last possible second. Her great-grandmother, twenty years old, saying goodbye to her mother. Perhaps for the last time.

Mary's own mother, Celestine, must have been named for her.

Now-Beatrice's living room faded back into reality, replacing the vision. Mary closed her eyes, breathing slowly and trying to absorb what she'd seen.

"It's a good trick," Rajni said, sitting back. "But what does it tell us?"

A lot, actually. When the Knife had come to Earth. Who had brought it—if not how, exactly, that had occurred.

But Rajni had a point. A small one.

"We're supposed to figure out why I can resist Sever's powers," Mary said, as Bradley sloshed his feet out of the water and began to dry them with the towel. His eyes were bloodshot, his face even paler than its usual pasty color. "We thought you might know."

Beatrice raised a painted-on eyebrow. "You can, can you? That's interesting, isn't it."

"Very," Mary said.

"Well, I don't know," Beatrice said. "But I could certainly take a guess."

Bradley slipped his feet into his galoshes. He looked about five seconds from passing out. "And that guess is?"

Beatrice shrugged. "Adina was betrothed to Sever, wasn't she? So Celeste could well have been his daughter."

MARY WAS ALL TOO aware that Sever's people would be looking for the missing guard by now, and that they'd probably be storming the house—with backup—any second.

And yet, Beatrice had just dropped some serious information in her lap. The kind of information that made it difficult to leap up and make a run for it. The kind that would make Eloise start talking about LIO recruiting a shrink. Or fifty.

Why was there never enough *time?*

"So you're saying I'm an alien," Mary said.

And here she'd thought it was bad when Sever had thought she was his fiancée.

"Don't be dramatic," Beatrice said. "Four generations on? Diluted by now."

Sure, except that Sever couldn't use his powers against her. Four generations or not, like couldn't destroy like. Apparently.

If Beatrice knew more, they needed to hear it. But for now, they needed to evacuate her before Sever's people did.

The front door flew open, and Beatrice squeaked in protest as it crashed against the wall, sending chips of brick scattering across the floor.

There was never enough time.

The Dallas Cowboys guard rushed into the room, a pair of new buddies close behind. Mary met them halfway, Rajni by her side. "Get Beatrice to safety," Mary called over her shoulder to Bradley.

He caught the older woman's arm and they ran, heading for the corridor that led to the back patio. And, Mary hoped, a good spot for Eloise to portal them the hell out of here. She'd better be sitting by her phone.

The Dallas Cowboy barreled toward Mary, like a linebacker rushing a quarterback—not that the guy would have any idea what that meant—and she met him with a heel to the gut. She couldn't feel any armor under there, but the kick hardly seemed to faze him, as if he was too big for the hit to resonate.

Also, he was an alien. But hey, so was she. Apparently.

Dallas tried to catch her heel, but she threw herself away from him and toward the stone fireplace, where Beatrice's statue collection waited, looking attractively heavy.

Across the room, Beatrice shrieked, and Mary looked back over her shoulder as she ran for the statue-weapons. Beatrice was grappling with Rocker, who'd slipped around the battle to grab her.

Must be nice to be able to have the ability to mimic a TV stand, or whatever he'd done. At least he couldn't shoot poison.

Beatrice was no easy grab—the older woman was slapping at Rocker's hands, scratching and screeching with her teeth bared—but she wasn't a trained fighter, either. Rocker must have been instructed not to harm her, or she'd be down by now, but he'd secure her. And he'd do it soon.

Rajni was fighting her own opponent, the water from Bradley's makeshift wading pool whipping around the guy's feet like a lasso. She couldn't help.

Mary's fingers closed around the stone lion's head, and she hefted it off the hearth—the thing had to weigh twenty pounds

—and slung it at her attacker. It hit him in the stomach, and he stumbled back a step. Stone lion, for the win.

Still, he didn't stumble quite as far as she'd have liked. And as she ran to help Beatrice, he threw the statue aside, chucking it hard enough to chip the stone, and caught hold of her arm, wrenching her painfully back into a fight. Why did it always have to be *that* arm?

She flung her weight toward the tile, hoping to shake off her attacker, but he hung on. Like he meant to flick her away. Mary swung for his neck and missed. As robotic as Dallas seemed, she was pretty sure she heard him laugh.

She was still halfway across this too-huge living room, too far away to help Beatrice. Rajni was still sloshing water in her opponent's face, leaving puddles all over the tile.

And then Bradley stepped forward.

Mary was dodging punches and trying to land kicks, maybe knock Dallas off his feet. But she saw Bradley's bootless toes touch one of Rajni's puddles. So she was ready when he touched an index finger to Rocker's shoulder. Kind of.

The room flickered.

A golden-threaded portal, with Dolly ushering people through.

Flicker.

A restaurant with ivy crawling up white columns, people dancing to a muted song.

Flicker.

A dingy living room—Mary could smell the years of smoke embedded in the carpet, the drapes—and a woman begging. *Don't go, don't go.*

Flicker.

Dallas abandoned his fight with Mary and doubled over to empty his stomach. She couldn't blame him. This wasn't the ease of blinking into Beatrice's memory. Disconcerting as that had been, this was worse. A stomach-lurching carousel of memories, moving and stopping, then moving again. The floor shifted with the walls, giving her an almost weightless feeling. As if she'd been shot unceremoniously into zero gravity.

The scenes from Rocker's mind flipped by with clock-ticking precision, as if Bradley were scrolling through an old paper rolodex, the index cards pausing, then passing by.

A room at LIO HQ, the bed messy, magazines strewn across the coffee table. Diana, with no white in her hair yet, pacing and yelling. Venting.

Flip.

A boat, with mountains in the background, a woman in a blue sundress at the wheel.

Flip.

A baseball stadium, with red concrete floors.

"Ah," Bradley said. As if he'd found the magazine article he'd been searching for. The not-camera of his perspective followed Rocker's head into a ballpark suite, the kind Mary had visited plenty of times while surrounded by actors and producers. High-top counters aimed out at the baseball field, the view unobscured. Everything clean and neat.

In the vision, Rocker held a tray with a plate of eggs, and a cup of coffee. He set them on the kitchen island and fiddled with the utensils.

Mary was so focused on wondering why Bradley had stopped the memories to watch Rocker eat breakfast that she didn't notice Nathan until he said, "What, Starbucks doesn't deliver?"

He sounded like himself, and her breath caught in her throat, stifling a half gasp, half sob. She knew him, and she knew the tone was purposefully quippy. Startled, she whipped her head around to find him lounging on one of the couches that was right-angled around the TV screen, his feet propped up on the arm, his hands pillowing his head.

An angry bruise covered the left half of his face, the purple-red mark stretching from his jaw to his temple, reaching out across his cheekbone like it wanted to spread toward his nose. Or receding away from it, she hoped. His eye might have been swollen shut a day ago.

He'd made himself look casual, lounging there on the couch. But she'd seen Monster kick him in the stomach during the last fight at HQ. He had to be in pain.

Mary staggered away from her still-retching opponent and knelt beside the couch, reaching for Nathan's face.

He's not here, Bradley said. His voice was so soft, it might have been in her head. Maybe it *was* in her head. She wasn't sure she'd be able to tell the difference. It was like one of Goldi's illusions, only pulled out of someone else's mind.

There was nothing in the room to tell her what day this was. The light might have been dusk or dawn, and she couldn't wrench her eyes away from him to try and gauge which direction the sun was in. To collect any details.

She didn't understand Bradley's powers enough, anyway, to know how accurate these memories really were.

But Nathan was here. Alive. She couldn't touch him, but she had to believe he still was.

This isn't for you. Bradley's voice was still in her head, maybe, and sounded—felt?—strained enough for her to wonder how long he could keep this up.

Using the floor for leverage, Mary pushed to her feet.

Rocker was on the floor, hands gripping his hair, his mouth open in a silent scream. Beatrice had retreated behind Bradley, her own hand to her temple. As if wondering how easily his powers might have twisted her own memories into physical pain.

The would-be Dallas Cowboy staggered to his feet and roared across the room toward Mary, clearly ready to resume the fight. She just had time to raise her fists in defense before water gushed across the ceiling from the kitchen, joining another stream from down the hall behind her.

The streams met above Mary's head and hit Dallas straight in the chest, knocking him back into the wall. And holding him there.

"Sorry," Rajni said, breathing hard. "Took a second to burst the pipes."

Sure. Why wouldn't it? "Well done," Mary said. "She'd be proud."

Rajni nodded in thanks as Bradley waved them down the hall. Beatrice was already running for the patio door, where a silver-bordered portal waited.

With Rajni at her side, Mary followed.

Nᴀᴛʜᴀɴ ᴋᴇᴘᴛ ᴡᴀɪᴛɪɴɢ for a good time to cause a distraction.

The night after his spying expedition, he'd lain awake on the couch, expecting Sever's people to slam into the room, demanding an explanation for the tear in Nathan's jeans. Even when dawn found him safe and unbothered in his room, he couldn't quite gauge the right timing. Should he wait until they were distracted with something else to cause his own? What would that be? And how long would it take?

He couldn't wait forever. Sever wanted the Pearl Knife, and soon he'd go on the offensive to get it. Mary and Eloise needed all the intel they could get before they had to face him in battle.

Just as pressing—moreso, perhaps—was the frozen crowd outside the gates. They haunted Nathan's restless dreams, and he found his thoughts returning to them with more and more urgency. If they couldn't eat, would they waste away where they stood? Or was it more like a magical spell—one that, if broken in a hundred years, would release them all at their current ages?

Mary would say that even if it did work that way, it would be science—not magic. Nathan had, so far, managed to avoid telling her that to him, the inner workings of her gadgets might as well be sorcery. Though it was possible she already knew that. After all, she knew him better than anyone ever had.

Science, magic. It didn't matter. Those people were hurting, and he needed to help them. The sooner he could get a message to the League, and describe his theory about the Knife draining Sever's power, the better. If Nathan could distract Jenna and the others for long enough, one of Caldwell's people could sneak up to the press booth and find a way to send a message to Eloise.

Unable to sleep, Nathan had again crept out of his room—this time in the early morning hours—to visit with the president's people. They'd all agreed; Nathan would do the distracting, and Caldwell would send a team to the broadcast booth to contact the League. If all went well, Sever's grunts would be too busy dragging Nathan back to his cell to notice the broadcast-booth side quest.

Now, Nathan waited for a lull in guard check-ins, then let himself out through his secret door.

When he slipped into the president's suite, though, he found himself in the middle of an argument.

Vice President Grafton had her hands on her hips, her tight ponytail swinging as she shook her head adamantly at the president. The secret service agent had his lips pursed, and was shaking his head practically in time with the VP.

"You cannot go yourself," Grafton said. "Louis is trained for these things."

"He certainly is not trained to swing around baseball-park balconies like a monkey." President Caldwell's eyes were wide, almost as if he were surprising himself by making such an argument. "My face, my name, will patch me through to anyone I need to reach. It has to be me."

It was a fair point. From what he could tell, Nathan didn't

think Sever had cut communication with the outside world. Why would he? Sever controlled this place. If anything, he'd probably been broadcasting threatening messages to the whole world. On the hour, every hour.

And if Caldwell had to broadcast to get his message out, the press would allow it. Hell, they might even leap at the opportunity.

"Why not me, then?" Grafton pushed. "My face, my name—"

"Because you opposed the executive order," Caldwell interrupted. "Your hands are clean."

The risk here was implied. Whoever made the call might well find themselves facing Sever's wrath. Caldwell was taking the job on himself—because if the worst should happen, she'd be the one to end up in power. Nathan could respect that choice.

It was still strange, knowing that Sever—he seemed all too human, and almost refined at times—could crush this planet to dust. Was choosing not to, and could change his mind at any moment.

Nathan had seen his power, his fury, when he'd launched it against the EAEA. He could still hear the screams, the snapping bones, when he thought of it. And here he was, was about to go get caught on purpose. But hopefully, Caldwell *wouldn't* get caught. That was the whole point.

Nathan had to believe that his relationship with Mary made him valuable enough as a hostage to save his life. If not... If not, at least he'd have given her the information that would save *her* life. And everyone else's.

He couldn't say he'd die without regrets. He wanted, more than anything, to hold her again. But for now, he'd settle for trusting her enough to know she'd get him out of this. Until then, he'd do what he could to help.

Grafton pressed her lips together, like she wanted to argue but couldn't think of a reasonable angle.

President Caldwell nodded, as if all was decided, and stood, looking at Nathan. "Are you sure *you* want to do this? They won't give you a chance to escape again."

Didn't he know it. "I'll buy you as much time as I can."

Caldwell extended his hand to give Nathan's a firm shake. "Good luck."

And then Nathan was out the door, creeping toward his own suite as Caldwell slipped out behind him and disappeared in the other direction, the President of the United States crawling through old soda spills and remnants of nacho cheese in hopes of saving the world.

Nathan waited a breath, two, ten. And then, he moved.

It was a delicate business, pretending to slip up enough to get caught, and Nathan moved as if he'd been formulating a plan. He darted out from behind the seat and ran down the steps that led toward the baseball diamond. He heard a shout from behind as one of the guards noticed him, but he had to get farther, lead them away from the stands. He needed to draw as much attention as he could.

Nathan reached the bottom of the stands and vaulted over the rail. He landed clumsily, his ankles smarting as his injured body tried to keep up with the plan, but he used his momentum to stumble into a run. Pretending he'd spotted an exit beneath the scoreboard, he dashed across home plate, lungs burning as he skirted around the pitcher's mound and headed straight across the diamond toward second.

Not the way he'd wanted to tour a Major League Baseball park, but there was no denying that this approach fit his lifestyle.

Footsteps pounded behind him as Sever's people converged

on the field. He didn't turn to see who it was, but he hoped there were a lot of them.

He almost hoped it was everyone.

Nathan made a mad dash for the outfield, running with all his might to draw them farther away from the stands, from the broadcast booth, and from Caldwell's mission.

A wall of fire erupted from the ground in front of the scoreboard, pulsing out of the grass like a geyser made of flame. Nathan swerved as heat blasted his face and hands, and someone tackled him from behind. Claws sank into his back as he fell, long nails raking through fabric and skin.

Nathan hit the ground chin-first, his teeth cracking together, his shirt wet with blood. Monster landed on top of him to wrench his arms behind his back, growling low in the back of his throat. If he was saying any actual words, Nathan didn't understand them.

All he could think through the pain—his HQ-fight bruises weren't even healed yet, and his probably-cracked ribs were protesting angrily—was that they'd responded too fast. It hadn't been long enough, not nearly.

"Idiot," Monster said. "Did you think we wouldn't see you?"

The wall of fire disappeared, though the flames still beat behind his eyelids when he blinked, and then Jenna was crouching in front of him and peering into his face. "He knew we'd see him," she said. "Who's still guarding the concourse?"

She'd always been too observant, too savvy. Monster, as far as he could tell, just wanted to growl and claw things. Deeply. Painfully. As for Diana, she was always centering herself.

But Jenna took the time to figure out who people were.

Nathan's face was still pressed into the grass, and he couldn't see anyone but Jenna, couldn't smell anything but dirt and sweat and Monster's coffee breath.

But he could guess from the silence that the answer was no one. No one was left guarding the concourse.

As Monster hauled Nathan to his feet, though, a figure appeared behind the glass of the broadcast booth. It wasn't President Caldwell, but Nathan recognized the thin, upright outline clearly enough. It was Dolly Reyna.

Nathan's stomach sank. She'd known. Somehow, she'd known what he was going to do. And if Caldwell hadn't managed to get his message out, Nathan had a feeling things were about to get much, much worse.

Sever was dreaming of his chambers back in the Adu System, on a moon he'd never given any name besides 'home.' A tiny moon, it was full of yellow flowers and warm days, its marble-like home planet shining across the full sky come evening.

And his court. The orbiting hall where his people danced among the inspiring scents of freshly painted artwork, every melody bright and new. Sever had sat on a lofted pedestal, much too far above them to join the party. Too regal for the revelries. Only Adina had ever made him long to dance.

Now, Morik woke him with a hand to his shoulder. Despite the throbbing pain in his temple—always there, on this wretched planet—Sever immediately rose.

Morik ranked sleep alongside sear-weed tonic. He never woke Sever.

"What's wrong?" Sever asked, blinking away the still half-formed images of his whirling court. Homesickness. That was all it was.

Morik looked as though he himself had not slept in several nights. The corners of his mouth tipped downwards, worried. "Nathan Pearce," he said. "He attempted to escape."

Sever rubbed his face. He'd noted Nathan's torn pants during their last meeting and ordered an extra watch on his suite. "I thought he might have a way out."

"Yes, so you said. But he formed a partnership with the president. They've been working together."

Nathan should not have had any way of knowing the president was also a prisoner here. The man must have been moving around this facility longer than Sever had realized.

He rolled his shoulders back, attempting to loosen some of the pain that was working its way into his muscles. Once upon a time, he'd been little short of invincible. This planet was wearing on him, slowly shaving away at his power. "And?"

"The president managed to get a message to the League of Independent Operatives."

A spark of anger burst in his stomach, low and hot. A message? How? What *kind* of message? It took an effort to keep his voice level. "I take it they've been recaptured."

"Yes, my lord."

Of course they had. Of course. He wanted to fall back to the bed, to allow his pain to subside into visions of dancing. To deal with Mary's lover, and whatever message the president had sent, at a later time.

But Morik still stood before him, hands twisted, mouth tipping ever downward. And Sever felt the spark of anger grow, expanding into a hot sun. These people taunted him. They would not stop.

"There's more," Morik said, as if Sever had not gleaned that already. "Mary found Beatrice Carter."

33 / ELOISE

Hope. Eloise wasn't sure she'd felt it for some time, maybe not since the moments she'd learned of her mother's betrayal. Now, with the Pearl Knife singing its song to someone other than Eloise... Yes, it finally felt like they might be able to figure it out. Like they might be able to help it heal.

They could have waited for a team to help them move Tam's piano into the lab. Or Ire. But Agnes wouldn't call him, claiming she'd just helped him to bandage an injury and that he needed to rest. So while she, Tam, and Lucy carted Agnes's equipment, Eloise and Steve pushed the upright piano down the hallways of Wave's underwater hideout.

How, Eloise wondered, had they gotten the piano into the dome at all?

"This would be so much easier if their carpets weren't so soft," Steve said. Tam had forbidden him to take so much as one super-fast step, in case he should accidentally bash the piano against a wall and damage it irreparably. Eloise couldn't blame her for that.

So now, Eloise had the rare pleasure of watching Steve do manual labor without the help of his powers. Or Ire's. As much as the two used to bicker, they were pretty inseparable these days. Steve was pushing, while Eloise walked backwards to pull and guide.

Among its perks, the angle gave her an excellent view of Steve's arms. The man had nice arms.

"At least it has wheels," she said.

Steve huffed a good-natured laugh that sent a bolt of lightning through her ribcage, stealing the breath right out of her so forcefully that she actually had to stop walking.

When he looked up, a question in his eyes, she said, "We kissed."

Steve raised his eyebrows, just a touch, then grinned. It was his best smile, not his *this-is-my-charming-mask* smile. It was the smile that crinkled the skin around his eyes, lighting them up. "We did. A lot, actually."

Eloise rested her fingertips on the top of the piano. "So... Are we going to talk about that?"

He laughed, the sound like smoke in her ears. Good smoke, like campfires. and wood stoves and winter evenings by a fireplace. "I thought you'd forgotten. You know, with HQ collapsing around our ears."

Eloise swallowed. Yes, that was the gist of the timing.

Steve breathed a laugh and came around, leaning one elbow on the piano. "I'm kidding. But your plate is brim-full at the moment, El."

She couldn't disagree with that. "It's true. It might crack."

He curled a thumb around her ear, leaving her skin tingling. "Exactly. So I thought I should back off a bit. Give you some space while you save the world, and you know, make out with you later. If you still want to."

Eloise leaned into his touch. She did want to. She wanted him in her life, standing steady by her side, whispering encouragement in her ear. "I'm not saving the world *right* this second."

He cupped her cheek, drawing her closer. "I noticed that."

He kissed her, his touch gentle as he caressed her cheek. He pulled her closer, and she leaned into his warmth, the light smell of spiced coconut, the steady feeling of his hand on her back. He tasted sweet, like spring. She'd spent so much time feeling alone in all of this, and suddenly she had allies.

Maybe she'd had them all along.

Steve sighed into her, making a husky noise in his throat, and Eloise thought of dragging him through one of the doors in the corridor. They could ditch the piano for a while, just sink into each other. The others could wait.

But then Lucy darted by, her hands full of cords, her nose wrinkled. "Ew," she said, and Eloise broke the kiss, laughing at the little girl's disgust.

"Later," Eloise said.

Steve kissed her again, briefly. "Save the world, then make out."

Once they'd hauled the piano into Wave's laboratory—through a door that was barely wide enough to allow it through—Tam played, Agnes measured, and Eloise listened. Fran arrived and added her own exercises. Steve left to sleep, to train, to bring lunch. And then dinner. And then breakfast.

And through the dissonance, the Pearl Knife's melody began to emerge. Agnes began to talk about molecules and patches and healing.

Eloise didn't know how long they'd been working when Gail called. Gail had been stashed in a Wave safe house with Jeff Hayes and the other members of the team, blessedly safe from yacht attacks and ballpark battles. Her face on the screen looked calm enough, though she had to be feeling the stress. She knew what was at stake. Unless Eloise missed her guess, she'd be wanting to help.

Although if anyone in this organization needed—and deserved—a vacation, it was Gail.

"How are you holding up?" Eloise asked.

"Fine. Jeff's annoying."

"Tell me about it."

"Anyway, I've got a call to patch through," Gail said. All business, all the time. Eloise didn't know how Gail was working from wherever she was, or how she'd received a call—she assumed Wave had provided the patch-through information—but before she could ask, Gail disappeared.

And the President of the United States took her place.

"Um," Eloise said.

Caldwell cleared his throat, glanced over his shoulder. There was a wall of equipment behind him, alongside a bunch of baseball memorabilia. "Yes, it's me. Nathan's, um, well." He glanced past the screen, like he was looking out a window. "He's causing a distraction so I can call."

Eloise blinked, trying to reconcile the sound of Nathan's name coming from the president's mouth. "You're both being held prisoner in the same place? At Nationals Park?"

Caldwell raised a hand to his collar, tugging at it. Nervous, clearly. "Ah, yes. Yes, he figured out how to escape his suite, but the place might as well be a fortress otherwise. It was the best use of our resources, trust me."

Eloise didn't trust him. She did, however, trust Nathan. "Is he OK? Are you OK?"

Caldwell cleared his throat again. "Excuse me, Ms. Reyna. I don't mean to be rude, but I have reason to suspect my time in this booth will be limited. Nathan asked me to send a message."

It perhaps shouldn't have surprised Eloise that Nathan Pearce had convinced the President of the United States to personally act as a messenger. The man had made friends with LIO's Wave prisoners *while* they were prisoners. She nodded, aware that Tam had stopped playing and that Agnes and Fran were listening intently behind her. Even Lucy was staring curiously at the screen.

"The Pearl Knife appears to be draining Sever's powers," the president said. "It, uh, it hurts him. Sever believes that if he gets the Knife, his powers will return. But we—that is, Nathan —he thinks that Sever's illness coincides with the Knife's proximity. It hurt him at your headquarters—I'm so sorry about that, truly I am—and when the portals kept appearing at the park."

Interesting. *Intentional?* Eloise asked the Knife.

The Pearl Knife sent confusion back to her. Not this time.

"Are you sure it isn't the huge dome he's maintaining, and all those frozen civilians?" Eloise asked. "He seems to be using a lot of power."

"No," Caldwell said. "Not sure at all. But Nathan thinks his theory is sound. He—"

Something slammed into Caldwell from the side. He cried out, flailing for the phone, but the camera flipped and clattered around, showing the underside of the desk. Eloise squinted at the screen, as if it could tell her what was happening as people shouted and furniture slammed against walls.

Fran reached over Eloise's shoulder and ended the call. "No need to give them a place to portal to," she said.

Eloise wondered, distantly, if Gail had seen that. If she knew what was happening, and if she was safe. As safe as anyone else was, anyway. Which wasn't safe at all, until they'd defeated Sever.

She didn't want to think about Caldwell, about Nathan, and about what might be happening to them right now. Caldwell had clearly been caught, but how much had they seen? What did they know?

Sever might want them as hostages, but if they caused more trouble than they were worth, she doubted he'd hesitate to cut them loose.

Had Sever's people heard the message? Would he know now that the Knife drained his powers? Or would he still come looking for it?

Fran placed a hand on Eloise's shoulder. "Come," she said. "They risked everything to get us that message. Let's put the information to good use."

Eloise nodded, trying to breathe past her anxiety. She could use this to her advantage. She just needed the right angle.

The Knife sent cooling thoughts into her mind, and she thanked it. "Let's hope Mary finds something, too. Then maybe we'll be able to end this for good."

DOLLY INTERCEPTED Sever on his way up to the press box, falling into step beside him as Morik escorted him through the concourse. His dark hair was mussed, sticking up in every direction, and a film of sweat gleamed on his neck. She hadn't seen him looking less than perfect before; it was unnerving, and required a concerted effort not to stare.

"The League will not stop trying," she said, struggling to keep her breath even as he barreled ahead. She'd run from the broadcast booth to catch him. Everything hinged on this. Everything. "You need to do something drastic. Lure them here."

"Do not harry him," Morik said. "You're supposed to be checking in with our people in Oklahoma."

He said it like he was uncertain of its pronunciation, a long pause on the third syllable. Ok-la-ho. Ma.

"I'll check in," Dolly said. "But I need to talk to you first."

Sever stopped walking and spun toward her with a motion that would have sent a cloak swirling, had he been wearing one. His eyes were bright with wild light, the orange flames leaking through the irises like cracks. "What is it you would suggest I do?"

If he knew she'd been stringing this along, that she'd been aware of Nathan's ability to escape—if he knew that she'd been hoping, vaguely, to play him against the League so she could get the Knife for herself—if he knew, he'd kill her. There was no question.

But if he knew, she'd already be dead.

What was more, they would not have caught Caldwell without her. True, she hadn't gotten there in time to stop the message, but it hardly mattered. This was her chance to turn the situation to her favor.

Dolly swallowed, gathering her courage. "Threaten their lives, show your true strength. The League will come, whether they're ready or not. They'll have to."

35 / NATHAN

AT JENNA'S DIRECTION, Monster dragged Nathan back across the field. Nathan's shoulder stretched painfully as Monster pulled him by the arm—though he could have easily tossed Nathan over his shoulder instead.

But that wasn't what Jenna had ordered, and so it wasn't what Monster did.

Nathan scrambled to gain his footing, to push to his feet, but Monster was moving too fast. His hip caught on a base, the plate banging painfully into bone, his bruised ribs making it tough to breathe.

It would be worth it, if this stunt had bought Caldwell the time he needed.

Diana and Goldi flanked Monster, with Ranger a step behind. Everyone closing in tight, as if Nathan might try to escape again.

Escape had never been in the cards. Not really. Jenna seemed to be the only one who knew it. She sauntered across the field ahead of them without bothering to look back.

Apparently, Dolly had known it, too. How had she anticipated him?

Monster hooked his arms under Nathan's shoulders and

hoisted him up to the stands, where he managed to scramble to his feet mere seconds before the dragging started again, this time up the concrete stairs. Nathan stumbled, but he stayed on his feet, working hard to keep up with Monster's pace. A few more days of recovery, and it wouldn't have been a problem. Now, there were fresh wounds to contend with, layered viciously on top of the old.

Monster, for his part, seemed to be working to keep up with Jenna.

When they moved into the shaded part of the concourse, Jenna didn't lead them back to the suites. Instead, she headed for the stairs and led them up, past the nosebleed sections and directly to the press box. Not the glassed-in broadcast booth where he'd sent Caldwell, but to the open-air section below it that was reserved for newspaper and magazine writers.

Dread coiled in Nathan's stomach as Monster pushed him into one of the small cubicles reserved for reporters. A table, an outlet, and a short wall. That was all that separated him from a long drop to the concrete.

"Nice workspace," Nathan said, but he was breathing too hard for the quip to land. Jenna just smiled and folded her arms over her chest. Like she was waiting.

Nathan didn't need to ask what she was waiting for. The seconds ticked, and Jenna drummed her elbow with her fingertips. Diana stood poised at the door.

Monster watched Nathan, his incisors cutting through his bottom lip, his eyes dark and beady against his blue-gray scales. He looked ready to throw Nathan to his death.

When Sever came, he came like a storm.

In their meetings so far, Sever had seemed contained, his energy carefully controlled. A dangerous energy, yes, but one that had always felt leashed. Restrained.

Even without his pupils burning orange, Nathan would

have been able to read the difference. Static crackled at Sever's fingertips as he swept into the room, fury painted across his dark brow, his pinched-thin lips. He seemed, suddenly, about five times taller than his actual height.

In this man, Nathan could see the monster who'd split Niagara Falls open like an eggshell. It was difficult not to imagine the entire stadium collapsing on top of them all. Sever, no doubt, would rise from the ashes.

Behind him, Morik entered, escorting a handcuffed Caldwell. The president looked pale, his chin trembling, but he twisted to meet Sever's gaze as Morik led him to another booth.

"Masterminds, are you?" Sever said. "Heroic spies? Legendary heroes? I can guess *who* you contacted. You're that predictable, at least. But what could you possibly have had to say?"

Spit flew as he spoke, his voice raw and rambling, as if the words were unspooling from the core of his rage. And Nathan understood, through the fog of pain and fear, that Caldwell had indeed managed to send his message. At great cost, that much was clear, but it could mean the battle won. It could make every difference, and even with Sever raging before him, Nathan wanted to sag with the relief of it. Some hysterical part of him wanted to cheer.

"A mayday would be useless," Sever continued. "They already know you are here."

Jenna unclasped her arms, then hooked her thumbs through her belt loops. "They think they know something."

Sever motioned to Diana, and she followed him to Caldwell's booth, one level above Nathan's. The president had seated himself on the desk, where he was twisting his hands in his lap. Though otherwise, he looked calm enough. "I don't know anything," he said.

Sever snapped his fingers, and Caldwell's fingers stopped

moving. Still, Nathan couldn't tell for sure that the president was frozen until Sever nodded to Diana.

With a slight twist of her lips, as though trying to hide her distaste, the Trap pressed a poison-tipped thumb to Caldwell's temple.

Nathan couldn't imagine that Diana objected to torture. She'd certainly not hesitated to torture Mary, when she'd had the chance. Maybe she preferred the thrill of the chase.

Whatever her objections, Diana kept her thumb anchored at Caldwell's temple as she raked the rest of her fingertips along his cheek. It almost looked like a caress, except for the oil-slick poison she left behind.

And Caldwell couldn't move. He made a strangled noise, as if even his vocal cords were frozen. Tears streamed down his cheeks, catching at the corners of his mouth, but Diana didn't let up until Sever gave her a wave.

Caldwell collapsed forward, clutching his face, and Diana actually used her knee to keep the president from falling off the table. Nathan felt air leaving his own lungs, too, his stomach turning in disgust.

"I don't know anything," Caldwell said, his breath coming fast, his voice thick with tears and suppressed screams. "There was nothing to tell them."

Before today, Nathan would not have thought the president had it in him.

"I've been patient," Sever said. "But my generosity begins to wear thin."

Nathan couldn't help thinking of Travis Bertram and the bone-cracking attack at the restaurant. If that had been Sever's idea of patience, he didn't want to see the opposite.

"Generosity," Nathan repeated. He couldn't help himself, couldn't keep the word back. And when Sever looked at him, giving Caldwell a reprieve from his hot gaze, he couldn't stop himself from continuing. "Like murdering our people? Like destroying our headquarters? And leaving a graveyard of statues outside the stadium?"

"Your world needed a lesson," Sever said. "Those people are collateral. Behave, submit, and I'll let them go free."

Would he? Nathan could picture Sever's fist closing over the world, his fingers in every nation, every resource funneled toward his vision. Whatever that might be. And he could imagine, too, these people frozen in perpetuity—a warning, a reminder, a testament to the dangers of rebellion.

Sever nodded to Diana to continue with her interrogation. Before she could touch Caldwell again, the door swung open and Dolly escorted a quivering Rocker into the room. His long gray hair was stringy and damp with sweat, his skin flickering to match the beige walls and the blue carpet before settling back to its usual white color.

Sever motioned for Diana to wait. "You have an update?"

Dolly actually took a step back, leaving Rocker on his own to face Sever. Nathan didn't know if he'd ever seen the woman retreat.

"Adina's neighbor." Rocker's words were hardly coherent, his voice shaking too much to be easily understood, hands quivering violently. As if he'd just spent a week out in the cold. "She got away."

Nathan didn't dare move. He hardly dared to breathe. Someone knew the story of Adina's presence on Earth, and thus Mary's connection to Sever. And the League had reached her first. That had to be a win. It *had* to be.

Sever stared at Rocker in silence. Such a long silence that Rocker actually let out a sob, clearly aware of the reaction this news was about to illicit. "They came. Mary, and two others. We tried to stop them, but one of them... He gets into your head... He just..." Rocker made a circular motion with a wavering finger, as if that could explain it.

If Sever understood the motion, he didn't let on. He curled his fingers into a fist, and the orange spots exploded across his irises, bleeding into the whites of his eyes.

Rocker's feet left the ground. Not slowly, not gradually, but as if an invisible giant had picked him up and begun flinging him about the room. His head cracked against the nearest cubicle wall, and he cried out.

Sever stood completely still as Rocker sailed out the open window, arms flailing. Nathan could hear him screaming, a stomach-curdling wail that cut short with a sickening crunch.

"Keep them here," Sever said to Jenna, starting for the door.

Nathan's own knees wanted to give out, and he wasn't the only one looking toward the edge of the booth, shock numbing his thoughts to near whispers. Diana was staring after Rocker, white-faced, while Dolly held her stomach like she might be sick. Monster peered over the side of the booth, lips moving silently as if in prayer. Ranger had come up here, too, but he'd disappeared.

Rocker had been their friend, their colleague. But he wasn't Jenna's. Unmoved by the murder, she said, "What are you going to do with them? The prisoners?"

She was too bold for her own good. Too foolish. Nathan half expected Sever to fling her out the window, too.

But Sever just paused. "I've been too patient with this world," he said. "It's time to demonstrate what happens when people get in my way."

WHEN THE PORTAL dropped Mary and Bradley in Wave's underwater base, Eloise took one look at them and dashed off looking for Agnes, shouting orders over her shoulder for them to go to the infirmary.

Bradley handed Beatrice's care over to a Wave operative, while Mary ignored Eloise's instructions, instead heading straight for the engineering lab.

"I believe they'll want to test you," Bradley said, practically tripping over her heels as he hurried to keep up. His breath had a raspy edge, and she slowed her pace a tick.

"Agnes will be here soon with all her monitors and needles," Mary said. "But if we don't build something that can trap all the retirees, we'll fail before we get close enough to Sever to test it."

Rocker was one thing. His powers hadn't been enhanced, that she'd seen. But if Dolly could increase Diana's abilities, and Monster's and Carlisle's, then they'd get their asses kicked. Mary doubted Bradley could tap into all their minds at once, or he'd have done it already.

Mary flung the lab door open, startling several Wave engineers. One of them dropped a vial, which thankfully didn't break when it hit the floor, instead rolling under a nearby table.

"I can't help feeling that you're avoiding the main point here," Bradley said, following her inside.

"I can't help feeling that you're being less helpful than you could be."

Bradley sighed, as if he were capitulating to a tantrum-throwing child. "Fine. By all means, let's focus on the retirees instead of on your world-saving alien blood. What could possibly trap them?" Bradley banged open a cabinet door, shut it, banged open another one. "The enemy formerly known as the Pearl Knife can wormhole them out of trouble at any second."

"I made a device that blocked her powers at HQ."

"Congratulations, it worked splendidly."

Mary ground her teeth. Her arm was smarting where the Dallas Cowboy had twisted it, her stomach queasy from the flickering tour of Rocker's mind. "It did work. Dolly couldn't portal them into HQ. Sever had to break it open."

Which didn't exactly make it sound like a pro-jammer argument, now that she said it out loud.

Bradley opened another cabinet and snatched a box of bandages. He pulled himself up to sit on the counter while the other engineers watched with obvious concern, and started to wrap his hand.

Mary hadn't noticed he was injured. She paused in her search for tools, ready to ask if he needed help. And then he opened his mouth. Again.

"What are you going to do, then?" Bradley said. "Build them a cage?"

Mary hadn't formed an exact plan yet, her brain still a whirlwind of ideas and concepts and theories. She'd thought, vaguely, of making some kind of net. If they could get the retirees to cluster into a group, she might be able to trap them.

How she could herd them into a cage, well, that was something she'd need to figure out. Invisible walls like one of her forcefields, maybe? Or something she could drop on them? But from where?

The creative process had its stumbling points.

Bradley was still looking at her, like he expected her to say something snarky in response.

"That's a great idea," she said. "If I can get the walls or bars resonating with the portal-blocking frequency, Dolly won't be able to get in or out."

Bradley shrugged, but he didn't argue.

One of the Wave engineers tapped Mary on the shoulder, and she turned to find a woman with a blonde braid and a sprinkle of freckles across her cheeks. "There's electrical equipment in the tall cabinet, and we might have some tech compacters we could use. There's definitely a frequency jammer."

Another tech was nodding, pushing glasses back up his nose. "Four metal strips, maybe."

"They could interlock," the braided woman said, excited. "Catch the group like a ring toss, then unfold the walls."

It took a concerted effort for Mary to keep her jaw from dropping. She hadn't pictured Wave running with a staff team behind it. She didn't know who'd she thought all these people *were*, but she hadn't imagined this. She only wished her friend and fellow engineer, Luke, could be here. He'd love them. But he was hiding out in a safehouse with Gail and Jeff, and the rest of the LIO support team.

Both the techs looked at her, as if for approval. "Yeah," she said. "Go ahead, design the apparatus. I'll get the vibrations coded."

Bradley finished wrapping his hand as she made her way to the tall cabinet with the electrical equipment. He was staring off into space, and she made a note to send him to Dr. Gordon later to make sure his injury was clean.

"So," she said, "the galoshes?"

He smiled, a pinched twitch of his mouth. "I can't control it," he said. "And yet, I'm *adept* at controlling it."

Bradley was nothing if not a man of contradictions. Mary waited. If he wanted to tell her more, he would.

"If my feet touch water, I'm in people's minds," he said. "Can't help it. Shoes don't help. Socks don't help. Just the galoshes."

He clicked his heels together, Wizard-of-Oz style. The motion made a dull clang, like a tamped bell.

"Reinforced?" Mary asked.

He nodded. "If the Pearl Knife really gave me these powers, as everyone seems to think, it's got a sense of humor."

Mary rummaged through the cabinet, looking for parts that could help her build her machine. She remembered the frequencies she needed to use, but she'd have to collaborate with the others to make them work with whatever compact-able metal they were imagining. Not that she couldn't do it on her own, if she had the time. But the Wave team would help her whip up the tech at double speed.

Bradley was still watching her. She said, "You spoke into my mind. Back there, at Beatrice's."

"I did, and I apologize. As you may have gleaned, I don't like to do that without permission."

"Don't apologize. It was good."

Bradley brushed his fingers against the bandage, tapping his heels against the cabinet. "I was a kid when it happened. I was stomping in puddles all the way home from school, and I remember." A husk of a laugh. "I remember I knew, with crystal certainty, that I'd be in big trouble when I got home. For ruining my shoes. So I took them off and hopscotched through the puddles in my socks."

She could picture it, a mini Bradley Archer with his shock-blond hair. Probably in a yellow raincoat, too.

"There was no lightning strike, no sudden jolt. Just the ability, during my bath that evening, to read my mother's thoughts. And her relief that I hadn't ruined my shoes, because she couldn't afford to buy me another pair."

It reminded Mary of Dawn Kimble's story. The reporter's ability to track people by location had appeared overnight, too.

"When did it happen?"

Bradley twitched an eyebrow. "And where? St. Louis, Missouri. About the time Dr. Gordon was arrested."

Mary nodded. There'd been a cluster of powers that'd cropped up in St. Louis at about the same time. It'd helped clue the League in about the Knife's connection to enhanced abilities on Earth. Mainly, that it created them. Not Agnes's, which the scientist had created herself, and not Ire's, which had come from a chemical weapons test gone wrong. But many.

And Bradley Archer's were among them. What was it like to live with such an isolating power? To have to wear those heavy boots all the time? A year ago, she'd have said that Bradley Archer would do anything for power. But that wasn't true at all. He could enter anyone's mind whenever he wanted, yet he chose to live in discomfort to avoid intrusion.

"Maybe I can improve your shoes," she said. "Make them lighter, but still protective. If you'd be willing to run some tests after we kick Sever's ass."

Bradley inclined his head. "Much obliged, Coral."

Mary carried her equipment to the nearest lab table. Before she could dig into the project, Eloise opened the door.

Mary expected Agnes to be two steps behind her, ready to

poke and prod at Mary. While she worked, hopefully, because she needed to finish this project almost as much as she needed to share her Sever-defying powers.

But Agnes wasn't there, and Eloise had her bottom lip wedged between her teeth, her index finger pressed to her temple.

"Where's Agnes?" Mary asked. "We got the info."

"And we're going to need it." Grimly, Eloise handed Mary her tablet.

Sever's face took up the entire screen, except for a ribbon of text at the bottom that declared the broadcast was a replay. The alien-god looked puffy and pale, his eyes brimming with fire. Swallowing hard, Mary tapped the play button.

"I came here to help this planet," Sever said. "But you don't appreciate my intervention. I've been lenient, hoping you'd come to understand."

He cleared his throat and glanced behind him, and molten fear cut through Mary's stomach. She didn't know what—or who—Sever was looking at. There was no way to know. And yet somehow she did know, was certain, that Nathan was there. Just past the edge of the scene.

"Your League attacks my people," Sever said. "They kidnap those in my care. Even your civilians storm my fortress."

Fortress? Mary wanted to laugh. She could feel it, bubbling up from the fear in her stomach, the lava threatening to explode. It was ridiculous. He'd stolen every inch of Earth that he controlled, and he thought it belonged to him?

Sever's eyes burned orange. "Clearly, my leniency has been misguided."

Sever moved away from the camera—was Morik filming him? Jenna?—allowing the Nationals press box to come into view behind him. Nathan was there, as she'd known he would be, his hands tied behind his back, the bruises on his face more faded than they'd been in Rocker's vision. President Caldwell slumped beside him, with ribbons of bloody tracks slicked across his cheek.

They were worse off than they'd been with HQ collapsing on their heads.

"An example must be made," Sever said. "This world must capitulate, or submit to the fate I've levied against so many others. And so as your final warning, at dusk tomorrow, your country's leader and your League hero will die."

ELOISE WOULD HAVE LIKED to spend some time contemplating the fact that her great-grandmother had been best friends with Mary's great-grandmother. And that they'd somehow forged a path to another galaxy, where they'd stolen the Knife out from under Sever's nose.

Of all the revelations—the constant, never-ending revelations—that one, outlandish as it was, somehow seemed to make the most sense. The friendship part, at least.

But Eloise didn't have time to contemplate her family's history with Mary's. There was no doubt in her mind that if they failed to meet Sever's deadline, Nathan and Caldwell would die.

So now, they had to move.

Agnes had relocated her test materials to the engineering lab, where Mary was fiddling with her retiree-cage—that didn't sound doable, but few of Mary's schemes did at first—while Agnes drew blood and measured cell counts and did something to DNA that Eloise hadn't quite caught.

She'd also hooked up a screen that was somehow projecting the Knife's messages, though not in a language Eloise understood as well as she understood what it said in her head. All she knew was that Agnes and Tam were getting better at reading it.

They'd moved Tam's piano into the corner, too, and she played on and on in elegant bursts of melody, with Lucy on the bench beside her. As long as she played, the screens kept translating ideas, instructions, and stuttered ideas from the Knife about where to look for the gene—or whatever it was—that made Mary immune from Sever's control. They came in images, most of them foreign to Eloise, but Agnes seemed to understand. She looked back and forth between the screen and her microscope for what felt like hours, searching for the answer.

With the technicians helping Mary with her project, it might have seemed crowded. But something about it felt comfortable to Eloise. Like they were finally working toward a common goal.

"Ironic," Mary said, "that my power turns out to be a *lack* of powers."

"Or not ironic at all," Bradley said. Eloise had forgotten he was there, but he stood with the technicians, assisting them with their wires and hammers and screws.

"Ha, ha," Mary said. And then she actually smiled at him. *Smiled.* Yes, it was a tight smile, but Eloise thought that part was more about the general situation, her worry for Nathan, than it was about Bradley. Her eyes kept flicking toward the clock on the wall, and she was tapping her foot under the table.

And yet, she was joking with him. With Bradley Archer.

Wonders. They truly never ceased.

"Is it strange?" Mary asked. "That other people can talk to the Knife now?"

It took a second for Eloise to realize that Mary was talking to her. Eloise considered, trying to put the feeling into words. "Mostly it's like finally getting to introduce a friend."

"You still understand it best," Agnes said. "Can you look at this, please? I think it's referring to something on this slide, but..." She shrugged.

Eloise leaned over Agnes's shoulder to look at the screen, the Knife pulsing a flurry of feeling into her mind. She moved to the microscope and back to the screen.

"There." She pointed to the screen, to the Knife's projected image. There was a tiny sparkle, like a snowflake glinting in a lake of lava. When Eloise peered into the microscope to look at the drop of Mary's blood, the same white fleck was shining there on the slide. An anomaly, or so the Knife claimed.

Agnes compared the two, then gave a brisk nod. "All right," she said. "I can work with that."

"Is it a gene?" Mary asked.

Agnes shook her head. "I don't know what the hell it is. But I'm going to isolate it, and I'm going to find out what it is. And then I'm going to produce enough of it to storm that alien's baseball castle."

Saving the world, one impossible task at a time.

Did it really have to be so impossible? Eloise's emotions felt raw, overused, and she kept pushing her fatigue down. There was no place for fatigue here, no place for a break.

Maybe there was another way. She kept thinking of Dolly's face on the yacht, the way she'd been yanked through the portal against her will. Could it be that she feared Sever? That she could want out?

Eloise slipped out of the lab, where Agnes and Mary were discussing equipment and whether Agnes was concerned about the snowflake-gene thing containing materials she couldn't replicate on Earth.

Eloise made her way back to her room. It was too dangerous to make a call with a portal—Dolly could track them here, and it would be much more difficult to evacuate the underwater base than it had been to submerge the yacht—so she opted for a video call.

She didn't bother to wonder why there was such good service down here. Wave was Wave. LIO had always been able to do the same; Mary liked to make jokes about which service providers would be willing to install fiber optics beneath Niagara Falls.

To Eloise's surprise, Dolly answered the call on the second ring. She appeared on the screen, her eyes wet and hungry, and searching. If she could leap through the screen to snatch the Knife, she absolutely would. The sight made Eloise want to throw the phone away. This call was a waste. She could already tell.

But she couldn't stop herself from trying, anyway.

"How can you let this happen?" she asked. "How can you let him murder people?"

Dolly licked her lips, eyes still searching. "It's the only way."

Eloise kept the camera tilted toward her, away from the Knife. It was cowering in her mind, whispering. She could feel its desire for her to close the connection. But she couldn't. She had to try.

"You've always claimed to be a hero," Eloise said. "How can you pretend that's at all true, if you're willing to let him execute Nathan?"

"And the president, don't forget him." Dolly said it like a taunt, but there wasn't much heat behind it. As if she baited by rote.

How could Eloise forget about Caldwell? Of course she couldn't. But Nathan was the member of their team, the one whose face she saw, whose death she feared most. She didn't want anyone to die, but Nathan... Nathan was a friend.

"OK," Dolly said, as if Eloise had answered. "Turn the Pearl Knife over to me, and I'll stop it."

Eloise blinked. Her eyes were dry, and she wanted to rub them. She didn't. "What?"

"If I have the Knife, my powers will be limitless. I can grasp Sever's powers. I can stop him."

Eloise's throat went dry. She swallowed. "You know that?"

Dolly waved a hand. "I assume."

She shouldn't. Sever's powers played by their own rules. The Knife fit with them, but in ways none of them could predict. Sever's powers didn't work on Mary, but the Knife's did. Unless Dolly knew far more than Eloise thought she did, it could go either way.

It was clear, however, that Dolly was only allying with Sever out of a desire to meet her own goals. She wanted the Knife back. She didn't want Sever to win.

"The Knife won't go," Eloise said.

Dolly scoffed, lips twisted in derision. "You are its *mistress*, Eloise. It answers to you. You can make it go."

The Pearl Knife shuddered in her mind, as if imagining itself once again at Dolly's command. Eloise supposed it was possible to grasp it as tightly as Dolly suggested. She supposed she'd even tried to, once upon a time.

"And why shouldn't I take Sever's powers, if it's so easy?" Eloise asked. "You've given me important information."

Dolly just laughed, a harsh sound that crackled through the line like dry paper. "You don't have the nerve."

Didn't she? Eloise had come so far. She knew the Knife more intimately than Dolly ever had, because the Knife let her know it. She'd learned to use it in ways Dolly had never imagined.

And yet, she still resisted using the Knife to control others' powers. She still feared that doing so would make her too much like her mother.

"Come, Eloise," Dolly said. "Your pride, or the fate of the world? Think carefully, daughter. Is it worth it?"

Eloise didn't bother to answer. She ended the call and set the tablet on the bedside table, rubbing a hand across her face, her mother's derision echoing in her ears.

When she dropped her hand, Fran was standing in the doorway, leaning both hands on her cane.

"I suppose you heard that," Eloise said, deciding not to point out that they were in her private room, and that knocking was a thing. Fran would only stare at her, say something about it belonging to Wave. Or secret phone calls necessitating supervision.

"I heard it," Fran said. She gripped the top of her cane, her bone-white knuckles giving away her tension even though her expression remained smooth. "So? What're you going to do?"

Direct to the end. What *was* she going to do? Why had she even come here? Some part of her had still hoped Dolly could be reasonable—or maybe that she was regretting her partnership with Sever. That she wanted an out that Eloise could provide, and take advantage of.

"I can't just hand it over to her," Eloise said.

"But?"

Eloise could almost feel the phantom thump of the cane punctuating the word. But Fran stayed still. No anger, no annoyance. Curiosity. Maybe some fear. But no anger.

"But," Eloise said, "on the other hand, maybe it's foolish not to. She might be able to stop this."

Fran crossed the room slowly, leaning on the cane. She eased herself onto the bed beside Eloise, bringing a light floral scent with her. "Perhaps Dolly can stop Sever," Fran said. "The question is whether she will. And, if she does, what the cost will be."

Eloise tried to follow the path in her mind, imagine what her mother would do with the Pearl Knife back in her possession. She might defeat Sever, accept the accolades. Become a hero again.

And then what? How would she use her new status as Earth's savior?

Dolly had always been thirsty for power, and willing to do whatever it took to grasp for more. Holding schools hostage, murdering Mary's parents, and framing Wave for every crime she committed. While abusing her husband's powers, and using them to hurt people.

If Dolly had the Knife again, she'd be as unstoppable as Sever.

Fran put a hand on Eloise's shoulder, startling out of her thoughts. "You've been shouldering too much by yourself, for too long. Not by choice, not entirely, but by circumstance. You're a capable woman, Eloise, more than capable. But you're still just one person."

Eloise sucked in a breath, let it out slowly. Between negotiating her own operatives, dealing with anti-enhancement government policies, and facing one public disaster after another—not to mention the implosion of her own family, the reappearance of the father she'd thought was dead, and the obliteration of her life-long home—she truly had reached her limit. How had she not realized it?

Fran sighed. "I didn't see how overburdened you were when Mary tried to form an alliance with us months ago. I could only see my own history with LIO. For that, I apologize."

Eloise felt a tear run down her cheek, and she brushed it away, horrified. Fran was apologizing? To *her*? "I didn't see it, either."

Fran let go of Eloise's shoulder, handed her a tissue, then rose. "We've all made mistakes, then. So, my dear, this decision is yours. But your friends are with you. And that means you don't need to make it alone."

Every moment Mary spent in the underwater base was a moment she wasn't rushing to free Nathan. Every cell in her body—the newly discovered alien ones included—wanted to rush to that ballpark *now*, with or without backup.

But she knew better. Sever would be expecting them. This was certainly a trap, and Agnes needed time to work her Sever-stopping magic, with help from Mary's intergalactic cells. Or whatever they were.

She'd have to square with that reality later. Preferably with Nathan by her side, and a gin and tonic in her hand.

In the meantime, Mary and Eloise had to get everyone on the same page.

There was no room for rogue maneuvers here, for manipulations or political hemming and hawing.

So naturally, Mary and Eloise were headed to meet with the Committee, along with Rajni to represent the recruits.

Why not? If they wanted a democratic system, might as well set it up now.

The Committee's underwater-bunker conference room wasn't nearly as spacious as their throne room back on the yacht. It was just a regular conference room, like the one she and Eloise had used to call Sloane, with a big oak table and mismatched chairs squeezed around it.

Still, Mary couldn't help the twinge of nerves that fluttered up her spine as she sat down to face Wave's leadership. If they refused their help, the mission would fail. If they insisted on cowering in the shadows, Nathan would die. Caldwell would die. And Sever would essentially have claimed the country.

After that, he'd claim the world.

The Committee faced them with their usual unreadable expressions. Was that because Mary's nerves were thrumming too hard to figure them out, or because they'd all studied up on how to appear wooden? For all she knew, there could be enhanced abilities at work here.

Eloise propped her forearms against the edge of the table, her face a perfect match for the Committee's smooth, calm appearance. Mary knew El's talent for negotiation, but she wasn't sure she'd ever truly appreciated it until this moment. El's heart had to be hammering as hard as Mary's was, but she radiated confidence.

"Well? What's the plan?" Sitting at the other end of the table, Fran punctuated the question with a rap of her cane against the floor. If her time mentoring Eloise had opened any doors, Mary couldn't see it. The old woman looked as severe as ever.

Eloise pressed her palms flat against the table and leaned forward. "The plan is a full-scale attack. We portal to the main entrance of the baseball park with everyone we've got. Agnes is working on a gas to dilute Sever's powers."

The corner of Fran's mouth twitched. It might have meant anything. "On the basis of?"

Mary raised her hand. "My blood. I'm part alien, apparently."

"Part Sever," Rajni added. "He's her grandfather."

"Great-great," Mary said. "And for what it's worth, my great-great grandma was an alien, too. But yeah. Essentially."

Jian leaned back in his chair. Gem's eyes widened. Fran pressed her lips together and frowned.

Mary waited for them to demand an explanation, with evidence and details, but Fran just said, "Go on."

Eloise dipped her chin toward her chest, the barest hint of a nod. "The civilians—the frozen ones—are surely guarded, but we need to get them out of harm's way, too."

"Sever is no doubt expecting us," Jian said, still leaning back in his chair. He'd ditched the suit he'd worn on the yacht, replacing it with a maroon sweater and corduroys. He looked comfortable, and a bit... teachery. "They'll meet us and fight."

"Yes," Eloise said, "they will. But we'll choose the battle-field. We'll save the civilians, then portal into the park and get the prisoners."

Matthew tapped his fingers on the table, watching Eloise closely, his lips pursed. "Wouldn't it be better to split up? Send some for Caldwell and Nathan while the others take care of the civilians?"

Yes. Mary did want that. More than anything, she wanted that.

When Eloise glanced at her—probably feeling how much she ached to follow that plan—she shook her head. "We don't know what Sever will throw at us. We should start together."

How five people could all maintain such identically inscrutable expressions, Mary had no idea. Matthew kept drumming on the table, while Jian cradled his chin in his fingers. One of the others, whose name Mary had never learned, sighed audibly.

Fran turned her gaze to Rajni. "And the recruits?"

Rajni started, as if surprised to be addressed. She licked her lips and squeezed her fingers into a fist. Mary could almost see her thoughts turning to the friend she'd lost. The action she'd want to take. "We agree to the plan."

Fran looked to each of her colleagues. Each of them nodded.

"All right," Fran said. "We're in."

Mary blinked. She and Eloise had discussed all the arguments the Committee might throw at them, all the different protests they might raise. They'd been ready for a fight.

Worse, they'd been ready for a three-hour discussion.

She exchanged a glance with Eloise, who shrugged. "Good," she said. "It's about time we all worked together."

THE D.C. HEAT lasted into the night, the dense humidity coating Nathan's skin, and his shirt, with a layer of sweat. He hadn't truly appreciated the air conditioning in his VIP prison until it was gone, replaced with the open-air cubicles of the press booth. The fresh cuts on his back were a constant throb, and yet somehow the heat felt worse. Near unbearable.

When he risked turning his head to catch a glimpse outside, he could see the distant wink of the sky's brightest stars. Or planets, probably. He could never remember which were supposed to be the brightest. Or did it change? His head swam, somehow desperate to remember. It seemed wrong to die without the knowledge. It seemed impossible.

Morik had escorted Caldwell away before nightfall, leaving Nathan alone in the box with Monster, Jenna, and Sever. Jenna was lounging on the desk across from him, picking at her nails, while Monster kept a vigilant watch on the open windows. As if expecting some attack.

As for Sever, well. Sever was coming undone.

The alien demi-god paced across the back of the press box in a wild, weaving pattern. His skin was pale and clammy, shining with the same layer of sweat Nathan felt. He muttered to himself, occasionally lashing out to hit the wall with a fist. Whenever he did that, Monster glanced over his shoulder, as if to check that Sever hadn't killed Nathan ahead of schedule.

There was no doubt in Nathan's mind that Sever intended to follow through on his threat. At dusk tomorrow, he would put Nathan and Caldwell to death. Would he make the entire country watch him do it? Nathan didn't want to picture Mary, to think of what her reaction would be. Would she watch his death, like everyone else?

No. No, Mary would intervene, as Sever must hope she would, and the League would help her. But whether they'd succeed, well... That was another question entirely.

Not that he was ready to give up. He wouldn't willingly bare his neck for Sever's blade, or however they executed people in demi-god land. He'd fight until his last breath.

But he didn't see how they could win, either. No matter their allies, no matter their tools, Sever was just too strong.

They could lose. They probably would. And Nathan would die.

He wanted to write a message to Mary, in case she survived. In case he didn't. He wanted to make sure she knew that he was thinking of her, that he would think of her, until the very last. He wanted to make sure that, if he hadn't said the words enough, she would know that he loved her to the end.

But he had no tablet to tap out the words, no pen, no paper. Just the steamy breeze and Sever's meandering footsteps.

Breathing deeply, Nathan closed his eyes and composed the letter in his head.

THE ARMY ASSEMBLED in the underwater bunker's version of a garage. The place was full of submarines, instead of cars and vans, but it was still a garage.

And they were definitely an army. Agnes couldn't deny it. There were LIO's recruits, lined up in the back; Wave operatives, including everyone Agnes had helped on the island, led by Fran and Jian; and of course, the League. Steve, Ire, and Will; Eloise, poised to make a portal; and Mary, muscles coiled as if she planned to be the first to step through, even if she had to shove everyone else out of the way to do it.

Agnes had made more of the anti-Sever gas than she'd anticipated she'd have time for. Still, it wouldn't be enough. She'd had to guess on the concentration, on the exact makeup. She'd loaded the red-tinged vials into dispensers and distributed them, begging them to work the way they were supposed to.

By the time Tam had come to drag her out of the lab, she'd been convinced they should just ditch the whole thing. She knew the gas wasn't toxic to her people, but beyond that, it was anyone's guess if it'd do what it was supposed to.

She'd kissed her wife goodbye, and her daughter, not at all

certain that she'd be returning. She hated going on missions, hated fighting. This time, though... This time, she couldn't even protest. Humanity was at stake, Tam and Lucy included. And Agnes could help to save them all.

Now, she wove through the group and stationed herself near the front, taking up a spot beside Ire. Just like old times.

"Got your magic gas?" he asked.

"It's not magic," she said. "It's chemistry."

He grinned down at her. "Sometimes, it feels like the same thing."

He'd spent enough time helping her in the lab to know the intricacies of it. Still, she knew what he meant. But she couldn't return his smile. "We didn't have any way to test it. We're going in trusting something that we whipped up five minutes ago."

"We're going in trusting you," he said. "That's enough."

Agnes hoped it would be.

Lifting the Pearl Knife over her head, Eloise seared a silver portal line into the air, pulling the thread down with expert grace. She'd been practicing, working, leaning into her relationship with the Knife. And it showed. Even from the outside, it showed.

The portal bloomed open, the edges uncurling toward the walls like a scroll unfurled, like waves washing across sand. This doorway was wider than any Agnes had seen her make before. Wide enough to get them all through, and quickly.

Ire grunted, a surprised sound, and Agnes stopped observing the portal's expansion long enough to notice what was on the other side.

Through the growing window, jungle-thick trees were crowded together. The sweet smell of coconut and mango drifted through, along with thick, humid air—which was about the only thing that resembled Washington, D.C.

"Not that I'd mind a side-trip to Bali," Mary said, "but are you sure that portal's opening in the right spot?"

Eloise nodded, lips pressed into a grim line. "He's already throwing us curveballs."

And then she was stepping through, side by side with Mary and Steve. Agnes exchanged a glance with Ire before following, taking care to step over the edge of the portal.

The trees closed in tight around her, undergrowth grasping at her ankles as she moved away from the portal to let the others in. Already, she and Ire had to separate to navigate around ivy-covered tree trunks, their line weakened if not broken.

Agnes reached out to squeeze the a leaf on a nearby fern. It felt as real as her own hand. "How did Sever do this?"

"Goldi," Mary said. Agnes had never seen the retiree's illusions, had never quite imagined them on a scale like this. Mary certainly would have, though. She'd grown up with these people. Goldi had probably conjured unicorns for her as a kid.

OK, it was difficult to picture Mary requesting a unicorn. The inside of an engine, maybe, or the Large Hadron Collider.

"How are we supposed to find our way?" Ire asked as the recruits left the portal and Eloise zipped it shut behind them.

"We find Goldi," Mary said, "and we stop her."

Her voice was grimly determined. She'd had her own run-ins with the retirees this year, and Agnes couldn't help wondering what she'd seen. What she'd done. And whether there was actually any reliable way to locate Goldi in this mess.

They trekked through the too-real illusion, none of them dressed for jungle exploration. A fist-sized spider skittered up Agnes's leg, and she shook it away, trying to tell herself it was just an illusion, just an illusion.

If she could feel the fern leaves, though, could she feel a spider's bite? What about its venom? She wavered between wanting to squish it and wishing she could trap it in a specimen jar for further investigation.

Eloise shouted, and that was all the warning Agnes had before a group of armored soldiers crashed through the jungle ahead.

Ire whirled around, catching a soldier's metal-encased arm in his fist. Only Ire could force back a robotic arm like that, muscles straining, teeth bared in concentration. To her right, Will blasted a stream of fire directly at an attacking soldier, filling the air with the smell of ozone and singed electronics.

And then Agnes was facing her own opponent. The silver-armored soldier swung for her, and she dodged, all too aware of the precious gas she carried at her back. It was protected by metal tubes—like a fire extinguisher, or a scuba pack—but still vulnerable.

Agnes could call light to make her invisible. She could call air to pull her above the fight.

Instead, she tugged at the molecules in the armor.

It wasn't as easy as pulling at water or light or air. They were packed in tight, and mixed with metals she didn't recognize. Metals from another galaxy. But after working with Wave's submarine dome, Agnes felt more confident. She teased the metals, poked at the joints. Finessed them. Eroded them. And as her attacker swung another punch, the armor crumbled away from his body like a cast-off shell.

He lunged for her, anyway, sweat popping up on his face as his armor fell away, exposing his skin to the hot D.C. jungle. Agnes called the wind, and it lifted her just high enough to kick the soldier soundly in the teeth. He staggered back, clutching at his mouth.

"Missing your armor?" Agnes asked.

He started for her again, but she kicked him again, this time in the temple. He fell, clutching his head, and didn't rise. One down.

The battle raged on around her, though, with plenty more

soldiers closing in from unseen places. If she didn't find Goldi, they'd lose the fight before she ever had a chance to use her anti-Sever gas.

An image of a rainbow flickered into her mind, cutting through the jungle with glittering precision as it reached for something she couldn't quite see. Agnes looked around, searching for Bradley—she understood his powers now, that he might be able to speak into her mind—but only one entity had ever sent *images* someone's way.

Agnes glanced at Eloise. The Knife was shining in her hand, winking with prismatic light. And speaking to her—to *Agnes*—without the assistance of music or machines.

Agnes looked back to the jungle and saw it in reality. The rainbow. The path, if she understood the Knife correctly, to Goldi.

A soldier stormed her, and Agnes used the air to wrench him out of her way. The time for subtlety had passed.

The underbrush snaked up to snatch at her ankles as she dodged through the trees, immune to the invisibility she wrapped around herself like a cloak. She yanked herself free with each step, her eyes locked on the rainbow.

The arch ended abruptly, and Agnes stumbled through the wall of the illusion to crash straight into Goldi. The retiree screamed as Agnes knocked her to the ground, still invisible, and the illusion shattered.

One of the recruits—Quin, Agnes thought—appeared at Agnes's side and plunged a syringe into Goldi's neck while the retiree continued to scream. Quin bound her hands as Agnes staggered to her feet and let her invisibility drop away.

They were still standing in a forest, of sorts. Only this one was made of people.

The civilians who'd marched on Sever stood like statues around her, their faces frozen in rage, or fear, or open in mid-shout. One held a sign above her head. Another pair were bent as they attempted to crawl beneath the turnstiles that lead into the park.

Their eyes were open, and glassy in a way that made Agnes swallow hard. But when she touched a woman's wrist, her skin felt warm, her pulse beating strong beneath Agnes's fingertips.

Agnes was aware, vaguely, that the fight was ending; with visibility restored, LIO and Wave could stop Sever's soldiers. They weren't endless, after all. In the distance and well behind her, Sever's dome glittered like a translucent orange wall. It looked like it was made of light.

Agnes closed her own gentle dome over the heads of the crowd, hardening the air into a shield, and released the anti-Sever gas.

A breath, then two.

The woman whose pulse Agnes had checked shuddered, then gasped. Agnes caught her elbow as she wavered on her feet, ragged breaths following from all around her. People were coughing and collapsing to the ground, sobbing with relief.

It worked. The gas could protect against Sever's powers, even reverse their effects. Agnes's heart soared with triumph. They had a chance now. They might actually win.

"Thank you," the woman said.

Agnes nodded. "We need to get you to safety."

And she'd need to examine them, too, to make sure that there were no lingering side effects from Sever's spell.

A flicker of movement sparked in the corner of her eye, and Agnes looked back at the walls of the dome.

They were moving. Rushing closer.

She shouted to the people to duck, to cover their heads as the orange wall fell toward them. She didn't know what good it would do, if any, but instinct was instinct, and she threw herself to the ground along with the crowd.

The dome passed by with a pulse of energy, and Agnes leapt to her feet, anxiety thrumming through her chest. But the people were OK, straightening slowly, helping one another. The League was behind her, and Wave, all of them unharmed.

But the dome had collapsed inward to re-form itself on the inside of the park. Ten or fifteen feet past the turnstiles, she could see it—thicker now, but not entirely opaque. Like dark orange jello.

Standing in lines before it were LIO's retirees, and Jenna. Sever's allies. Ready to fight.

"Agnes."

She turned to see Eloise and Mary striding up to her, as the LIO-Wave army reformed its ranks behind her.

"I'm ready," Agnes said. "Do you want me on Diana? Or Jenna?"

Eloise shook her head. "Go back to the lab."

Agnes looked around at the League operatives, all ready to fight. "But you need me."

Eloise nodded. "Yes, we do. We need you to save these people. And to prepare more of that gas in case things go wrong here."

In case things go wrong. Things always went wrong, had *already* gone wrong. But Agnes didn't want them to go wrong in the way Eloise meant. She tried to imagine continuing the fight without Eloise, without any of the people here. She came up short.

Agnes threw her arms around Eloise, who let out a breath of surprise before hugging her back.

Agnes shrugged the bottles of gas off of her back and passed one to Eloise, another to Mary. "Do me a favor and save the world, will you?"

Mary saluted, El cut a portal, and Agnes began escorting the civilians to safety.

ELOISE COULD SEE shapes through the thickened dome, the edges of their silhouettes clear through the orange-tinted force-field. The entrance to the gift shop, the steps leading up to the spectator seats. An unlikely place to save the world.

President Caldwell was there, too, his hands roped behind his back and securing him to a pole. A flagpole, maybe. Eloise wondered if Sever planned to burn Caldwell at it, or shoot him into space. She craned her neck, hoping for a glimpse of Nathan. If he was there, though, she couldn't see him.

She was going to save Caldwell, and find Nathan. And save him, too. Along with everyone else.

But first, they needed to outsmart LIO's retirees. They stood in formation, guarding the strip of courtyard between the now-concentrated dome and the turnstiles leading into the park. Diana and Jenna stood at the front of the group, flanked by Monster and the twins. She didn't see Dolly.

"We don't have to get past them," Eloise said, "we just have to cut a portal."

Mary was standing to Eloise's right. She'd somehow dredged up another Coral outfit—how many of those did she *have?*—and she looked no worse for the wear after the fight in

Goldi's jungle. When Eloise mentioned the portal, however, she frowned. "I think it's—"

Eloise jammed the Knife into the ether before Mary could finish her sentence, as she'd done a hundred times before. Perhaps more, now.

This time, the ether pushed back. Shock reverberated up her arm like an electric shock, knocking her off her feet. Mary caught her before she could fall, grasping her arm.

"It's too strong," Eloise said. "It's blocking my portals now."

She had the distinct sense of being played with. Sever must have known they could portal to him, that he could stop them from crossing the border into his territory. And yet, he hadn't. Until now.

To her credit, Mary didn't say 'I could have told you that.' She just nodded. "It's more concentrated," she said.

"It's a good sign," Dad said. He'd appeared on Eloise's left, and he looked half ready to grab her elbow if she needed steadying. "Means he's consolidating his power."

At his side, Steve nodded. The retirees, for their part, just stood and watched them. Jenna was smirking. Diana cracked her knuckles. One of the twins bent down to knot a shoelace.

They certainly didn't look like they planned to attack. Which meant they needed to defend the wall. It only seemed like an impossible barrier; there had to be a way through it.

"We have some gas left in case Sever tries to use his powers on us," Eloise said. "I don't see him, though. So wait to use it until he's in sight."

The Knife thrummed in agreement. Eloise had never understood it so clearly, its thoughts nearly as crystal as her own. It sounded like water. It sounded like chimes in the wind, or a melody that she'd been trying to place for ages, one that finally clicked into place. It was still sick, still struggling—

there'd been no time to fix that—but for the first time, it could actually *tell* her.

"So," Steve said, "we attack."

Mary ticked her chin at the retirees. "Herd them together so I can cage them."

"How close?" Steve asked.

"As close as you can get."

And then they were rushing toward the retirees, who were rushing to meet them, fists and powers raised. Eloise vaulted over the nearest turnstile, Mary in sync beside her, footsteps landing all around her as they hit the courtyard.

"We really have got to choose better locations for battles," Mary said. "Or at least, less weird ones."

Rajni and Jian surged forward, bringing a torrent of river water to wash the retirees off their feet. Jenna took to the air, rockets of flame jutting from her palms and throwing a cloud of billowing steam up out of the water. It smelled like the river, earthy and thick.

Monster, too, managed to leap high enough to avoid the current, launching himself above the wave to attack Mary with nostrils flared, rage painted across his face as she deflected his blows. Still bitter about her kidnapping crusade, perhaps.

The rest of the retirees toppled as the water pulled at their ankles, though Diana was quick to leap back to her feet. Then Fran was there, arms raised like a sorceress, her cane whipping around Diana's head and twisting to grab at her arms. Diana coated it in ink-black poison, but the cane kept going, unaffected.

Eloise scanned the chaos for Dolly, hoping to get close. Yes, her mother appeared to be stronger now, but the Knife might be able to drain her powers again. If they got close enough.

But the twins, Brenda and Donny, broke free of the chaos to rush toward her, looking eager for a rematch after their defeat on the yacht. Eloise abandoned her search for Dolly to face them as they read each other's minds, allowing them to fight like two very blond, very angry clockwork soldiers.

Eloise barely managed to avoid Brenda's first blow, and her dodge sent her straight into Donny's kick. Their moves were coordinated to bat her around like a toy.

The Knife left her hand to carve a protective circle around her, forcing the twins to back off a step. She could feel the blade's energy, the deep fatigue that pulsed beneath its surface. It was trying to rally, and doing admirably. But how long could it hold out?

Donny threw himself into a somersault to evade the Knife, grabbing for Eloise's legs. But the Knife anticipated his movement, and Eloise felt her foot land in Donny's neck, almost before she knew she was moving. He fell back, clutching his throat, and his sister abandoned the fight to check his injuries.

"Eloise," Steve shouted, his voice rising above the chaos, "there!"

Eloise caught his eye and followed his gaze across the ball park's courtyard. Dolly stood at the edge of the fight—whether she'd been there all along or whether she'd just materialized, Eloise couldn't say—watching the battle with her eyes narrowed in a calculating gaze. The dome glittered at her back, and Eloise considered for the first time that Sever had locked his allies out of his protective sphere.

It didn't seem to matter. They fought for him, just the same.

Eloise called to the Pearl Knife, and together they cut a short portal across the square. When she stepped through, Dolly was disappearing through her own doorway and reappearing in the spot Eloise had just abandoned.

The battle raged in the space between them, Mary and Steve fighting Monster together, Rajni and Jian working to dowse Jenna's flames. Fran and Diana still grappled near the center of the fight, and Diana's lips were pressed together, her nostrils flared in frustration as her poison pounded uselessly against Fran's powers.

Dolly waved to Eloise. And then, she lifted both her hands above her head and closed her eyes.

Coated in Diana's poison, Fran's cane suddenly withered, drying to a husk and dropping to the ground, defeated. Fran staggered, but Quin rushed to her side to steady her.

Dolly was grinning. So she really could enhance their powers, then. That would certainly explain the depth of Goldi's illusion.

Dolly sliced a portal open, and Eloise had only a second to absorb the fact that Ranger was joining the fight. And that he was flanked by a pair of gray-coated wolves, their teeth bared. Mountains rose up in the distance behind him, and Eloise had a split second to wonder where he was portaling from before the rest of the pack materialized behind him, a gray-and-white cluster of muscle and sharp teeth. They looked... hungry.

Eloise had never seen Ranger speak to so many animals at once; he looked positively giddy beneath his cherry-red Nationals cap.

Eloise had studied tactics for so many scenarios—even for evacuating HQ—but this was definitely a new one. She didn't want to fight a pack of animals that were born to hunt. And she definitely didn't want to hurt the wolves Ranger was manipulating.

Also, she wasn't entirely sure she *could*.

The wolf to Ranger's left lunged at Rajni, who stood closest to the oncoming animals. She pulled up a wall of water, but the wolf splashed through it, apparently unconcerned about waterfalls—or at least, it was brainwashed to be.

Rajni stumbled back, and Eloise saw Steve blur toward her,

knocking her out of the wolf's path. But Steve couldn't rush everyone out of the way. Another pair of wolves stalked toward Quin, jaws snapping.

Eloise started forward—she didn't know what to do, only that she had to do *something*—and then the air twisted, spitting a figure out of nowhere to whisk Quin away from the danger.

Eloise gasped as Quin reappeared across the square, with Phil, the tall, gangly teleporter from Philadelphia, at their side.

Across the square, thick plants shot up out of the concrete to form a thick wall between the animals and the League operatives.

Phil was grinning as Rose and her plant-wielding family entered the courtyard, followed by Dawn Kimble, who'd probably tracked them all here, and Liz, who could bend shadows to her will—and all of them, everyone they'd rescued in Philadelphia. They were all here.

"How did you get here?" Eloise said. "I know how *you* got here, Phil, but how did—everyone else is—"

"We set up camp outside D.C., soon as the dome went up," Phil said. "Thought you might need some backup."

Eloise couldn't help it. While the retirees regrouped on the other side of the square, she threw her arms around the teenager. He laughed before awkwardly returning the hug.

Shadows pooled around the wolves, dark and disorienting, and Liz dropped them into darkness. Eloise could barely make out their silhouettes as they hesitated, apparently against Ranger's commands. He was squinting into the shadows, confused, as if the smoke-like clouds obscured his powers. Perhaps they did. Or perhaps the wolves' survival instincts were just stronger than a little bit of mind control, or persuasion, or whatever it was Ranger did.

Thick stalks shot up out of the ground, branches twining out in every direction to embrace each other and form thick cages around the pack. The courtyard filled with the earthy smells of plant life, thick and heady in the humidity.

Rose's family had been working on their powers since Eloise had last seen them. Which hadn't actually been all that long ago.

Or maybe they'd been able to do this all along. It was the EAEA that had forced them to tamp down their powers.

Skirmishes continued on the borders of the courtyard, but two of the recruits—Elle and Len—had been able to join Mary against Monster, and Ire had backed Diana into a corner. She seemed to be working hard not to touch Sever's dome. Eloise couldn't blame her.

Jenna was blasting the other plant wall, the one Rose and her brother Ethan had thrown up in front of the wolves. Her flames tore ragged holes into the barrier, but Rajni and Jian sent spurts of water at each spot of fire. Jenna was gritting her teeth like she intended to send the next blast straight at them.

Good luck with that, Eloise thought. Jenna and the retirees were outnumbered. They couldn't win. If Eloise's team could herd them together, Mary would be able to lasso them with the contraption she'd worked up with the Wave scientists.

They were winning.

Next, they'd take down Sever.

Dolly portaled into the center of the action, shearing the end off the burning plant wall and missing Rajni by less than a foot. Rajni jumped back, and Jian grabbed her arm to keep her from falling.

Eloise started toward her mother, the Knife drumming a beat into her mind, but Dolly threw her arms out wide.

The Knife screamed feedback into Eloise's mind as a wave of power washed through her, hot and brimming with static. Her knees buckled, and she barely managed to stay on her feet. It was like the feeling of cutting her portal through Dolly's, only it was ten times worse. She didn't understand what was happening.

Carlisle followed Dolly through the new portal. His curls were wet, his eyes wide with their usual sorrowful expression. In the sky they'd left behind, lightning skittered across the clouds.

"Take cover!" Eloise shouted. The people closest to her dove for the few available overhangs that weren't blocked by the dome, but she didn't know if anyone else could hear. She didn't know if the flimsy shelter would protect them, anyway.

And she felt trapped, suddenly, with her people filling the courtyard around her, water pooling beneath their feet and lightning cracking its knuckles in the distance.

We have to get to Dolly, she said to the Knife. *Can you still drain her power?*

Dolly had so *much* power now, and the Knife was still recovering. Still not itself. It seemed impossible.

The Pearl Knife sent back a song, clear as a crystal ball: *She doesn't know he's alive.*

Not in words, but in feelings. She knew it as well as she knew her own thoughts. Dolly had no idea that her father had survived, and Eloise could use that.

Eloise made herself hold Knife lightly, a caress rather than a grip. She raised her hand, and the Knife lifted her feet out of the water as the first bolt of lightning cut out of the sky and burned the remaining limb of the plant wall to the ground.

DOLLY'S POWER WAS INFINITE. The forces of the Earth bent to her will. She could create, and she could destroy. And when the Pearl Knife was once again hers, she would defeat Sever and take her rightful place as the hero of Earth's people.

And they, too, would yield.

Yes, Carlisle was wielding his own abilities, but Dolly was feeding him the strength he needed to call the forces of nature to his aid. She could pull them away at any moment. She could leave him with nothing.

She felt Eloise rising toward her as Carlisle fired his warning shot at the wall of plants. The smell of scorched vegetation filled her nostrils, and she was vaguely aware of an oncoming sneeze crawling through her sinuses.

It didn't matter. Her power was limitless. She didn't need the Pearl Knife, but she would have it just the same.

43 / MARY

Cold rain pattered down from the sky as Carlisle's clouds streamed out of the portal and into the D.C. heavens. Mary was almost thankful for it, actually; it broke the heat. The courtyard steamed as the drops hit the hot pavement, and if not for the threat of the lightning, she would have turned her face toward it.

She might do that, anyway. It wasn't like she could stop the lightning.

But she *could* stop the retirees. Nathan was so close, she could almost feel him. *Stay alive,* she willed him. *Just a few more minutes.*

If they could herd the now extra-powered retirees into a pen. And if her gadget kept them from portaling out. And if it worked against *all* their powers, if it could prevent Monster from bashing down the walls, and Jenna from incinerating them.

Mary hated 'ifs.' She pushed them all away as Ire ran over to crouch beside her, Steve a few steps behind. Ire's red hair was flat against his head, water streaming down his face, and he wiped his forehead with the back of his hand. He was favoring

242 / KATE SHEERAN SWED

the other one, cradling it close. Diana must've gotten a poisonous hit in.

"What's the plan?" Ire said.

Eloise was flying away to face her mother. Mary had never seen the Knife lift her straight up from the ground like that—usually it guided a jump, say between two moving airplanes—but it was pulling out all the stops today, apparently.

"Eloise is dealing with Dolly," she said. "We need to get the rest of the retirees close to each other."

Ire shook his head to dislodge the streaming drops. "Why couldn't your gadget do that part?"

"Oh, I'm sorry, I ran out of time to make a chasing *and* capturing cage. Maybe next time." Mary pointed to Steve. "You take the turnstile side of the courtyard. Tell Will to take the far side. Rajni and Jian on this side. A plant barrier against the dome. We'll force them together."

Steve nodded, then took off to get everyone in position.

"What about us?" Ire said. "Do we build a wall with our muscles?"

Mary grinned. "I wish. But no, we harry them inside, and then we spring the trap."

"The easy job, then."

Mary shrugged. "Get a degree in accounting."

"I might. Not sure it'd be easier."

"Bit less deadly, though."

A fountain burst up out of the stones, and steam fogged the courtyard as Will's wall of fire roared to life across the way. Steve was running a tight circle in front of the turnstiles. Anyone who could fly well would be able thread the space above his head and escape through the narrow gaps above.

But this was the best they could do.

From her corner, Mary could make out the scene through Steve's blurred side of the power-box.

Some of the retirees had already been caught inside. Diana was turning a frantic circle, unsure of where to aim her poison. Steve might've been the best bet, but he was moving too fast to target. Monster was considering the plant wall like he might've scaled it, had Sever's dome not been pressed flush against the other side. Seemed he didn't want to touch it by accident.

Rajni and Jian pushed their wall forward, and Will's fire moved forward, too, like a magnetic opposite, to squeeze the retirees closer together.

Ire was fighting the twins on Mary's side of the water. They both rushed him at once, and Mary saw their mistake before they did; even with one injured hand, Ire swept them up by their collars and dragged them off their feet like naughty kittens, one in each massive hand. As she watched, Rajni opened a narrow gap in the water wall, and Ire tossed them inside.

It was always fun to fight with Ire.

"Well, Mary, it comes down to us. Again."

Mary turned to find Jenna Carpenter, standing behind the water wall, her hip cocked, her dark hair frizzing out of its ponytail. She flipped a spark of flame along her fingertips the way someone else might play with a coin.

And she was right. The courtyard had emptied of the other retirees, all of them trapping between fire and water. It wouldn't hold them forever. It would have to be long enough.

"If you really wanted to hurt me," Mary said, "you'd have burned me from behind, instead of warning me."

"See, that's why we've always misunderstood each other," Jenna said. "I'm just here for the party."

"I don't even know what that means."

Jenna grinned, then reeled back as if to throw a pitch. Mary threw herself to the ground as fire blasted over her head. She really hadn't missed Jenna's flame-throwing.

Jenna laughed. "Sever's going to love this. I'm already his favorite. I might just let the others die. Tell him you did it. Why not?"

Fighting fire was the worst. Of all the people to be left skulking outside the box. Why couldn't it be Ranger? Without the wolves, though.

Mary picked herself up and clicked her dart gun out of her belt. Best option with this one would be to sedate her. The only option, maybe.

Jenna just laughed again, as if she knew it.

A thread of water reached out of the wall and grabbed Jenna by the ankles. Jenna pinwheeled her arms, trying to keep her balance, but she couldn't fight the water. She landed on her back, and Rajni pulled her straight through the wall of water.

Mary clapped the girl on the shoulder. "Thanks," she said. "Exactly what Tally would have done."

Tears sprang into Rajni's eyes, and she nodded.

Mary squeezed her shoulder. "Give me a boost?"

"My pleasure."

Rajni lifted Mary off the ground in a surge of water, and Mary felt it turn to ice as the League's ice-wielding recruit used her powers to solidify the top of the wall. The recruits were already aces at the teamwork thing.

Will, Steve, Rajni, and Jian had done their job, along with Rose and her family. The retirees were hemmed in close, standing-back to-back as if they didn't know what to expect. Carlisle kept staring at the sky, as if trying to call down lightning, but nothing happened. Mary didn't see Rocker among them; she supposed he could be waiting elsewhere, camouflaged, but if so, they'd deal with him.

Mary pulled the sleek stick the Wave scientists had built for her. "I really hope you work," she told it.

When the pole hit the ground, it unfurled. That was the

only word for it, as it snapped out to build a border around the now-panicked retirees, clicking loudly as it assembled itself. A beautiful piece of tech.

Diana tried to kick it away, but it was too late; the walls were already popping up, the cage growing up around her. Monster tried to leap out, but the ceiling closed over his head before he could clear the wall.

Will's fire wall disappeared, and Steve stopped running as Rajni lowered Mary to the courtyard. Jian was on his knees, wavering like he might pass out, but he was smiling.

Mary couldn't smile. Not yet. Because across the courtyard, Dolly was facing Eloise. And she looked pissed.

As the walls of water and fire dropped away, Dolly stared at the box that contained every single one of her allies. The Knife set her down, and Eloise kept her attention locked on her mother.

"Clever," Dolly muttered. "It's blocking my portal."

"That would be Mary's design."

Dolly turned to her. "If you recall, it did not keep us out last time."

Eloise took a step closer to her. Dolly took a step back. "I don't see your pet alien god here," she said. "Or are you his pet? I can't tell, Mother."

Dolly huffed out a breath that might have been a laugh, but she didn't smile. Eloise thought there was fear in her eyes. Eloise didn't know how her mother expected to take the Knife without getting closer than ten feet. She could feel the Knife reaching for Dolly, could feel the wall her mother had erected to keep it out.

She didn't know Dolly's plan. She wasn't even sure Dolly *had* a plan, beyond 'step one: get Knife, step two: win.'

Dolly's eyes were trained on the Knife, and the blade shouted a warning into Eloise's head a moment before her mother's mental attack hit. She groped at Eloise's power, and Eloise had to fight to stay on her feet as Dolly delved into her mind, picking at her powers as if she meant to take control of them.

"The Knife is mine," Dolly said. "It was my mother's, and her mother's, and they gave it up only after they were gone."

Eloise gritted her teeth, the Knife screaming into her mind to get close, get close. It needed to touch her. It needed to end this.

"Aren't you wondering," Eloise said, through her gritted teeth, "where we got a fire-starter?"

Dolly narrowed her eyes, the attack easing up slightly. And then she turned.

Dad had extinguished his wall of fire, yet he stood watching Eloise's exchange with Dolly. From a distance, but poised, she thought, to leap in if he had to. She wished she could have warned him, but there was no time.

Dolly's mouth actually fell open. The color drained out of her cheeks, and the last tendrils of her attack drained away as she stood there, as frozen as one of Sever's statue people. "Will."

His name came out so quietly, she might not have said it out loud at all.

Eloise didn't wait to see Dad's reaction. She darted close to Dolly, moving fast enough to take her mother's wrist. Holding tightly, she pressed the Pearl Knife's blade flat against her mother's skin.

Dolly fell to her knees, gripping her head in her hands as the color leeched out of her hair, her face, the Knife taking back what it had never freely granted, drawing her energy, her youth, along with it. She never took her eyes off of Dad.

"The Knife gets to choose, Mom," Eloise said. "That's what you never understood."

Dolly was sobbing, her face a mask of pain, and Eloise had no doubt that her powers were gone, drained away by the Knife's presence. She couldn't stand, let alone strike a portal into the air.

Gone for good? Eloise asked.

The Knife beamed back confidence. Gone for good. What the Knife could give, it could take. Not easily, perhaps, but with finality. Eloise hoped it was true.

Across the courtyard, past the black box that held the retirees—they'd either gone silent, or Mary had wisely made a soundproof box—Sever's dome shuddered, then collapsed in on itself. Like it had done before, kind of, only this time it was a stuttered movement, barely controlled.

The orange wall rushed inward, passing the outer walls of the ball park and exposing President Caldwell, who was still tied to his flagpole. The Vice President was tied up behind him, along with a man Eloise didn't recognize.

Leaving Dolly for Steve to handle, Eloise jogged across the courtyard and used the Knife to slice through the prisoners' ropes. She returned to Caldwell, crouched in front of him. He rubbed his wrists, then his upper arms.

"Nathan Pearce," Caldwell said. "He's in the press box. But Sever's with him."

Eloise blinked. She knew Caldwell had tried to help by contacting her before, but it was still a surprise that the injured President of the United States—especially the man who'd ordered enhanced humans to register—was focused on someone other than himself.

"Thank you," Eloise said.

Caldwell nodded as Fran limped up to stand behind her, the un-enhanced side of her cane still usable.

Eloise hesitated. "I assume we're no longer enemies of the state, then?"

Caldwell shook his head. He was dry, as if the dome had protected him from Carlisle's rain, but there were tears brimming in his eyes. "Of course, of course. The League is officially back, with my apologies. Official ones. As soon as I can make them."

Eloise glanced at Fran, who looked back with her steely blue gaze. She turned back to Caldwell. "And Wave," she said.

Caldwell sputtered. "Well, you know, I see... They're here, I see that, but they're criminals. I don't think... That is, the League has always..."

Eloise stood and brushed her hands on her pants. Her head was aching from Dolly's attack, and there was still Sever to face. "There's no more League," she said. "There's no more Wave. We're the Enhanced Abilities Coalition, and we protect everyone with powers. No matter who they are."

Caldwell rubbed his palm across his forehead. He'd atoned for his mistakes, but he still had to understand. "Yes, yes. Fine. Are you a government office?"

Eloise smiled. "No, Mr. President. We're independent."

SEVER'S STOMACH clenched and roiled in turns. He couldn't take three steps without retching, so he'd curled up in the corner near the window, where the breeze broke in occasionally. It felt like hot breath.

The League had broken past his defenses. His soldiers. His allies. It was incomprehensible. It was unprecedented.

Impossible. It was *impossible*. And yet so it was; he could not deny it. They were here; they were coming.

His dome glittered close to him now, so close that only he could see beyond its walls. He hadn't wanted to pull it in, but this was his best chance of survival. His best chance to beat them.

Perhaps Dolly had been right to warn him against this League, after all. The realization smoked through his thoughts like poison. They were stronger... But no.

It was impossible.

The nausea was thick, disorienting. He hadn't seen Morik in hours. Where had he gone? Where had everyone gone?

He'd sent them away. But Morik should be here. Morik should know he was needed.

"Maybe Morik knows a lost cause when he sees one."

Sever hadn't realized he'd spoken out loud until Nathan Pearce answered him. Or perhaps Sever had beamed his thoughts into the human's head; it was hard to tell, sometimes.

Sever staggered to his feet and turned to face his last prisoner. His last piece of leverage. His last revenge.

No, not revenge. That implied a loss. He would rally, and he would win. Because he always won. He would win forever.

"No one wins forever," Nathan said, but Sever hardly heard him. He would win, and he would take back every promise he'd made to protect this world.

He could see now, even through the fog of this poisonous rock of a world, that he'd once again tried to be what he wasn't. He'd once again tried to hide his true nature, to bend as he once had for Adina.

The entire Parse Galaxy had shunned him, had forced him to hide away. They'd built their trade routes around his system; they'd feared him. And they'd been right to.

Sever had thought to make a new start on this world, this Earth, but he'd been wrong. He was what he was.

And when he forced Mary and her friends to their knees, this world would burn. Just like all the others.

TOGETHER, Mary and Eloise made their way up to the press box. Sirens called out in the distance, getting louder by the second as they rushed toward the ballpark. Ire and the others would coordinate, take care of injuries, and figure out where to keep the retirees.

Mary and Eloise would take Sever.

They couldn't risk anyone else. Water and fire were all well and good, but it was the Pearl Knife that could take Sever down. And if somehow it didn't, the world would need *all* their heroes alive to fight.

"Are you sure you want to be here?" Eloise asked, as if she could read Mary's thoughts. They'd made their way past the popcorn-scented lower levels and up to the press box, where musty carpeting and closed doors defined the space.

Mary could only nod. Sever's powers didn't work on her. If they somehow ran out of the Sever-proofing gas, she would still be able to fight.

And Nathan was here. Her heart thrummed in her throat, painful and swollen. They weren't too late. They *couldn't* be.

On a count of three, they kicked the door in together.

The dome was entirely inside the press box now. It

shielded Sever alone, and it was so bright that Mary had to squint to see his form pacing behind it. He'd walled himself in at a desk near the window, leaving Nathan alone and unguarded at the station beside his.

Nathan startled awake at their entrance, or maybe just opened his eyes. His face was still bruised, and she couldn't stop herself from moving toward him as the Knife spun out of Eloise's hand to attack the dome. The tip cracked into the shield with a fizzle of orange sparks, and sweat beaded along El's hairline as spiderwebbed fissures curled up the blade.

But they were also curling into the dome, black threads of poison weakening Sever's shield. Given time, the Pearl Knife would break through.

Mary just hoped it wouldn't destroy the Knife, too.

While the Knife battered at the dome, Mary ducked around Eloise and knelt beside Nathan. His lip was swollen, his jeans torn, but he was here. Breathing. When she sliced through the ropes to free his hands, he lifted a trembling palm to her cheek. When had he last eaten?

"You," Nathan said, "are very late."

She let out a laugh, then realized it sounded like a sob. And that her cheeks were wet.

"Seriously," he said, "you were supposed to pull some kind of rogue maneuver, make everyone angry, and win anyway."

"I did do that. For a second. Except for the winning part."

He grinned, then winced. "I saw."

She kissed him, unable to stop herself, her heart too crowded with fear to make much room for relief. Sever was weakened, but they still needed to beat him. She still didn't know if they could.

She thought Nathan might be in too much pain, but he kissed her back, then pressed his forehead against hers. They couldn't be reunited like this only to die again. They just couldn't.

The Knife was bleeding sparks now, red ones mixed with the orange as Mary helped Nathan to his feet.

Behind the dome, Sever was rallying, straightening his back and pulling himself upright. She could only make out his outline, but she recognized the way that Nathan stiffened at her side, the way Eloise's fingers stopped moving on the hilt of the Knife. Sever was controlling them.

Not this time. Mary dispensed the last of Agnes's gas, and Nathan's muscles relaxed. Eloise nodded, lips pressed tight, her eyes locked onto the Knife.

"Cool trick," Nathan said. "How'd you do that?"

"Oh, you know, I'm part alien," Mary said.

The Pearl Knife pierced through Sever's dome with a crash like shattered glass, drowning out Nathan's response as they both staggered back in the wake of the energy pulse.

The dome flickered, flashed, then disappeared. The Knife clattered to the ground, and Eloise collapsed, too, though whether because of sympathetic weakness or to crawl after it, Mary wasn't sure.

Sever wavered on his feet, his face thin and starkly pale. He stayed standing for a beat, two, then fell to his knees.

He might have looked at the Knife, or at Eloise. Instead, his orange-flecked eyes bored straight into Mary's. "Part alien?"

His voice sounded far away, like an echo. Mary nodded. "Apparently you're my great-great grandfather."

Sever crumpled to the floor, as if this information was too much for him to handle. Though Mary suspected it was the presence of the Knife that had weakened him—the blade still lay motionless, just out of reach of El's fingertips—rather than the news of their familial connection.

El's eyes were closed, but she was breathing. Mary didn't

think she was unconscious. Talking to the Knife, maybe. She hoped.

So Mary went to Sever, with Nathan at her side.

Sever's face flickered, his long nose replaced with a snub one, his thin lips growing thinner and then thicker, his ears curving to points like Morik's and then smoothing back out into rounded shells. His skin, too, flashed from white to green to blue and back to white again, his hair doing the same. She blinked, trying to understand, trying to pin down the real Sever.

Through all the different faces, his eyes remained the same. Black, with a spark of flame in the center. He watched her.

"What will you do now, granddaughter?" Sever asked, his voice a rasp. "How will you save your world?"

"No offense, but you don't look very capable of crushing it at the moment," Mary said.

"Give me a moment."

She didn't dare. The Knife still lay on the blue carpet, and though Eloise's lips were moving now, like a silent prayer, it hadn't twitched. The tip was as black as Diana's poison.

Sever was a monster, one who would destroy the world as soon as he regained his strength. He didn't deserve her compassion, or anyone's.

But Mary had already tried to take justice into her own hands, against the LIO operatives who'd murdered her parents. Sever wasn't human, though he looked it, but what did that matter?

She was supposed to be a hero, not an executioner.

She'd have to sedate him. Failing that, she'd have to wrestle him to the ground and tie his wrists and hold him here until someone more powerful could deal with him. Maybe Agnes could keep him in a box made of air.

They'd figure it out.

"I can't kill you," she said.

Nathan leaned into her arm, just slightly, and she pulled out a syringe. Darts were all well and good, but nothing beat a good dose to the artery.

She leaned over Sever to plunge it into his neck.

"That's really too bad," Sever said. "The feeling isn't mutual."

He reared up, a jagged dagger in his hand, and Mary barely had time to dodge as he lunged toward her with it. Nathan tried to dart forward, but she shoved him aside—no one was going to pull a Tally today, least of all Nathan—as Sever staggered forward, murder plain in his eyes.

A searing white line cut through the air between Mary and Sever, and the Pearl Knife whipped through space to plunge itself into the alien-god's belly. Sever screamed, clutching at his gut, but the Knife dragged itself up his body, fizzling with incandescent color as it sank into its maker.

Sever's skin charred, inky lines carving through his flesh like veins. They snaked out of his collar and up his neck, crawling toward his face and down his bare arms at the same time.

When he fell, he shattered against the carpet, like a glass vase.

Mary only realized she was stumbling back when Nathan caught her by the arms, wavering only slightly as she fell into him. She waited a beat, then another, half expecting Sever's body to re-form. But the pieces stayed where they were, scattered like ashes on the carpet.

They'd won. They were free.

The Knife lay flickering in the ruins of Sever's body, and Eloise stumbled toward it from somewhere behind Mary. With a cry of pain, she fell to her knees beside it.

Still gripping Nathan's hand, Mary went to Eloise, looping

her arm through her sister's. Eloise squeezed Mary closer, her hands shaking, tears pouring down her cheeks. She didn't look away from the Knife.

The Pearl Knife blinked blue, then red, then blue again. For a brief instant, it shone with its old milky white beauty, luminous in the dusk-blue twilight of the room.

And then, with Eloise weeping over it, the Knife went dark.

WAVE HAD NICE THINGS. A yacht, apparently, which could dive down to an underwater bunker. It was currently bobbing above the waves, though, which Nathan was thankful for. He wasn't sure he was ready for enclosed spaces after HQ's collapse, and the ballpark ordeal. Even with Sever and the retirees out of the picture.

It was good to see Dr. Gordon again, though Nathan wished he'd find someone else's minor injuries to fuss over. He'd already spent an hour in the infirmary while the doctor cared for Monster's cuts and made absolutely sure he didn't have any internal bleeding. Apparently he needed to know that before he could actually heal the rest.

"Bad bruises," Dr. Gordon said finally. "That's all."

"Excellent," Nathan said. "Fix me up, doc. I want to see that horizon."

Dr. Gordon chuckled. "I'm sure you do."

"How're you feeling about the whole LIO plus Wave equals a new organization thing?" Nathan asked. LIO had held the doctor, along with a number of Wave operatives in their underground prison, and it was easy to imagine him objecting to a partnership.

"Oh, I imagine it's a positive thing," the doctor said, the skin at his eyes crinkling slightly as he smiled. He'd always been gentle toward the League, despite their crimes against him. No doubt some of the other Wave operatives would be feeling a bit differently.

Or maybe not. They'd all come together for that last battle. Maybe they could come together for this, too.

The door opened, and Mary stuck her head into the room. The sight of her still made Nathan's stomach flip. For a while there, he'd truly thought he'd never see her again.

To Nathan's surprise, Dr. Gordon stood. "I'd better check on President Caldwell. I'll be back."

Mary watched him leave, then settled on the edge of Nathan's bed, curling a leg up under her. She had on soft pants that hugged her body at the hips, a white T-shirt doing the same for the top of her. He couldn't look away. Not that he wanted to.

"Am I really that scary?" she asked. "Chasing the doc away?"

"Um, yes."

"Good." She leaned forward to twist her fingers into his hair, and he pulled her into a kiss. She smelled fresh, like ocean breezes and crisp apples. Her hair was soft against his cheek, her body warm as she leaned into him.

"I wrote you a letter," he said, when she broke the kiss.

She was still just a breath away. Maybe they could lock the door and talk later. She kissed him again, lingering, the taste of some sweet fruit on her lips. "Oh yeah? Let me see."

"I can't," he murmured, teasing the back of her shirt between his fingertips. "I didn't have any paper. And my hands were tied up."

"So you thought me a letter."

"Yes."

"Tease."

He'd missed everything about her. The way she leaned into him, dragging a hand across his chest as she kissed him. He felt like he could melt into her and stay there, maybe forever.

Mary sat back abruptly and took his hands. "Let's hear it, then."

He licked his lips, aching to pull her back to him. "Now?"

She smiled. Nodded.

He cleared his throat. "It sounds a bit ridiculous in my head now. It might have been romantic, if I'd died and you'd found it—"

"Opposite of romantic."

"—but now it just seems... Not enough."

She swatted at his shoulder. "You brought it up, so just tell me before I get Bradley to project it on the wall for you. We're friends now, you know."

She'd need to explain that one later. But it didn't sound like something he wanted, in any case. "All right," he said. "Before I met you, I only ever wanted to be an independent operative. To help people. To make up for my past. And then we were apart, and all I wanted was you. And then we were apart again—"

"You skipped some drama in between."

"—and I thought, if I live through this, I'd better make sure she knows. It's only her. It's only *you*, forever."

Mary blinked at him. She looked beautiful, her curls messy around her face. She always looked beautiful. "Nathan, are you proposing to me?"

He realized he was gripping the bedsheet, and he made himself let go. "Yes. I mean, I was. Before you interrupted."

Her hand was back on his chest now, her lips hot on his neck. "You paused."

Nathan swallowed and brushed his fingertips down her

neck, running them along her collarbone. "I was reading the room."

"So you could back out if I looked horrified?" Her voice was a throaty hum in his ear.

He was probably a second away from losing track of the English language entirely. He cleared his throat. It didn't help. "Precisely," he said, then paused again. She was hovering over him now, her lips no longer teasing his neck, yet still close enough to catch. But he had to know her answer. He had to. "So?"

She pressed her forehead to his. "So, what?"

"Are you horrified?"

She laughed. "I don't know, you haven't asked me anything."

"But you know what I'm going to... Will you marry me, or are you going to drag this out forever?"

"Yes, and no," she said.

This time, he did pull her back to him.

And this time, they locked the door.

IT FELT RIGHT, somehow, to stand beside the ruins of Niagara Falls. Like a memorial, a visit to an honored grave. The wind tugged at her hair, the falls rushing a new song into her ears.

Eloise still had her own powers, bestowed on her by the Pearl Knife, and she'd portaled here from the yacht at dawn to stand beside the falls. It had only been a week since HQ's collapse—two days since they'd defeated Sever—and the visitors' center was closed, the whole street roped off as engineers tested the safety of the area. Eloise highly doubted anyone would kick her out.

It was funny. From up here, the falls didn't really look ruined. Different, certainly. But an alien visiting—a friendly one this time, like Sloane—wouldn't know it had ever been a different shape. They would just see the blue-white water, rushing along to fill the gorge.

Still striking. Still beautiful. But, like LIO and Wave, forever changed.

Steve meandered over from the other side of the visitors' center and came to stand beside her at the rail. She'd woken him this morning, asked him to come with her. And here he was, by her side, warm and smiling, and smelling of spiced coconut.

He nudged her with his elbow. "What now, boss?"

How could she begin to know? She still had her powers, yes, but grief coursed through her body with every breath, every step, every word. She missed the Knife's voice, its song. She missed its images, its companionship. It had understood her in a way that no one else ever had.

In the end, she thought she had understood it, too.

And it had sacrificed itself to save them all.

"Now," she said, "I guess we build a new era."

She could see the way forward, in theory. A new headquarters, a new mission. Supporting enhanced humans, training them—not for fighting, unless they wanted to fight, but to handle their powers and excel in whatever they wanted to do.

She could see the way forward, but it was hard to feel it. The grief made her numb.

Steve tilted his head toward the sky, and Eloise looked up to see Agnes descending to meet them, her curls whipping around her like a halo. "Think I'll go for a run," Steve said. He winked and kissed her cheek, and then he was off, speeding down the riverside as if to chase the wind.

Agnes landed with a few graceful steps. "It's so pleasant here in summer," she sighed.

"Not in winter, though."

"No."

They stood there together for a moment, looking out at the falls. More companionable than awkward, now, though Eloise couldn't begin to guess why Agnes had come. "Did you fly all this way?"

"Not exactly."

She didn't elaborate. Mysterious. "How are the civilians? The ones Sever froze?"

"Oh, they're fine. Dr. Gordon and I are keeping them under observation for a few days, just in case."

They must be anxious to get back to their families, too. Eloise was grateful for Agnes, for her quick thinking in defeating Goldi's illusion. She had no doubt that the scientist would make sure the civilians were completely recovered before she let them go.

"Make sure you speak with Will and the architects," Eloise said. "Get the lab specs you want in the new building."

Agnes smiled. "The Enhanced Abilities Coalition, eh?"

Eloise wrinkled her nose. "Fran's grumpy about the name, but I came up with it on the spot. Seemed... fitting."

"Bringing everyone together. I like it." Agnes was still staring out at the falls, giving her head an occasional shake, as if she couldn't reconcile the new shape of the place. It would take some getting used to.

Eloise rubbed her hands on her pants, suddenly feeling nervous. "So... Are we good now, Agnes? Everything that happened, it's... I'm sorry."

Agnes smiled. She reached into her bag and pulled out a very familiar box. There were etchings engraved along the sides, silver-white designs that had been carved long ago, in another world. Another galaxy. Eloise had last seen this box in Sloane Tarnish's hands.

"I'm sorry, too," Agnes said. And then she handed the box to Eloise.

Eloise was afraid to hope. Afraid to breathe, as she opened the latch and pushed open the top.

The Knife's consciousness flooded into her mind like an embrace, the blade beaming with silver light, and she had to grip the rail to keep her knees from buckling as she cradled the box close to her chest.

"How?" she gasped, the word barely a whisper.

"We coaxed one last pair of wormholes out of Sloane's scientist friend. Apparently Mary has a way to contact them now? It took a couple days to get a response on the stolen tablet, but she did get one." She shrugged. "Mary had a theory that the box might be able to help us revive it. Tam helped."

Eloise's head was too full of emotion, too full of the Knife's familiar flow of song. Still, she managed to say, "A pair of wormholes?"

Agnes tucked her fingertips in her pockets. "The second one was for Morik. He's safe in the Parse Fleet's custody, it seems. Whatever that means."

Eloise doubted he'd cause any trouble without his tyrant of a boss. She shook her head, unable to contend with the flood of emotions that crashed into her. The Knife was alive. It was alive, and Agnes had helped her to get it.

She threw her arms around Agnes, who laughed and hugged her back, and finally, Eloise could feel the way forward.

49 / MARY

THREE MONTHS LATER

"IT'S GOT TOO MUCH GLASS," Nathan said.

He was standing next to Mary, on the steps of the newly erected Enhanced Abilities Coalition Headquarters, and he wasn't wrong. The entire wall was glass, a huge window that opened out to a garden with fountains and flowers and tons of open space.

And it was all open to the public. Anyone could come and visit the interactive exhibits, and they were already flocking in droves—there was a school bus pulling into the parking lot even as they spoke, Dawn Kimble ready to take pictures as the kids disembarked. Mary could see Ire standing in the lobby, preparing to greet them for a tour.

"I like the glass," Eloise said. She'd been walking in the garden behind them, while the Knife cruised by a wall that commemorated the people they'd lost in relief-carved scenes. Mary's parents. Tally. Even Jenna's father, Mange, who'd once tried to do the right thing.

Worlds were colliding. So many worlds. But it was a good kind of collision.

This place reminded Mary of her beach house in Malibu, in some ways. Only this time, the display was actually real.

"Villains like to crash through glass," Nathan continued. "I think it's a rule."

"Tell your government friends, then," Mary said. "They can fund an indestructible-glass study."

Nathan had taken on a position as a liaison to the U.S. government, to make sure communication continued openly. At least, as openly as it could where the government was concerned. And Mary was scheduled to meet a brand-new group of recruits. The ones who wanted to learn combat.

She wasn't sure how she'd do as a teacher, but Rajni had talked her into it. So she figured she might as well try. She hoped the newbies were ready to spend some time in the garage, too, because she planned on teaching them everything she knew.

"Indestructible glass. The villains will bounce right off the walls," Nathan said.

"Exactly."

Eloise came over to watch the kids as they hopped off the bus. She rested an arm on Mary's shoulder, the Pearl Knife levitating by her waist. More and more, the blade reminded Mary of a puppy.

Nathan slipped his hand into hers. "Off to work, then?"

She nodded. Maybe they wouldn't have to save the world for a while. But maybe, just maybe, they could make it a little bit better.

THE END

Thank you so much for reading the *League of Independent Operatives* series!

Before I go off on a mushy tangent about the end of the series (and I will, I promise): Sloane and her crew are taking off on their own space opera adventure in 2022. The first book, *Chaos Zone*, is already available for preorder. Find links on my website at katesheeranswed.com/parse-galaxy

Here's the description:

Space isn't Sloane Tarnish's thing. She's a med student, not a planet jumper. And she's definitely not leadership material.

Unfortunately, her outcast uncle has decided to disappear, saddling her with his questionable crew -- a cranky pilot and a mad scientist -- plus a ship that only answers to Sloane.

Sloane just needs enough cash to find her uncle and get back to

her life, so she takes on a bounty job in an abandoned system. No one else wants to go there, but how bad can it be?

When a Galaxy Fleet Lieutenant shows up on her bounty's tail, pushing for her to abandon her quest and let the Fleet handle the job, Sloane ignores him. The reward is too big to give up. But as dangers close in on all sides, she can't help wondering if she'll live to claim it...

Order here: katesheeranswed.com/parse-galaxy

AFTERWARD

I've been putting off writing an afterward, because it's so hard to sum up the experience of finishing this series.

First, let me thank all my loyal readers, and my new readers, and everyone who gave the *League of Independent Operatives* books a chance. When you picked up book one, then two, and so on — when you wrote reviews, told your friends, emailed me about how much you loved the Pearl Knife or Jeff Hayes... Any time you participated in the process, you kept me excited about the story. You made me believe in it even more, and I can't thank you enough.

This is the longest series I've finished yet. It was a challenge, and a labor of love.

From the moment I realized that Wave wasn't just a mustache-twirling eeeeevil organization (and yes, I wrote several drafts of *Alter Ego* before that came into focus for me) the *LIO* books have been about bringing enemies together to fight a threat to everything they love. They needed to find common ground; they needed to accept their pasts and banish their biases.

Not "the enemy of my enemy is my friend," which is a fine saying — until the Big Enemy is vanquished and we then turn on one another. But actual collaboration. Healing. In my opinion, we need it more than ever.

My books are always about escape, first and foremost. But I

can't help reflecting our world in them; I can't help hoping for something just a little better, and envisioning that on the page.

I love stories about redemption. I love big bad guys facing their due.

I also love humor and silliness and happy endings.

I hope I've provided all these things in this series.

It is not easy to write a series that essentially has 100 different magic systems working in it (one for each unique enhanced ability). Or, if you like, 100 different sci-fi principles. The two genres truly blend in the superhero realm, which is part of why I like it so much.

But I enjoyed the heck out of it, and I hope you did, too.

I want to thank my parents and sisters for always supporting me.

I want to thank my son for his enthusiasm and for saying "whoa!" whenever I showed him a new cover design. And my daughter, for being a tiny bean. I also want to thank my husband for all his support, and for protecting my writing time.

And again, thanks to all my readers! I hope you'll stick with me to see what happens next :)

-Kate

P.S. If you turn the page, you'll find a bonus short story — from IRE'S point of view!

BONUS STORY: POWER FAILURE

A LEAGUE OF INDEPENDENT OPERATIVES
STORY

McCallister would've laughed at him for wedging himself into a back alley like this. Even before the swollen muscles and the magical-beanstalk-like height—he stood above seven feet now, it was unreal—his bright red hair tended to make it impossible to blend in. His tendency to scowl didn't help, either.

In other words, he'd never been much for skulking.

Even if he had been an ace at navigating the shadows, McCallister would've found something else to rib him about. The fact that he was tiptoeing around piles of garbage would do; the air back here was thick with the smell of fried oil and week-old beer spills.

What, McCallister would say, *can't you find a decent gig? You gotta harass the brass where they drink now?*

McCallister was always saying stuff like that. Jobs were gigs, officers were the brass. If there was a slang term for it, McCallister would throw it around, guaranteed.

"I don't talk to ghosts," Ire muttered, stepping around another pile of garbage. It wasn't strictly the truth, and McCallister's ghost knew it. He could hear his friend laughing at him, even as the words crossed his lips.

Most businesses wouldn't keep their back alleyways so filthy, but Ire happened to know that Cordy's Bar and Grill used this street less for trash management and more as an office for backroom deals that needed to spill out onto a private street.

Nothing said 'private' like an alley packed with rotting trash bags. He didn't know why the city didn't crack down on them.

He did know, however, that General Lerner made use of that back door once a week. He wasn't sure why, exactly, only that the general met a contact outside of it every Wednesday night at 11:12pm on the dot.

Tonight, Ire had detained the usual contact, temporarily. He needed to take the guy's place.

What do you think they meet for? McCallister mused in his head. *Drugs? Prostitutes?*

Ire wanted to believe it was something admirable. He ignored the ghost and took up his position by the door. The general would come, Ire would have his say, and everything would be OK. He wouldn't need to skulk around anymore.

"Who are you here for?" The woman's voice came out of nowhere, and Ire started so hard he nearly slammed his head on the brick wall behind him. He looked around, squinting into the shadows, but there was no one in sight.

"Not more ghosts," he said. He knew McCallister was in his head—that had never been in doubt—but the woman's voice had sounded real.

"Oh, sorry." On the other side of the doorway, the woman materialized. He didn't have another term for it; one second there was a wall of dingy bricks, and the next, there was a person standing in front of it. "I forgot I was invisible."

She was a petite woman, with brown skin and a halo of springy black curls framing her face. A gold wedding band glinted on her left hand when she lifted it up to give him a wave. Ire felt like he should know her face, but he couldn't quite recall her name.

"Are you an independent operative?" he asked. He knew he wasn't the only person in the world with enhanced abilities. Who didn't? There were IOs everywhere these days, would-be heroes who could fly and turn invisible, and who even knew what else. They were loners, the lot of them. Just like him.

She hesitated, then nodded. "In a manner of speaking. I mean, I have the powers. I'm not big on all the punching stuff."

He snapped his fingers. "Agnes Jenson. The scientist."

She raised her eyebrows, a smile touching the corners of her mouth. "You know who I am?"

"I read your paper." He tried to dig back in his mind for the title and came up blank. "It was something about... using individual powers for the better of society. Developing them into technology."

She touched a finger to her bottom lip. "Such a dry one."

"I didn't think so." He'd been digging for information, any information that could help him understand who he was now, what these abilities were good for. If he could reverse them, he would, but if he was stuck living with bulked-up muscles and superior punching power, he figured he might as well do some good.

Agnes tilted her head toward the door. "You need some help?"

Yes. Desperately.

But she obviously meant in this moment, on this mission, not in general. He stuck his hands in his pockets, unwilling to tell her what he was doing. The IOs, they were do-gooders—rescuing people from flaming buildings and crashing planes and all that—but his mission wasn't for the good of everyone. It was only for the good of a few.

And when it was done, he planned to disappear, the old-fashioned way. Cabin in the woods. Maybe a desert island somewhere.

"I'm an independent operative now," he said, though the words tasted strange on his tongue. "I guess that means I work alone."

She shrugged. "Suit yourself."

Before he could ask why she'd been waiting here in the first place, she vanished.

A beat later, the door clicked open and General Lerner stepped out into the alley. His dark hair was slicked tight against his skull, and he craned his neck to squint up at Ire. "You," he said. "What'd you do with my guy?"

Ire had been imagining, vaguely, that he'd have to introduce himself to the general. But of course Lerner knew who he was. Ire had been careful since the accident, operating on the assumption that they'd be looking for him—he'd disappeared in the middle of his service—but he hadn't really thought it through.

The general had been there. He knew everything.

A beat too late, Ire clapped his feet to attention. It felt wrong, his thighs pushing back against the movement, his spine working harder to lift more his new height. "Your contact is fine, sir," he said. "I needed an opportunity to speak with you in private."

General Lerner lit a cigarette, and the glowing tip cast his features in a strange wave of orange light that melted into murky shadows. He took a breath of smoke, let it out, then flicked the ash away.

Ire decided to take that as an 'at ease.' "Sir, I'm here to talk to you about Captain McCallister's family."

"Who?"

Ire had been about to explain who, but something about the

way the general barked the word made him bristle. He clenched his teeth, took a breath. "Captain McCallister, sir. He didn't make it out that day." Ire pointed to his bicep, hoping that was enough to tip the general off as to what *that day* meant. "But his family hasn't received any of the benefits they're owed. None of the others have, either."

He'd visited them, one by one. Carefully. Quietly. The silent houses, the crying kids. He'd seen the bills stacked on counters, the houses in foreclosure.

General Lerner flicked another bit of ash off the end of the cigarette. "That's because *that day* never happened, soldier."

Not a soldier anymore, pal, McCallister's voice said in his head. Ire nodded in agreement.

General Lerner tossed his cigarette on the ground without bothering to stamp out the burning tip. "Get my guy back," he said, and reached to open the door.

Ire touched a fist to the door. He'd only intended to hold it shut for a second, to give himself another moment with the general, but the touch—which he'd swear had been light—left a dent in the door the size of a tennis ball.

He wasn't used to his size. Needed to move more carefully. "That's it?" he asked. "You're just going to leave them to suffer?"

"Careful, son," Lerner said. "Far as I'm concerned, you're government property."

A pair of rough hands grabbed Ire from behind, and only the surprise of the moment—their owner *was* good at skulking —allowed them to wrench Ire away from the door. Lerner slipped inside, and Ire whirled around to face a pair of soldiers in fatigues.

They'd been ready for him. Had Lerner known he would come?

The soldiers rushed him, but Ire knew how they'd fight. One threw a punch, and he caught it while kicking the second in the groin. He stood more than a head taller than the bigger of the two, and they couldn't match his strength. He grabbed them both by the collar, one in each hand—they were as light as dolls —and bashed their heads together.

He threw them back against the wall, then leapt up to grab the edge of the roof. He hauled himself up without bothering to look back and see if they were alive, and he ran.

◁▭▷

McCallister had been the first one inside.

Their squad had been called to a chemical weapons plant, a boxy building that practically screamed 'military factory.' It was belching acrid black smoke into the air to the tune of screaming alarms and flashing red lights. General Lerner himself had been outside, along with a pair of corporals and a white-coated scientist with flyaway curls and a curious, squinting expression.

His squad had kicked open the door and rushed the place, not knowing if it'd been compromised, if they should be expecting to face fire, or if the whole thing was an accident.

There'd been no bullets, no attacks. Just the red-hot blaze that needed extinguishing, an onslaught of nostril-searing chemicals that'd knocked him back against the wall.

Months later, the smell still assaulted his senses with every breath. No mater how many showers he took, no matter how many oils he smeared on his upper lip, he could smell the memory of that day as if it'd just happened. It sometimes felt that if he could wash it away, he might undo it.

He didn't know why his friends had died, didn't know why

he'd lived. He only knew the raging fire of those last moments in the lab, and the feeling of McCallister's limp body in his arms.

He only knew that he'd stormed out of the facility with McCallister slung over his shoulder, feeling like his own limbs were on fire. He remembered the feeling of his lips, swollen over his teeth, the painful stretch of his back as his body mutated into something... more.

When no one came to help them, he'd lifted a Humvee off its axels. He'd rushed for the general and the corporals, screaming for help, but they'd all run away. Like cowards.

Unmatched Ire, McCallister's voice had whispered in his head, like he was writing a headline.

So he'd taken the name, wrapped himself in it. His armor. His mission.

———

"I've been thinking."

The woman's voice spoke into his dreams, but it sounded real. A bit too real, tugging him out of the blackness of sleep.

Ire risked opening his eyes.

Agnes Jenson was sitting on a crate in the corner, a laptop open in front of her, the screen reflecting in her black-framed glasses. "Was it really an accident?"

Ire sat up, blinking sleep out of his eyes. "How did you get in here?"

She didn't look up. "You're squatting in an abandoned warehouse. How could I not get in here? So anyway, I've been looking at tapes from that day—"

"You have tapes? How?"

"—and I think the general knew what was going to happen.

See this man?" Agnes turned the laptop to face him, tapping the scientist's face. "He's a chemist. Works with enhanced abilities. He'd not considered to be very ethical."

She pinched her lips, clearly disapproving. Pretty rich, coming from a woman who'd crashed a guy's bedroom. Squatting or not, it was bold.

Still half suspecting that this was a very lucid dream, Ire slipped his T-shirt on, all too aware that it had been several days since his last shower. "What are you saying?"

"I'm saying I think the general knew exactly who he was working with." She leaned forward. "If they wanted to create super soldiers or something, they'd have come to me."

She said it with full confidence, like it was pure fact. It probably was. He'd come across her name so many times during his own frenzied research. "So why didn't they come to you?"

"I don't know. Maybe he was cheap. Or maybe he agreed to rush it. Test on humans before they were ready. Or maybe..." She tapped her lip with her finger. "Maybe they were testing a product, not a weapon."

After that meeting in the alley, Ire could imagine it. Maybe General Lerner didn't see them as soldiers at all. Just expendable test subjects. Just a way to profit.

Agnes was watching him, waiting for a response. He knew he probably shouldn't trust her; he was hiding out, though clearly she'd found him easily enough.

But the truth was, he could use the help. And he couldn't help the curiosity that made him want to know more about her work. "The general won't compensate my friends' families," he said. "If your theory is right, it's because he wants it covered up."

In a way, Ire was surprised it hadn't occurred to him before. But he'd been focused on his own recovery, on staying safe.

Maybe some part of him *had* suspected; if he hadn't, he'd have turned himself in months ago.

He might even take it further and come after them. McCallister's wife and kids, Gordy's aging parents, Peshlaki's little brother.

"We can find out," Agnes said. "Together."

"I thought independent operatives worked alone. What's in it for you?"

Agnes gave him a sunny smile and slapped the laptop shut. "What do you say? Should we go capture a criminal?"

———

"This is ridiculous," Ire said.

They were crouched side-by-side on the beams above the doctor's shiny new lab, which was once again conveniently tucked away in the middle of the desert. In case something else exploded, perhaps.

Agnes looked perfectly comfortable perched on the beam beside him. Ire, on the other hand, felt precarious with his enormous frame balanced on the narrow strip of metal. And a bit surprised that his weight hadn't bent the thing.

"This is the job," she said.

Below them, the door swung open and the chemist sauntered in, carrying a cup of coffee and whistling tunelessly. He was looking at his phone as his kicked the door open, a black backpack slung over his shoulder like a high school kid in the nineties trying to look cool.

Ire shimmied toward the middle of the beam, aiming for the right spot to jump down.

Agnes tapped his shoulder. "I'm going to go invisible. Like you said, we work alone." She winked, then disappeared.

"I wish I could do that," Ire said. "What am I supposed to do?"

"Distract him."

It was a good thing he had practice talking to ghosts.

Ire felt the hush of air as she leapt down from the beam. He'd have liked a little more preparation, but he supposed he might as well follow. Sighing, he dropped down after her.

It was still something of a surprise when he landed on the concrete without cracking his ankles. Or the concrete, honestly; he could feel the way his weight punched it, and wondered if some training would actually increase his abilities. He hadn't given training any thought.

And now wasn't the time for it. The chemist was staring at him with that same squinty expression he'd had outside the facility.

"We've been looking for you," he said. "How are you feeling?"

Pissed off, actually.

The chemist set his coffee down on the floor and bustled over to a desk that was covered in papers. "If you'll bear with me, I'd like to run some tests."

Ire watched the man scurry around, arranging things as if unexpected company had dropped by. Ire supposed he was unexpected company, though he doubted this man intended to offer him any refreshments.

"So you did know," he said.

"Know what?" The chemist was distractedly shuffling papers. He reached for a briefcase, snapped open the double latches, and pulled out a syringe.

"That the explosion would kill them."

"Oh, that." The chemist waved the question away like it was a bad odor. "We knew there'd be some casualties. It was a great step forward when you survived. Not when you escaped, of course—we didn't anticipate desertion—but a triumph, truly. Especially now that you've returned."

Thoughts whirled through Ire's mind, dark and bitter, and Ire's newly powerful body propelled him across the room in three steps before he'd quite realized he was moving. When he reached the scientist, he lifted the man up by the collar of his white lab coat. "You murdered my friends."

The chemist flailed, but his feet were several inches off the floor. "Let's be reasonable. You're a medical marvel!"

Ire didn't want to be reasonable. He wanted his friends back.

The chemist's briefcase slid open, and invisible hands began lifting papers out, tucking them away into the ether. Agnes Jenson, gathering evidence. Good thought.

"Please," the chemist said. "I have money."

"I'll bet you have a lot of it right now," Ire said.

The door crashed open, and Ire dropped the chemist to face a squad of soldiers that looked all too much like his fallen friends. Only they had black masks pulled over their faces, and guns pointed in his face.

Ire threw himself to the ground, and the chemist scurried behind a crate as the masked newcomers opened fire. Ire crawled for the crate, expecting to feel the bite of bullets, the burn of blood filling his lungs. A fitting end, but too soon. He'd die without avenging his friends. Worse, he'd die without helping their families.

But the bullets didn't come. He paused, looking back to see a shimmering wall of energy shining in the air between him and the attackers. As he watched, their guns jerked out of their hands and went flying across the floor.

"That wall blocked the bullets." The chemist was peering

out from behind the crate. He looked like he wanted to start taking notes. "Did *you* make a shield? That wasn't in the plans at all. Incredible."

It was definitely Agnes who'd made the shield, but Ire didn't feel like correcting the guy, especially since he'd referred to 'plans.' As if Ire were a building he'd remodeled. Personally, he was more impressed by the flying guns.

The soldiers seemed undecided about their next move—retrieve the guns, or get Ire—which gave him a chance to move. Agnes dropped the shield, and he rushed them.

They went down like dominoes. Crashing, flailing, shouting dominoes. One of them tried to run for the door, screaming something about Frankenstein—Ire decided not to correct him on the whole doctor/monster thing—but he was too late.

Ire's new muscles were big, but they moved fast. He caught the fleeing guy buy the back of his jacket and jerked him back into the room, using his feet to knock down the one other soldier who'd tried to get up.

From there, it was easy.

When the bad guys were trussed, the police on their way—or so he assumed—Ire met Agnes behind the building. She brushed off her hands, looking entirely satisfied with her work for the day. "Drink?" she asked. "It's on me."

He'd have liked to know how she planned to handle all the law enforcement stuff. The evidence. The lab work. He'd have liked to know what else the chemist had planned, who else he'd hurt.

But he still hadn't nabbed the general. He still didn't have money for the families. He could picture the road ahead, a dark period of months hulking in back corners and peeling safes apart with his bare hands.

Agnes wouldn't help him with that. And he didn't want her to see him do it. Hell, in a few months she might be saving someone else from *him*.

"I appreciate the help," he said, "but I can't. I work alone."

———

She showed up at the bar, anyway, in jeans and a T-shirt, her curls flying free around her face. She slid into the booth across from him with a smile and a wave at the bartender.

"I said I work alone." Not that he was sorry to see her. In fact, he thought he'd be sorry if she hadn't come.

Ire drank from his Guinness, then looked back at the glass, surprised that he'd downed half of it in one sip. He still wasn't used to this body. He wasn't sure he'd ever be.

A tall Black woman joined Agnes on the other side of the booth. She had on a pinstriped suit and heels, and the way she carried herself made Ire sit up a little straighter before he'd quite realized why. He didn't slump back, though; he had a feeling she'd notice that. Had a feeling she'd notice everything.

"Am I supposed to know who you are, too?" he asked. It wasn't easy to feign nonchalance with these two women staring him down, Agnes smiling pleasantly, the newcomer scanning him with her eyebrows raised.

"Not without my mask, no," she said. She must be another IO, then. But which one?

"I get it," he said. "This whole thing was a setup."

She gave him a faint smile, but didn't deny it. He could respect that. He drained the second half of his beer, stalling. "Why?" he asked.

The woman leaned her forearms on the table. "We'd like to recruit you."

He snorted. "Independent operatives work alone. It's in the name."

She slid a blue card across the table. He thought about ignoring it, but in the end he was just too curious. He picked it up. "The League of Independent Operatives," he said. "Seems like a contradiction."

"You have no idea," Agnes said.

Ire wasn't sure what that was supposed to mean. The card beckoned to him, and these two women—they clearly knew what they were doing. If anyone could help him to understand his powers, to use them for good, it would be them.

But he'd made a promise to a ghost—and his family. He couldn't abandon them, no matter what.

"Sorry," he said, "but I can't join your... I can't. I have to help my friends. Their families."

The Black woman tapped the card, still pinched between his thumb and forefinger. "I don't give that card to people I expect to refuse."

No kidding. That'd give them away pretty quick.

"We've already wired your friends' families the money they need," the woman continued. "And before you wonder if General Lerner's implicated in this whole thing, Agnes recovered ample evidence to send him away, too. You're free, Ire. We'd love to have you."

Ire's brain was still glitching over the idea that independent operatives weren't independent at all. And that they had business cards, of all things.

The woman leaned forward, her hands halfway across the table now, her dark eyes boring into his. "So? What will you choose? Revenge on people who are already headed to prison? Or a chance to make a real difference?"

Ire looked at Agnes, who gave him an encouraging nod. "What can I say?" he said. "I guess I'd rather be a hero."

THE END

To read more exclusive stories, including a LIO prequel novella, join my email list at katesheeranswed.com

ABOUT THE AUTHOR

Kate Sheeran Swed loves hot chocolate, plastic dinosaurs, and airplane tickets. She has trekked along the Inca Trail to Macchu Picchu, hiked on the Mýrdalsjökull glacier in Iceland, and climbed the ruins of Masada to watch the sunrise over the Dead Sea. Kate currently lives in New York's capital region with her husband and two kids, and a pair of cats who were named after movie dogs (Benji and Beethoven). She holds an MFA in Fiction from Pacific University.

You can find more of Kate's work, and pick up a free novella, at katesheeranswed.com.

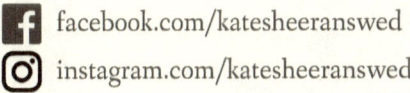

facebook.com/katesheeranswed
instagram.com/katesheeranswed